Sam had al. <!-- text obscured --> was doing before his head was yanked down and his lips met the sweetest-tasting mouth in Missouri.

He'd heard of your evasive moves, but this one won the prize. And what a prize. Del's lips parted and her tongue darted against his lips. Not being a man who missed an opportunity, he opened his mouth and welcomed the invasion.

Her hands were locked into his hair. Through the fog filling his brain it registered that he couldn't escape even if he wanted to—so, why fight it?

BOOK YOUR PLACE ON OUR WEBSITE AND MAKE THE READING CONNECTION!

We've created a customized website just for our very special readers, where you can get the inside scoop on everything that's going on with Zebra, Pinnacle and Kensington books.

When you come online, you'll have the exciting opportunity to:

- View covers of upcoming books
- Read sample chapters
- Learn about our future publishing schedule (listed by publication month *and author*)
- Find out when your favorite authors will be visiting a city near you
- Search for and order backlist books from our online catalog
- Check out author bios and background information
- Send e-mail to your favorite authors
- Meet the Kensington staff online
- Join us in weekly chats with authors, readers and other guests
- Get writing guidelines
- AND MUCH MORE!

**Visit our website at
http://www.kensingtonbooks.com**

Love Is All You Need

LORI DEVOTI

ZEBRA BOOKS
Kensington Publishing Corp.
www.kensingtonbooks.com

ZEBRA BOOKS are published by

Kensington Publishing Corp.
850 Third Avenue
New York, NY 10022

All Kensington titles, imprints, and distributed lines are available at special quantity discounts for bulk purchases for sales promotion, premiums, fund-raising, educational, or institutional use.

Special book excerpts or customized printings can also be created to fit specific needs. For details, write or phone the office of the Kensington Special Sales Manager. Attn. Special Sales Department, Kensington Publishing Corp., 850 Third Avenue, New York, NY 10022. Phone: 1-800-221-2647.

Zebra and the Z logo Reg. U.S. Pat. & TM Off.

ISBN 0-8217-7866-8

First Printing: May 2006
10 9 8 7 6 5 4 3 2 1

Printed in the United States of America

Chapter 1

Pearls before swine . . .

"You want me to buy a pig in a poke?" Del Montgomery twisted the necklace at her throat and struggled to remember that the man sitting across from her desk had the power to take away everything those pearls represented.

"Not just any pig in a poke, *the* pig in a poke. The Unruh Pig." Her boss, Benjamin Porter, couldn't have been any more condescending if she'd asked "Which Liberty Bell?" Of course, Del was used to his attitude. As creator of Porter Auctions, the premier auction house of the Midwest, Porter tended to address her with a certain level of disdain on a regular basis.

She was used to it, but she didn't like it.

"Ah, the Unruh Pig." Del searched her memory for mention of any swine in Unruh's history. The pottery company, though legendary, had enjoyed a brief existence in the early 1900s. They were best known for their founder's eccentric free-form designs—never had she heard of anything resembling a pig.

"That was before the second fire, wasn't it?" A safe question, since everything of any value was created before the second rebuilding of the factory.

"So, you have heard of it?" Porter beamed at her. "I was certain if anyone knew the history, it would be you."

Lucky her. Rolling her pearls between the pads of her index finger and thumb, she asked, "Who did you say tipped you off the Pig was back in circulation?"

Porter leaned against the worn leather of the one side chair allotted to her office and watched her over the top of his tortoiseshell glasses. "I didn't."

Ass. "Fair enough." She pulled a spiral notebook that served as her Day-Timer from her lap drawer. "So you want me to authenticate the piece before we accept it?"

"Yes." Porter adjusted his skinny butt, like he couldn't get comfortable in the hand-me-down seating. Del hoped both of his cheeks went numb.

Expecting more information, she waited, pen poised over paper. Nothing came.

Okay, try another tactic. "Is this to be an open auction or are we just acquiring it for a 'special' client?"

Apparently more comfortable with this topic, Porter replied, "An open auction. The tip was a personal favor to me, a repayment of sorts."

Del gave him time to continue.

He didn't. Fine, she wasn't in the "need to know" club. Hell, she got kicked out of Brownies;

she couldn't expect more from Pompous Porter. He had to give her something though.

"Did this person mention where the Pig is now?" He had to answer that—unless the thing was supposed to materialize at midnight under the light of a gibbous moon, or some other such nonsense. She tapped her pen against her desk calendar.

Porter took a moment to check his cell phone for text messages. Looking up, he seemed surprised to see her. "You were saying?"

That you are a complete moron, with a dick the size of a toothpick. She smiled. "Just wondering where the Pig is now. Did this person give you an address or just a contact name and number?"

"Neither, actually." He flipped his phone shut. "Just somewhere in southern Missouri."

Somewhere in southern Missouri? Del kept her face purposely blank. "Really. Do you have a starting point?"

"Allen County, that's where the rumors started. So, that's where we'll start—well, you, anyway. You can leave tonight."

Leave tonight? For southern Missouri? Del pasted a cooperative look on her face. "Are you sure I'm the right person for this? David has a lot more experience in acquisitions than I do, and this could be a big one. I don't want to step on any toes." *Or have my toes caught and hauled off.*

Porter stood. "Stomp on toes if you have to, but get the Pig. We have an Unruh collection slated for sale in one month. I want the piece by then."

"But David—"

"Will do as I tell him. He'd be as out of place in

southern Missouri as a Loetz vase at a five-and-dime. You'll blend right in."

Gee, thanks. Del's smile was getting a little tired. Porter didn't seem to notice. He headed for the door.

"Wait—do you have any more information other than just Allen County?" Was the frustration beginning to edge into her voice? "I mean, that could be a big area."

He halted. "Not so big, the place is a speck of dirt on the map—maybe five thousand people in the entire county. Good news for us."

"Good news?" Del didn't see how leaving the conveniences of Chicago for a half-a-horse town in southern Missouri could possibly be good news.

Porter slipped her a self-satisfied smile. "Certainly, think about it. Even if the Pig turns up, who there would have the sense to know what it is?"

Sam Samson gripped the head of his mallet and surveyed the crowd from atop a flatbed trailer. All the usuals were here: the rusty-junk crowd, the pretty-glass set, and even the I-can-make-a-buck-on-anything throng. Yep, the players were here, but their dollars weren't on the board.

He motioned for Kenny, who was sitting at the wheel of Sam's dually, to pull forward another five yards. His friend complied, towing the trailer over the rutted ground until Sam was even with a stack of discarded auto parts and old farm tools.

Sam studied the bidders digging through dirty boxes and dingy bedclothes. He spied a likely target.

"Earl, you got your number ready?" Sam called over the bullhorn.

A man in worn overalls and a greasy feed hat waved a white card with a black 87 on it.

Sam lowered the horn. "Where's Gail?" he called to Earl. The older man was almost always good for upping bids on auto parts. Sam had no idea what Earl did with the dirty crap he hauled home after a sale, but he did know he'd get a lot more action out of Earl if his wife wasn't around to smack down his bidding arm.

"She's in the house looking at fancy glass," Sam's pigeon yelled back.

"Lot of nice stuff in there," Sam replied, then searched the trailers for his assistant. Spotting Charlie, he motioned her over.

With his voice low and his gaze on Earl, he said, "Why don't you go in and help the ladies out? Get them started on the small stuff and I'll be in just as soon as we're done with this lot. But whatever you do, keep Gail inside." Sam nodded toward Earl.

"Will do, boss." Charlie all but clicked her heels together in a sign of false subservience. Grinning, she whipped her ponytail around and jogged toward the white clapboard house. Sam dragged his hand over his face. She might be cocky, but she'd do her job; now he just had to do his.

Thirty minutes later, Sam had unloaded two tons of spare parts not worth the gas it would cost to haul them to the dump and had made a thousand dollars in the process. Well, not a thousand to him; his cut would be more like three hundred, then he'd have to pay Charlie and the kids who helped out, sorting merchandise before the sale and holding up boxes during. Hell, when you thought about it, Sam probably lost money wheedling and cajoling every penny out of today's tightfisted crowd.

He needed a break. He was never going to get the money to set up a second office in Springfield at the rate he was going. One good break, that was all he was asking. Something simple like Jesse James's gun belt or a previously unknown novel by Mark Twain, anything really. Just something worth some decent cash and with enough mystique to guarantee him lots of bidders and plenty of press. Yep, that was all he needed.

He hopped off the trailer and trotted toward the house. His pointy-toed cowboy boots hit the kitchen's worn linoleum just in time to hear Charlie call a set of Pyrex bowls sold for one dollar.

Yep, he needed a break. Fast.

Del backed her Insight into the tiny space in front of a diner creatively named the Bunny Hutch. She'd bought the car the same weekend Porter had presented her with her pearls. Naively, she'd been under the impression that along with the pearls came a raise in salary, but no, she still had to prove herself for that. In the meantime, she was saddled with car payments she couldn't afford while she continued to fling herself into work and toward the as-yet-invisible brass ring. This search for the Unruh Pig was, she hoped, the boost she needed.

Porter had been no help whatsoever, not even a vague suggestion on where to start her search. Somewhere in Allen County—maybe. Talk about a needle in a haystack, and only a month to find it. Boss or not, the man was insane.

The thing probably didn't even exist. If she'd ever heard a tale, and she'd heard plenty, the Unruh Pig had all the markings.

She slammed her car door and went to feed the meter. Illinois plates, small Missouri town—the meter maid was probably salivating already.

It was early, not quite eleven. The lunch crowd hadn't arrived and the breakfast crowd was gone. That left the regulars—old men who did nothing all day but sit at a Formica-topped table and drink coffee, when there wasn't a sale within a sixty-mile radius, that was. If anyone could point her in the direction of the Pig, she'd find him here.

She loosened the collar of her silk blouse and slapped a smile on her face.

"What can I getcha?" The waitress had a coffee stain the size of a saucer on her white apron and circles the size of Utah under her eyes. Her name tag read "Becca."

"Hard day?" Del slid onto a stool at the counter. The seventy-something man sitting near her pushed back his feed cap and nodded. Not one to waste an opportunity, Del flashed him her brightest Crest Whitestrips smile.

"Nothing out of the ordinary." Becca rested her elbow on the countertop. "You want coffee?"

Del returned her attention to the woman. She couldn't be more than twenty-five, but Del knew too well problems didn't come just with age.

"Decaf, if it's fresh, and a doughnut." Del pointed to the glass display case that housed stacks of pastries in various degrees of wholesomeness.

"How about a tractor tire? They're the freshest." The waitress filled Del's cup and, at Del's nod, retrieved a three-inch high doughnut.

Del added cream to her coffee, picked up the dessert, and dunked as much as would fit into the hot liquid. For a few minutes she forgot her mission, the waitress's sad eyes, and her own problems. She hadn't had a fresh doughnut like this since, well, it seemed like forever, definitely a lifetime ago.

"Where you from?" The spark of interest brought Becca to life, telling Del maybe this one could still be saved, not that Del was in the saving business. She had her own hide to look out for.

"Not from around here, I'm guessing." Becca nodded to Del's silk shirt and A-line skirt. Del couldn't say why she'd donned her normal work apparel today. For some reason the business attire made her feel safe, distanced a bit, and she wanted to prove Porter wrong. She didn't blend in southern Missouri any more than David would have.

Glancing at the other woman's stained apron, she realized she'd made a mistake. She wasn't here to prove anything, even to herself. She was here to find the Pig and get back to Chicago—period. To do that she was going to have to build trust fast; looking like a foreigner wasn't going to help any.

"Not too far from here, just haven't been home in a while." Del purposely let the accent she had spent the past seven years stamping out of her voice seep back in. It was easy, too easy.

The waitress's smile warmed another degree or two. "You want another doughnut? How about a bear claw?"

Feeling smaller than a two-dollar bid, Del swallowed her last bite. "No thanks."

Becca grabbed the aluminum-bottomed coffeepot. After refilling Del's cup, she wandered over to a couple who had just come in.

Del refocused on her purpose. No time for morals—she had a room to work.

Again realizing she was sliding into old habits, Del winced but shook it off. There was no help for it. As Daddy always said, do unto others before somebody bigger comes along and kicks you in the butt. And she had no desire to be pulling Porter's Italian loafer out of her behind.

Her friend in the feed hat picked up a newspaper someone had left on the counter. He snapped it open and turned to the classifieds.

Pay dirt.

"Any good sales coming up?" Del turned on the swivel stool until she faced him.

"Missed a good 'un this Saturday, Delbert Perkins's place. His kin shipped 'im off to the home. Can't likely picture ole Delbert sitting in a rocker, sipping apple juice, and pissing in a diaper." Her friend clicked his false teeth. "Them young 'uns of his didn't hardly wait till his bag was out the door before they called in Sam and his outfit. Sold everything, even the family Bible." He adjusted his dentures with his tongue. "Now what kind of folks got that little respect for family, you tell me that."

Del made sympathetic noises in the back of her throat.

"I tell you what, anymores people think they can make two bits on somethin' and they get downright stupid." He took a loud slurp from his cup.

Shaking her head, Del added more cream to her cup. She could use a little stupid to good advantage right about now. "You get anything good?"

He grinned. "Lever action .22. Delbert was always right proud of that gun." Slapping his hand on the counter, he laughed. "I picked it up for only sixty dollars. Sam was madder than a tomcat with his tail caught in the garden gate."

Del smiled in appreciation. "Sounds like a good one. Was there not much turnout or just lazy bidders?"

"A bit of both. The regulars was all there, but they were keeping their hands in their pockets. Just the way I like it." He winked. "And there weren't no turnout from Springfield, either. Sometimes them dealers come over and you can't get a decent buy to save your granny's knickers."

"So this Sam, he any good?" A bigmouthed small-town auctioneer was just the kind of tour guide Del could use to her best advantage.

"Good enough. He's about the only game in town, 'bout run everbody else out. He knows how to work a crowd, gets people bidding so fast they lose track of what they're buying and for how much. Nobody seems to mind much, though, can't stay mad at Sam, especially the ladies." He threw her another wink. "You looking to go to a sale?"

Del picked up her cup. This Sam sounded perfect, a blowhard who imagined himself a charmer—an easy mark in Del's experience. "I might. Looks like I'm going to be here awhile."

"You a dealer?" Becca had wandered up with the empty coffeepot. She slipped behind the counter and grabbed another pot.

"Not exactly. I'm more looking to add to a collection." The Unruh collection for Porter to sell, but there was no need to explain that.

"Well, if you're looking for something special, you should see Sam. There's not a washboard in this county he doesn't know about. He scopes out his customers long before they're rolled feet first into Tyler's." Becca picked up a menu and wiped it with a wet cloth. "You want something else? It's getting close to noon. The lunch crowd'll be in soon."

Del glanced at the menu. One lonely little doughnut wasn't going to hold her any time at all. "How about chicken fried steak and mashed potatoes with gravy?" Del wouldn't be here long; she could afford a few extra calories.

While Becca scribbled her order on a pad, Del assessed her situation. She had one lead, this Sam. He sounded exactly the type she didn't want to deal with, but if you had to work a con, it was always better to target what you understood, and Del understood shysters.

"So you think this Sam could help me out?" She tapped her fifty-dollar manicure, a required expense in Porter's world, on the cup.

Becca raised one brow and looked Del up and down, pausing briefly on the pearl buttons of her shirt. "Oh, honey, he'll help you out. The only question is, out of what?"

Del smiled. She knew his type, all right.

"By the way, I'm Becca." The waitress pointed to her name badge. "I don't think I caught your name."

"Del, just call me Del."

"So what do you collect, Del?"

Glancing from Becca's stained apron up to her face, Del replied, "Pigs. I collect pigs."

Sam slung a bag of hog chow over his shoulder and slapped it onto the flatbed cart. Hog chow. Seemed like the animals in this county ate better than the people. Of course, eventually most of the animals got eaten by the people, so maybe it evened out.

He tipped his cowboy hat at the dirty-footed six-year-old girl who stood next to her father while he waited for their order to be rung up.

Tugging on her pigtail, he asked, "You taking care of them hogs for your daddy, Jenny?"

Twisting her neck to look up at him, she replied, "I can't. Eloise, she's fixin' to have babies. Mommy says she's feeling awful mean right now."

"Eloise?" Sam had known more than one woman who got a mite mean at about eight months along, but he'd never heard anybody say it out loud.

Jenny nodded. "Yep, she just lays outside her house in the mud and grunts at me." She leaned toward him and whispered, "If you look real close you can see the babies moving inside her." The girl seemed both fascinated and disgusted by the revelation. Sam understood the feeling.

"Eloise a sow?" he asked.

"Course." The look Jenny tossed him said he was four eggs shy of a dozen.

To be six again and so sure of your world.

"Daddy's expecting them piglets to come out any day now. I can't wait. They're Hampshires, you know."

At this proud declaration, Jenny's father gave her

a good-natured smack on the behind. "C'mon, girl, we need to get home and give Eloise a good spray with the hose. It's getting hot." He nodded at Sam and rolled his cart toward the parking lot.

Kenny nodded toward another cart loaded with dog food. "You mind rolling that out to the lot? Someone from the shelter's gonna stop by in a bit."

Free office space in the back of his friend's feed store meant a few unglamorous jobs now and again, but in addition to providing the free room, Kenny frequently helped Sam at the auctions, like he had on Saturday.

"Sure thing, boss." Imitating the tone Charlie'd used on him at the auction, Sam pulled his hat lower on his brow and sauntered over to the cart.

Outside the sun was bright and the air was crisp. Perfect day for an auction—too bad he didn't have another one scheduled for weeks. Sam let the cart roll down the cement ramp, holding the handle just tight enough to keep it from racing down and smacking into a blue Honda parked six feet from the door.

Wait a minute, what did we have here?

Peeking at Sam from behind the windshield of the car was about the finest-looking rear end he'd seen in . . . well, way too long. Covered in gray cloth, the butt in question wiggled and bobbed as its owner searched for something in the backseat.

Not wanting to get caught ogling a backside, Sam deserted the dog food. Whistling the theme from *Green Acres,* he hazarded one last glance and ambled back up the ramp.

* * *

Where were they? Wedged in between her bucket seats, Del struggled with her luggage. Somewhere in this mess she had a new pair of high-heeled sandals—strappy, completely impractical, and treacherously sexy.

Just the ticket for dealing with a womanizing shyster of an auctioneer, which is exactly how she had Sam Samson pegged. She knew his type, constantly hiking up his pants over a gut made bigger by the six-pack, winking and chuckling when he wasn't slapping backs (men) and butts (women). Yeah, she knew his type and his type called for man-eating shoes. The fat old codger wouldn't know what hit him.

Her fingers closed around white leather and beads. Bingo. Slipping back into her seat, she peered around. No one in sight. She hiked up her skirt and peeled off her pantyhose. This called for a bare-legged attack, a lot less ladylike and a lot more possibilities, at least in dirty old men's minds.

After tossing her jacket into the back, she undid three more buttons on her blouse and smoothed the material open until the hint of cleavage became reality. Perfect. After wiggling her toes into the shoes, she undid the snaps that concealed the slit in her skirt, swung her legs out onto the gravel lot, and headed into battle.

At the entrance to the feed store she hesitated. Was Samson's office really here, surrounded by goat chow and kibble? Sure enough, a letter-sized sign declared SAMSON AUCTIONS, IN THE BACK. She stepped inside.

The place was dark after the glaring sun of the parking lot, and it smelled of milled corn and animal by-products. The combination sent her whirling back in time to when she was maybe seven and waited for her daddy in a store just like this.

She'd perch herself near the door and wait while her daddy did whatever he did to con a few bags of dog food out of the owner. Daddy had a weakness for dogs, but there was never enough food to spare, not even scraps. When things got real lean, they'd head to town and after an hour or so he'd reappear grinning and laughing and towing a bag of kibble after him. There were days the dogs ate better than she did.

She shook her head to dislodge the memories. That was then. Now she could at least afford to eat, if not a lot more, as long as she kept her job.

To do that she needed to find the Pig.

First step that direction, Samson. Spying a blond surfer type in a cowboy hat behind the counter, she put a swish in her hips and sauntered over.

Hello.
The bodacious butt had made its way inside. Leaning on an old iron and wood scale, Sam took his time admiring the view. She was cast in silhouette by the bright sunlight outside, and every delectable inch of curve was revealed. Based on her outfit, he was guessing she wasn't here to load up on hog chow. No, she was looking for something, and if it wasn't feed, it was probably him.

He stepped back into his office and slid behind his desk. Let her come to him. Pulling out a folder, he slapped it open and strived to look busy.

It was less than two minutes before he heard the

clod of Kenny's boots followed by the "tap tap" of high heels.

"Sam, there's a lady here to see you." Kenny shot him a sullen look. The man needed to get over his Charlie-induced heartache so he could enjoy a few of life's simple pleasures—like Sam's visitor. Pushing his friend's problems from his mind, Sam gave her a quick glance.

A lady? He hoped not. That would be an awful waste.

Keeping his thoughts to himself, he lowered his pen and motioned her inside.

Blond hair, eyes the color of sweet tea, and breasts that peeped out of her shirt like they couldn't stand the containment and were aching to break free. Or maybe it was Sam aching for them to break free.

She cleared her throat. *Oh yeah, not proper to stare,* he reminded himself.

"I'm sorry. Did we have an appointment?" Sam pulled open his desk drawer and dropped the folder inside.

"No." She hesitated a moment as if weighing her words. "Do I need one?" Her hand drifted to the swell of her breasts. Sam swallowed—hard.

"Well, it's usual, but since you caught me here, why don't you sit down and tell me what I can do for you."

Or to you.

With a smile she slid onto the scarred wooden chair. She crossed her legs and let her foot bounce ever so slightly up and down. Her shoe, an impossible creation of twisted leather and beads, edged down her foot. She arched her foot and caught it, letting it dangle provocatively from her toes.

Those were not the shoes of a lady. No, those were shoes meant to be worn with red nail polish and nothing else—well, maybe the pearl necklace that hugged her throat. An image of her lounged in his chair wearing nothing but nail polish, pearls, and those do-me-now shoes slammed into him.

Damn, wasn't imagining the competition naked supposed to help negotiations? No, it was in underwear. Lacy push-up bra, thong, and a garter belt.

Not helping. Sam shifted in his seat. How about boxer shorts and a thin tank? His groin throbbed with enthusiasm. Definitely not helping. Maybe without the tank . . .

She coughed.

"Hmm?" He returned to reality.

Her sweet-tea eyes weren't looking too sweet right then. "Sorry, I've got a lot on my mind," he said.

"I can imagine." She drawled the words out like what she imagined was less than complimentary, but then smiled and leaned forward slightly, allowing another half inch of breast to peek out of her shirt.

"What can I do for you?" he repeated. Determined to maintain the upper hand, he concentrated on the light freckles sprinkled across her nose.

"Nothing too exciting, I'm afraid. I stopped in at that little coffee shop downtown—you know, the one with the cute crocheted bunnies in the window?"

Like there were a half dozen coffee shops in this town. Besides, of course he knew it; his cousin owned it. "I think I know the one you're referring to."

Her nose twitched, just like Samantha's on *Bewitched*. "Well, while I was there, I just happened to mention that I'm a collector and some folks there said I had to come see you, that you'd know just where I could find some nice buys."

Some folks, huh? What was Becca up to now? "That right? What is it you collect?"

His guest fluttered her hand in front of her face. "Is it hot in here?"

The movement broke Sam's concentration. His gaze drifted south of her nose. Lips, stop on the lips—full, with a perfect little bow at the top.

She puckered them, then fanned her shirt against her breasts. "Do you think I could get something to drink?"

His gaze locked onto the flapping material.

"Excuse me, do you think I could get something to drink?"

Startled, he grabbed some quarters from his lap drawer. "Sure, how 'bout a Coke?"

"Diet, please." Another nose twitch.

He wandered to the back, waving off a surly Kenny. After feeding the Coke machine, he returned with two ice-cold cans in his hands. He rolled one across his forehead before stepping back into the office.

His guest had moved. Now perched on the end of his desk, she looked flushed and a few strands of blond hair had fallen out of the silver clasp at the base of her head.

What was she up to? Sam glanced around the office, but nothing seemed out of place. Handing her the Diet Coke, he walked back to his chair.

"What did you say you collected?" he asked.

She tapped the top of the can with a perfectly

manicured nail. Watching him, she replied, "Pigs, I collect pigs."

Her eyes were alert, like she expected a response from him. "That's a pretty broad field, isn't it? Any certain kind of pig: cartoon like Porky and Petunia, or one to store your pennies, or maybe pigs on velvet?"

She hopped off his desk and dropped into a chair. "I take my collection very seriously."

Guess she didn't want any Elvis Porklies. "I'm sure you do."

"I collect all kinds, but since you ask, I do have a few holes in my collection—specifically pottery."

"Pottery pigs."

"That's right." The alertness was back in her eyes.

There was something going on with this woman, and her story was less believable than a politician's promise. "I don't think I caught your name."

"Del, Del Montgomery."

"You from around here?" he asked just to hear her answer. Everything about her screamed "city," but still there was a hint of country that popped up every so often too. The lilt of her voice and the way she didn't even question his choice of office space. Most city folks, especially ones dressed like her, wouldn't seem quite so comfortable wedged between sacks of chicken feed and a salt lick.

He really needed to make Kenny haul that crap out of here.

"Of course, you're Sam Samson, auctioneer extraordinaire."

Sam's eyes narrowed as he waited for a sarcastic

follow-up, but she just sipped from the Diet Coke can, then smiled.

"So, do you have any ideas of where I might find something for my collection?" she asked.

"I might." He didn't have anything to do, and this little number was just the ticket to get him out of his slump. "Why don't you let me make a few calls and I'll get back to you. My normal fee is thirty percent, but on a job like this I'd need to set a minimum, say a thousand?"

Her eyes flickered, and her fingers pinched the pearls at her throat, rolling them slightly, but she replied, "That sounds more than fair. I'll be staying at that little motel, The Ranch, I think it is. You can reach me there."

It wasn't until she had sashayed out that he realized she never told him where she was from. He picked up her deserted Coke can—still full. Origins weren't the only mystery surrounding his bodacious visitor.

Yep, she had a lot of layers, each one of them tantalizing. He couldn't wait to roll up his sleeves and start peeling.

Chapter 2

Silk purse or sow's ear . . .

Del yanked her shoes off and lobbed them into the backseat with a thump. Damn it. Where was the beer belly? The leering grin? The completely unattractive and totally malleable idiot she could twist around her high heel and wheedle into finding the Pig? Del whacked the back of her head against the seat, causing her vintage hair clip to jab into her scalp. She focused on the pain for a moment, blocking out how close she had come to screwing up.

Sam Samson was nothing like she'd expected. First, no beer belly, not even a pooch. And his grin? White, even, and annoyingly distracting. He didn't even leer. Okay, he looked and looked hard, but he covered well. She had practically popped a button shoving out her chest, and for what? Nothing. She was out of practice. There was a time that move produced visible drool in the intended victim, and today what—not even spittle.

Then, he'd almost caught her thumbing through his files. She'd been sure he'd take his time jawing with the surfer cowboy about her and her "assets." They always did. Heaven knew, there'd been plenty of times she'd wished men weren't such braggarts, but they were, and she'd learned to play it to her benefit. Then this one broke the rule—scurried right back with her Coke. She'd barely had time to hop onto his desk and, obviously, not enough to contrive a provocative pose. He'd just plunged on with the questions.

The worst of it was, now she was stuck with him. He was already suspicious. She knew it. If she tried to find the Pig without him, he'd be on her like cheap perfume on a cheating husband. She had no choice but to let him haul her to East Jesus and back, if that's what it took to convince him she was an empty-headed pig collector.

Pig collector—just thinking it made her cringe. Of all the things a person could collect, who in their right mind would collect pigs? And wasn't it reassuring everyone seemed to believe that she'd spend her time tracking down hog baubles and sow gewgaws?

Del twisted the key in the ignition and placed her bare foot on the accelerator. It could be worse. At least people seemed to like Samson. That might open some doors. There was always the possibility the pig in a poke would be tucked behind one of them.

Leaving the feed store and Samson behind in a cloud of dust, she shook her head. Problem was there was no telling what she'd have to look at, and buy, in the meantime. And all with tall, dark, and immune to her charms Sam Samson at her side.

* * *

Sam tipped his hat at a woman in a lime-green pantsuit he recognized from his auctions as he entered the diner. Becca was wiping down a table for two near the window. He strolled up behind her and tugged on her hair.

"What you been up to, cousin?"

Without looking at him, she slapped the dirty dishcloth into his hand and replied, "Make yourself useful and finish this table. Then you can tote that bin of dirty dishes into the kitchen."

Why did his cousin seem to think he worked for her? Maybe because growing up she'd hauled his butt out of the fryer on more than one occasion. Busing tables and hauling supplies was about the only way he had of repaying her right now, but when he got his auction house running and turning a profit, things would be different. Becca and her son, Clay, wouldn't want for anything—not if he had his way. Sighing, he wiped toast crumbs off the table and onto the floor.

The woman in green cleared her throat. "Son, that girl ain't gonna let you get away with that no more than she's gonna sprout wings and fly to Oz."

He looked from the woman to his cousin. Becca was pouring coffee for two octogenarian farmers, but her gaze was locked on him and the look wasn't friendly. He smiled at the woman and squatted down to capture the crumbs in the cloth. Tossing it in with the dirty dishes, he grabbed the bin and sauntered to the kitchen. Becca was right behind him.

"You raised in a barn?"

"I cleaned them up," Sam objected. "You fuss more than a mother hen one egg short." He leaned against a cardboard box. "Or maybe I should say a sow one teat short."

In her usual pragmatic manner, Becca shoved him to the side so she could reach the box. "Pigs don't worry about that. If their babies can't fend for themselves, they let 'em starve." She ripped open the carton and pulled out brown paper–wrapped packages. She shoved one in his hands and nodded to an empty napkin dispenser. "Fill that up."

"How'd you get so bossy?" he asked, his tone light.

Her hand on a carton of straws, she replied, "It's called survival. You know that."

When did her eyes get so sad? "What's wrong, Becca?"

She heaved out a breath and dropped a handful of straws into a round glass container. "Nothing new. This place isn't paying for itself. I'm working round the clock, 'cause I can't afford any more help, and I haven't got a check from Bud in six months."

Becca's good-for-nothing ex-husband had moved away eight months earlier. "He still in Festus?"

"Far as I know. He did send Clay a birthday card at least. Nothing in it but a five-dollar bill, but at least he remembered."

Sam put his arm around her and squeezed, talking into her hair. "It'll get better. You'll make it. We always do, don't we?"

He pretended not to notice as she wiped her eyes with the back of her hand.

"Speaking of money, I got a new job," he said.

She looked up at him, surprise brightening her eyes. "You quitting the auction business?"

"No, this is more a fill-in. Thought you might

know something about it, actually." He shoved a bunch of napkins into the black metal dispenser. "Woman came to see me, looking for pigs. You know anything about that?" He watched her out of the corner of his eye. His cousin was often guilty of hinting Sam should find a wife and a real job.

Becca shrugged and grabbed another box of straws. "Not much to know. She needed some help, and I told her about you. Said if anyone in this county had something to sell, you'd know about it. That not true?"

Sounded innocent enough, but if Becca didn't point Del his direction, who did? Someone with an old ax to grind? "So, she didn't ask about me first?"

Becca thought for a minute. "Not that I remember. She was talking to old Mr. Daniels when I walked up. I figured he told her about you. I just filled in the rest. Why?"

"No reason. Seems like a strange request from someone like her."

"You mean someone built like her." Becca grinned at him. "Don't think I don't know what you're thinking."

Glad she was smiling, Sam wiggled his eyebrows. "Oh, I noticed."

"You're terrible." Becca slapped his arm and reached for his now full napkin dispenser.

"It's not just her"—he cupped his hands over his chest, then got serious—"it's how she's dressed too and how she acts. There's something not right. All the pieces just don't fit together."

"And here I thought you figured out how to make the pieces fit together a long time ago." Becca winked.

Sam felt himself blush. For all his joking with her earlier, Becca had a talent for embarrassing him. He just wasn't comfortable talking about sex with his baby cousin.

Seeing his reaction, Becca chuckled. "You talk a big game, but when it comes right down to it, you've got less brass than a twenty-year-old doorknob."

Del unzipped her bag and pulled out her laptop. After unplugging the phone line, she attached it to her computer. While she waited for it to log on to the Internet, she unpacked. The Ranch Motel wasn't much. Sure wasn't going to be getting any five-star reviews real soon, but the room was clean and the woman at the front desk was friendly. In a town the size of Allentown that was about as much as you could hope for.

Del glanced at the computer screen—still chugging away. She shook the wrinkles out of three silk shirts and put them on hangers. Running her hand down one, she shook her head. What was she thinking when she packed? She couldn't go traipsing around town, routing through dirty junk dressed in silk. As soon as she got done with a little research she was going to have to find more practical clothes. In the meantime, she pulled on a T-shirt and knit shorts she'd brought to sleep in.

Her laptop finally finished its whirring and beeping, indicating it had established a connection. Pulling it into her lap, she prepared to explore. If she was going to impersonate a pig collector she was going to have to learn a lot more. Her knowledge of anything hog related was sadly lacking.

Two hours later she was a veritable pig pundit. Carousel pigs, advertising pigs, art deco pigs, all selling for thousands online. It was a hog-crazy world. Who knew? She snapped her computer shut and slid it into the bag.

Actually there'd been a couple things that were kind of nice. She was reflecting on whether a Shawnee cookie jar or a set of salt and peppers would look better next to her Goodwill cast-off dining room table, when her cell phone trilled.

Her boss's voice drilled out at her, "You found the Unruh Pig yet?"

Del reached for her pearls. The feel of the round, cool beads between her fingers reassured her. In a cheery tone, she replied, "Not yet, but I've found someone to help me in the search."

"Someone you know? Can we trust him?"

Porter *would* assume it was a man helping her. The fact that he was right just annoyed Del more.

"As much as anyone." How was that for a safe statement? No reason to give any more information than was one hundred percent called-for. Del had yet to meet anyone in her thirty-plus years on this earth she could trust.

"What did you tell him?" Porter's question mingled with muffled conversation from the other end of the line like Porter was holding his hand over the phone while talking to someone else. Nice to know she rated the same level of attention five hundred miles away as she did in person.

She waited for the sounds to stop before answering. "Nothing. He thinks I'm looking to add on to my pig collection."

"I'm glad to hear things are going as planned. They are going as planned, aren't they?"

Del opened her mouth to answer, but Porter continued, "Remember, the Unruh auction is in one month. You return with the Pig by then and it's yours. If you don't, it's David's."

On that sour note, he hung up. Del punched the "end" button. David's. A high-profile sale like an Unruh auction could make a career. Earn her some money to go with these pearls. She brushed her finger along the bumps. Porter had presented her with the pearls the day she completed her first sale. They were an honor, a symbol of the decorum and dedication it took for a woman to be successful in this business. They were her most treasured possession, but a little more cash wouldn't detract from them any, and a coup like the Unruh sale would secure her place as a full-fledged auctioneer, not just Porter's fill-in girl.

She had to find that Pig.

She glanced at her watch: seven. Wal-Mart would be open at least a couple more hours. She hadn't seen anything else in town except some dress shop that from the window displays catered strictly to victims of osteoporosis.

Wal-Mart would have to do for now. She hoped they had something to go with pearls.

The phone ringing woke her the next morning. Tangled in the sheets, she grabbed the thing seconds before she plopped over the side of the bed and onto the floor.

"Morning." Sam Samson's voice was cheery and loud, very loud. "You ready to start your hog hunt?"

Del didn't know about a hog hunt, but if it involved stringing up loudmouthed southern Missourians with no more sense than to call at—she yanked the sheet away from her face and glanced at the clock—six A.M. Son of a . . .

"You there?" the loud mouth bellowed out.

Taking a deep breath, she willed herself calm. Instinctively she reached for her pearls, but they were safely nestled in their velvet-lined case. She balled her hand into a fist instead. "Sure, I'm here. I was just untying my shoes. Just got back from an early morning jog."

There was a beat of silence on the other end of the line. "That a fact? You didn't strike me as the jogging type."

Del pushed herself to a sit. "And why is that?" One word about boobs and black eyes, and the loudmouth would be the first pig on her grill.

"Hard to say—the shoes, I guess. Don't imagine someone in shoes like that trotting around the block."

So, he'd noticed her shoes? "I don't jog in heels, you know." She practically purred in victory. Noticing was just a few steps shy of conquering.

"No, I don't imagine you do. Shoes like that are more suited for something else."

Del narrowed her eyes. What was that supposed to mean? What was he insinuating?

"Back to the reason I called," he continued. "Since you're up, I assume you can meet me in, say, an hour? At the Bunny Hutch. You can buy."

After flinging the receiver back on the cradle, Del

unraveled herself and went to shower. Promptly an hour later she stood outside the Bunny Hutch dressed in the cheapest, tightest denim to touch her butt in seven years.

She'd deliberated some on the shoes. Tennis shoes would have been practical and lent credence to her tale this morning, but, number one, she didn't own any and, number two, they were, well, ugly. She wasn't inordinately vain, but part of her plan was to distract Samson from her real mission. And despite the fact that she'd developed small but painful blisters overnight, she'd slipped back on the man-eaters from the day before.

Pausing in front of the window that housed the bunnies, she checked her reflection. Tight denim and high heels—all she was missing was the trailer-trash hair and the Tammy Faye eye makeup, but she had to admit the tight, stretchy denim held in her behind, making her look a full size smaller. That had to be good, as long as they held.

Feeling more than a little discomfited by the thought of her pants splitting and her lace undies spilling out, she pulled her shoulders back and yanked open the door. The cowbell dangling overhead clanked at her arrival, and a roomful of feed hats turned to stare.

Best cure for embarrassment—pure unabashed brazenness. She flipped her silver-blond hair over her shoulder and sashayed inside. Her target was sitting in a booth near the kitchen, his legs crossed and his cowboy hat hooked on one boot.

With each tap of her four-inch heels, her trepidation grew. Yesterday she'd been so annoyed to discover he wasn't the bumbling buffoon she'd expected, she hadn't spent a great deal of time analyzing too much more about him. Today, under the flicker of fluorescent lights he was impossible to ignore. His simple black T-shirt hugged his body, outlining a developed chest and stretching over bulging biceps. What did he do to earn those? Toting furniture to sales or slinging feed sacks? Either way, the results were impressive.

Look somewhere else. His face showed signs of his profession, too—tan and that killer smile. He flashed it again. As she approached the table, he grabbed his hat, stood up, and waved her into a booth.

He turned his back for moment as he signaled Becca to bring more coffee. Del took the opportunity to analyze him up close, strictly to size up the competition, of course. Broad shoulders tapered to a firm waist, adorned by a horsehair belt. She was in the process of rating his butt—mint or just near mint—when he turned back around and slid into the booth across from her.

"So, how far'd you go?" he asked.

She blinked. "Excuse me?"

"Your run, how far'd you go?"

"Oh, a few miles." Did that sound reasonable?

"You must have gone right past the store then, but I didn't see you." His blue eyes were full of innocence, just like a moonlit pond full of piranhas.

"I'm fast." She flipped her coffee mug over with a clink. "Did you have some places for us to go today?"

Sam waited for Becca, who had just walked up with the coffeepot, to fill their cups and leave.

"Hope you don't mind, I went ahead and ordered for us. Got a full day, you know."

Del did mind. She'd been looking forward to another tractor tire this morning. Maybe she could sneak one for the road.

She poured an inch of cream into her coffee. "Anything promising?" she asked, striving for just casual interest.

Sam stared at the pale liquid in her cup. "Guess you don't have to worry about your weight."

Not looking up, Del stiffened. Her hand went to her pearls. "Are you saying I need to?" Who did he think he was, making comments about her weight?

He set his coffee down with a thunk. Black liquid sloshed over the side onto the red Formica. "No, no, just meant with you running and all, then the cream . . ."

Del tapped her spoon against the china cup. Maybe he thought she was too heavy, maybe he didn't; either way she knew when to use something to her own advantage, even something she was as sensitive about as her dress size. Blinking a tear to the surface, she looked up. "Where did you say we were going today?"

Hell. Why had he said that? Why did women have to be so touchy about their weight?

A few extra pounds, especially in the right places, which Del's were, weren't something to cry over. He hadn't even meant that. He was just trying to catch her in a lie. She'd no more been jogging at six in the morning than he'd been warming a church pew. She was a fake and he knew it. But she was a fine fake, and now she was crying. He felt as worthless as cracked carnival glass.

"I got some real good leads," he hurried to say. "Don't know that we'll even be able to fit them all in today. You planning on staying awhile?"

She sniffled and dug into a tiny red purse. "Darn it. Where's my compact?" Leaning across the table, she said, "Is my mascara smudged?"

Sam fought to pull his gaze from her breasts, which were now pushed upward by the pressure of the tabletop beneath them. He could even make out the edge of white lace peeking from the top of her scoop-necked T-shirt. If she'd move just a little closer . . .

She heaved a deep breath. Almost . . .

"Is it?" she asked.

He jerked his gaze upward into those innocent sweet-tea eyes.

"My mascara, is it smudged?"

Who in the blue blazes cared? Who was gonna notice? Dipped in denim and balanced on those screw-me shoes, she was a walking invitation to riot.

"It's fine," he gritted out. "But those shoes have to go. We aren't going to the country club. You'll break an ankle wearing those things and we've got a lot of places to get to. You have to keep up."

Becca, walking up with a loaded tray, raised an eyebrow at the annoyance in his tone. He ignored her. He was in no mood for a lecture on manners. He had a day jam-packed with visits to every dirty hole-in-the-wall junk shop in a thirty-mile radius ahead of him, and the Ozarks's answer to Jayne Mansfield would be bouncing along beside him. It was like waving a ham hock in front of half-starved

hound. He was going to be growling and snapping
all day, and the rest of the world just better keep
the hell away.

Del was trapped in hog hell. She'd sucked down
more dirt in the past two hours than a Hoover in
a chicken coop. Why did the man insist on driving
with the windows down? Hadn't he heard of air-
conditioning?

The only plus was that the air blasting through
the cab took with it the scent of Sam's cologne. Not
that it was an unpleasant smell—no, unfortunately,
it was quite the opposite. Some kind of citrus blend
that reminded her of fresh-squeezed lemonade
poured over hand-chipped ice—tangy and sweet,
cool and tempting.

Not the way she wanted to think of Sam.

She wasn't sure the trade-off was a good one,
though. Her hair was knotted and there was enough
dust in her cleavage to grow corn. He had to be
doing it just to irritate her. Something he had a real
talent for. As she was picking a strand of dead grass
from between her breasts, he asked, "Is the wind
bothering you?"

Her, bothered? Moron. She pasted on a brainless smile, laughed, and replied, "No, I love fresh
air." Sticking her head out the window, she inhaled
deeply—just as they passed the feeder pig lot. She
snapped her mouth shut and yanked her head
back inside. "What the hell is that smell?"

"Pigs. I thought you liked pigs." He grinned at
her like the buffoon she wished he was. "Anybody

claims pigs don't stink hasn't gotten closer to one than a pork chop."

That was four chews closer than Del wanted to be to anything hog related right now—unless it was made of pottery and capable of bringing in six-figure bidders.

Sam had dragged her down every gravel road and into every glorified yard sale in the county. To keep up the pretense, she'd shelled out two hundred dollars of Porter's cash on anything that even hinted of hog. At least she hoped it was Porter's cash. If she didn't find the Unruh Pig, there was no way she was seeing a reimbursement check. She'd be the proud owner of pails of pig paraphernalia and no job to pay for them.

She glanced at her tour guide. His straw cowboy hat was pushed back on his head. Smiling to himself at some private joke she suspected involved her, he flipped on the radio. Hank Williams Sr. began serenading them, claiming a "new dog's moving in."

Sheesh, this was more than she could handle. Not only did she hate the twangy tunes, but they also brought back discomfiting memories of riding in a much older truck down similar roads as a child. "Can't you find something from this century?"

Sam tipped his hat even farther back on his head and turned his blue gaze on her. "This is classic."

"If you want classic, let's talk Zeppelin or Lynyrd Skynyrd, not this crap." She flicked off the radio.

"My truck, my music." He flipped the radio back on and rolled the volume a few notches higher. Hank was now busy inviting some sweet mama to go stepping out.

Thinking she'd like to do some throwing out, if not up, Del crossed her arms over her chest and slumped in her seat. Her act was wearing thin and she was beginning not to care. So what if Samson figured out she wasn't some bimbo with no more sense than to wander the countryside with him hunting pigs? So what if he found out about the Unruh Pig? His office was in a feed store, for God's sake. He couldn't offer the seller the big-money buyers Porter Auctions could, and if the seller just wanted hard, cold cash, Samson would never be able to outbid Porter.

Her tormentor slapped his hand against the steering wheel in time to the music. She rolled her eyes in response. He was a confident son of a bitch, that was for sure. And knowing him, if she stiffed him, he'd make a stink that would bring every Unruh collector and beady-eyed auctioneer in the country down on them. No, she had to keep up her act. She had to act sweet—damn him to hog hell and back.

"Last stop of the day." Samson bumped to a halt in front of the biggest, sorriest excuse for an antiques shop east or west of the Mississippi.

A hand-painted sign, declaring their latest stop as IZZY'S HOUSE OF ANTIQUES AND COLLECTABLES, teetered above a ramshackle porch. The main building was roughly only fifty feet by fifty feet, but additional structures had been tacked on willy-nilly as the inventory grew. Izzy, being a resourceful sort, had used anything and everything at his disposal to enhance his domain. The latest seemed to be an old railroad refrigerator car. Another hand-lettered

sign propped by the steps declared the establishment was OPEN.

Del snapped her gaze from the shop down to
her hands. She'd been so preoccupied with Sam
and his complete lack of musical taste, she'd completely missed where they were headed. Izzy's.
Who'd have thought the old trader would still be
in business? And who'd have thought by the
roundabout way Samson got here that this was
where he was headed, anyway?

No hope for it, she was going to have to brazen
her way through—what else was new?

She tilted her head upward and eyed the dilapidated monstrosity with what she hoped was
trepidation. "What is this place?"

"You mean you've never heard of Izzy's? I thought
you were from around here." He assessed her for a
moment before pulling the keys out of the ignition.
"Oh, that's right, you never said where you were
from, did you?"

About now she should twist a lock of hair around
one finger, or chew on her lower lip, or whip off
her shirt and show off Victoria's Secret, but she was
dirty, tired, and in no mood whatsoever to play the
vamp. Instead she shot him an irritated look and
hopped out of the cab onto the rutted dirt. Maybe
if she was rude enough, he'd get ticked off and
leave her—or at least leave her alone long enough
to search out Izzy and convince him not to blow
her cover.

One step onto the wooden planks that led to the
railroad car and the heel of her man-eaters, which
she'd refused to change, lodged into an open
knot. Losing her balance, she fell face forward

onto her knees. A slew of cuss words she usually re-
served for private flew out of her mouth.

"My, for a lady like yourself, you have quite an
impressive vocabulary, don't you? You learn those
words the same place you got those pearls?" Sam
stood behind her, not bothering to help her up.

She had yanked her shoe from the board and
was considering nailing him right between his
bright blues with it, when his comment on her
pearls registered. What was she doing? She was letting him get to her, that was what. She had to be in
control. Talking trash and throwing shoes was not
how an auctioneer from one of the top auction
houses in the country comported herself.

Pearls—decorum and taste. Hurling sandals—
improper and unemployed.

She stroked the pearls for her benefit, then for
his, raised her leg, and, resting her bare foot
against his thigh, said, "Would you mind?" She concentrated on making her eyes round and innocent.

His mouth fell open and his gaze dropped to
her magenta-tinted toes. She waggled her missing
shoe at him, then in a delicate motion tossed it
into his open hand. He stared at the sandal, then
her foot, like he wasn't sure what to do next.

She fluttered her toes. When he still seemed
frozen in place, she leaned back, showing her
pearls, and what was under them, to full advantage.
He wanted war; she had all the ammunition.

Chapter 3

Everything but the oink . . .

What was going on with her? Sam had never seen
a woman switch from victim to vamp as quick as
this one. One minute she was fixin' to cry, the next
she was fluttering her eyelashes and flashing her
cleavage. That was hard enough to handle, but this
new trick—hothead to hoochie in three seconds
flat—was a head-spinner. He wasn't sure he even
knew some of the words she'd been spewing, and
the look on her face had been deadlier than a two-
headed rattler. Now she was melt-in-your-mouth
sweet and her pink-tipped toes were kneading his
leg just inches from his crotch.

He didn't know whether to jump on her or
run for the hills. Course, he was a man willing to
live dangerously if the payoff was big enough
and, looking at Sweet Tea here, he had no doubt
it was.

Why was he grinning at her? What happened to
the hunted-rabbit look of just seconds before? Del

started to jerk her foot off Sam's leg, but before she could pull it to safety he wrapped one sturdy hand around her ankle.

"I thought you wanted me to help." His voice was soft, smooth, and more dangerous than a Gatlin Gun at a preschool picnic. After dropping her shoe to the ground, he kept one hand on her ankle and used the other to massage her calf. "You didn't pull anything, did you? That looked like a rough spill." His eyes flickered like the flame in a stove.

Del's heart picked up its pace and a strange exhilaration started building deeper in her chest. What was he doing?

Whatever it was, it felt grand. She relaxed her foot against his leg, and he shifted his grip so both hands were kneading her calf. Del was not used to four-inch heels. They were get-what-you-want shoes, not all-day-long-tramping-around-the-country shoes. The feel of his hands on her calf was about the best thing she'd felt in . . . she couldn't remember when. And she couldn't help but imagine what those hands would feel like climbing higher and higher on her leg, until he was forced to kneel down onto the ground, hover above her, and . . .

She moaned.

The flicker in Sam's eyes shot to a blaze. He lowered her leg and bent forward as if he'd read her thoughts and was ready to join her there on the dirty walkway.

"You'uns got a problem?"

Izzy Malone leaned against a nearby oak. Hanging from the hook that served as his left hand was a bucket of roots. He used his other arm, which ended in a stump, to push a short-brimmed hat off his forehead.

Sam, halfway to the ground, grabbed Del's arm and yanked her to her feet. Unable to balance on one heel, she stumbled against him. She pressed her face against Sam's shirt and peered at Izzy through a curtain of fallen hair. He hadn't recognized her—yet.

Izzy squeezed one eye shut and spit a brown line of tobacco into the dirt at his feet. "Didn't recognize you, Sam, what with you being all busy when I walked up." He grinned, revealing surprisingly white, even teeth. "Who's that you got with you? That's not—"

Del slipped out of her lone shoe, stepped away from Sam, and shoved her hand out to Izzy. "Del Montgomery. It's nice to meet you." She kept her gaze steady, willing him to play along.

Izzy looked from her hand to her face, then at Sam. Looking back at Del, he said, "I'm not much for hand shakin', but in your case I'll make an exception." With a wink at Sam, he held out his arm.

Del grasped the leathery skin in her hand and gave it a squeeze. She was going to pay for this favor, but whatever the cost, it was better than Sam discovering her past and leaking her presence in southern Missouri to her family, or the authorities. Izzy she could handle. She hoped.

She sneaked a smile of gratitude at her father's old crony.

In return, Izzy gave a small shake of his head, then turned to Sam. "I'm glad you stopped by. I been meaning to call you. I got a mess of stuff in that shed." He pointed to a small freestanding building.

It would take Sam an hour just to get through the debris piled in front of the entrance, never mind sorting through whatever he found inside. Del hoped he'd had a tetanus shot recently.

"You look around in there," Izzy continued. "See what you think you can sell for me, and I'll show the little lady around. Take right good care of her." He effectively dismissed a dumbfounded Sam by turning his back on him and nudging Del up the plank walkway into the railroad car.

With the door snapped firmly behind them, Izzy turned on her. "Lilah Mont, what are you up to? Your daddy know you're this close to home?" He wandered over to a hot plate, where a kettle of water sat warming. "You want tea? It's Earl Grey."

Del nodded.

He poured the water into china cups adorned with roses and, balancing one on his stump, handed it to her.

Del needed time to think. "You're looking good, and I see you've added on some." She thumped on the wall of the train car.

"New teeth." Izzy pushed his dentures forward, out of his mouth. "Guy over in Daisy Creek charged me just ninety-nine dollars for them."

"They're nice. Probably beating the ladies off with a stick, aren't you?" Smiling, she took a sip of tea. So far, so good.

"No more'n usual." Flashing her a wink, he continued. "You want sugar?" He shoved a silver bowl full of white cubes her direction.

She took one along with a sigh of relief. This

was going to be easier than she'd imagined. Izzy might be a tough old bird, but he had a weakness for feminine wiles. She'd charm him into seeing things her way.

He slurped from his cup. "Your daddy know you're here?"

Old coot. What did it take to shake him? She deserted her tea to wander around the room. "This train car is a nice touch. You ever think of painting the outside red?" Turning toward him, she tried her perkiest smile. "It would look really pretty red."

"I ain't seen him in a bit." Izzy kept talking. "But I run into your mama just t'other day. You take after her, you know."

Del wished she took after her mama, but she was afraid most of her genes fell from the Mont side of the tree. She pressed her palm against the painted wood of the train car wall. The last thing she wanted to discuss was her family, but she couldn't resist hearing more.

"Where'd you see her?" she murmured.

"Down to Henning. First time I'd seen her at a sale in twenty years."

So now Del's daddy had her mama up to his crooked tricks. "She buy anything?" Del asked.

"Not that I saw."

If she was doing the job Del suspected, Izzy wouldn't have seen her buy anything—just bid and only then when her mama was confident that some sucker wanted the item bad enough to lose track of value and sense.

Del dropped all pretense. "What's it going to take for you to forget you saw me?"

Izzy slipped off his hat and placed it on a set of

steer horns that hung near the door. "Well, now your daddy's never done me wrong, and he can be a real good customer, not to mention contact. He's nosed out more than one deal I got a piece of." Returning to his seat, he took a sip of tea. As a child, Del had been fascinated by how he could handle such delicate china with just a hook and a stub where his hands should have been. Now, she just watched with the wariness of a cornered cat. He was going somewhere, and she was pretty sure it wasn't going to be to her liking.

"What I'm wondering is what brought you back, seeing as how you aren't wanting your daddy to know you're here."

As far as Del was concerned, he could keep wondering. Telling Izzy about the Unruh Pig would make as much sense as setting a coon loose in a corncrib.

"Yep, you show up here with that young feller, Samson, calling yourself some citified name, and you seem real eager to hush me up before I can twist the top off your jar of worms."

He set the cup down and pulled a foil pack of tobacco from his pocket. "You gonna tell me what kind of worms you're digging for?"

"It's nothing like that. I started collecting some since I moved, and Sam's helping me hunt down some pieces."

A stream of tobacco juice shot from Izzy's lips into a dented brass spittoon. "How's about the name?"

"I changed it." Her arms crossed under her breasts, she kept her expression firm.

Izzy stared her down.

How much to tell him? Too much and her daddy'd find out she was working at Porter's. He'd show up at a sale and ruin everything she'd worked to create. Del's hand jumped to her throat. The pearls were still there. Just thinking about her daddy and past mistakes made her doubt their existence. Real or not, word of her earlier life reached Porter and she and her pearls would be pitched to the curb.

Clasping her necklace, Del took a deep breath. "There are a few things in my past I'd as soon didn't get out, okay? Changing my name was one way to keep it from coming back and biting me."

"Changing your name don't change who you are or where you come from. Besides, I don't recollect you doing anything too bad."

He wouldn't. Izzy's moral yardstick was missing a foot or two.

Del shrugged.

Switching his chaw from his left cheek to his right, Izzy sighed. "So, what you collecting? If you ain't going to be upfront with me, might as well make a sale—or thirty."

Great, more pigs and, knowing Izzy, they weren't going to be cheap. Of course, there was always the chance he'd be the connection to the Pig in question.

"Pigs. I collect pigs." No matter how many times she said it, she still felt like an idiot.

To her continued annoyance, Izzy didn't seem surprised. "I can see that. When you was little you toted that toy hog everywhere you went, then there was that runt. What was his name?"

"Toadstool." Or as daddy had called him, ham. Del didn't want to discuss Toadstool any more than she wanted to discuss past business ventures with her father.

"So, you have any pigs?" she asked.

Izzy tilted back in his chair. She could see the cogs spinning. If there was a slice of bacon to be found within a twenty-mile radius, he'd sniff it out and sell it to her—for three times its worth.

She picked up a miniature stoneware jug and turned it over—no mark. She set it back down. "I'm particularly fond of pottery. You know of any pottery pigs?"

Izzy scratched his chin with his hook. "I think I got a McCoy cookie jar, and maybe some little pigs what come from England."

Del's hand tightened around a perfect example of an advertising mini jug. She glanced at the price— two hundred dollars. Late 1800s saloon piece, it would easily sell at auction for seven hundred.

"Then there's some kind of vase thing, it's what you might call unique." Izzy paused and Del froze, forcing herself to pick up a different tiny jug.

"What makes it unique?" she asked as casually as she could.

"I'll dig it out and you'll see." As Izzy pushed himself out of his chair, the cowbell clanged, announcing Sam had finished with the shed, or let what Del suspected was his untrusting nature get the best of him.

The way Sam's gaze snapped around the room, Del felt safe in her assumption, and based on his appearance, she was willing to hazard another guess, that Izzy's shed housed more trash than treasure. Sam's face was red, his Levi's were covered in dust and oil, and a cobweb dangled from his hat like a medieval princess's veil.

"You find anything good?" she asked, barely containing a grin.

He turned his gaze on her. Frost replaced the blaze from earlier.

Touchy. Del did grin this time.

"What you find out there, son? Anything you're interested in?" Izzy poked his tobacco package into his shirt pocket.

Sam stayed focused on Del. "If you want to haul it to my next sale, I'll sell it. What you two been discussing in here?"

Izzy strolled toward the far end of the room where a door led into the rest of the shop. "Just jawing. The little lady says she has a fondness for pottery pigs."

Sam raised a brow. "That's right. She mentioned that before. With any luck you'll have as much to offer Del, here, as your shed offered me." He continued to watch Del, the look on his face almost taunting.

Why did he have to be so suspicious? Time for another diversion.

Del ambled closer. Brushing her hand up the back of his neck, she snared the cobweb. "I'm full of surprises," she murmured.

The blue flame returned and Sam took a pace toward her. Stepping back, Del dangled the cobweb in front of his face. "Don't want to be tracking dirt into this fine establishment, now do you?"

"You'uns comin'?" Izzy peered at them from the doorway.

Sam snatched the cobweb from Del's hand and

whispered in her ear, "You keep this up and there's no telling what I'll be wanting to do in this fine establishment." As he sauntered past, Del caught another whiff of his lemony cologne, made even stronger by the physical exertion of clearing out the shed.

Nothing beat a tall drink of lemonade on a hot day, and Del had a feeling this day was about to get a lot hotter.

What games was this woman playing? Sam was tired of trying to figure her out and was about ready to launch a counteroffensive.

In addition to the sexual innuendos targeted at him, she and Izzy were up to something. Sam knew it. There was nothing in that shed worth more than a ten-spot, and Izzy had never consigned anything with Samson Auctions before. Funny how right after he got a glimpse of Sweet Tea he'd want to. Course, Sam couldn't blame any man for wanting to be alone with her, but he had a feeling Izzy's motive was something other than getting an eyeful of Del's cleavage.

Sam was on to them. It was just a matter of time before he figured out their game.

He followed Izzy into the next building, not sparing a glance at Del. Time for her to wonder, maybe even worry, a little.

Entering the main structure of Izzy's complex, Sam paused to let his eyes adjust to the darkness. Fluorescent lights struggled to illuminate the space, but major portions were abandoned to gloom. Izzy scampered ahead, weaving in and out of the mess of antique furniture like a squirrel dodging traffic on a busy highway. Behind Sam, Del wasn't having as easy a go of it.

She thumped into something. "Shit," she muttered.

Sam smiled. Teach her to go around barefoot. He'd thrown her shoes into the cab of his truck after she and Izzy had deserted him outside. Not that those shoes would be much use in here, but Sam for one was happy to be fully shod.

"Now this here's a nice one." Izzy held a pig-shaped pitcher in his hand. "I've got twenty-five on it, but I'd be willing to come down a little for you."

Del stumbled up and removed the item from his hand. While she examined it, Sam scanned the contents of the room. In a dark corner he noticed something hanging from the rafters.

"What's that?" He interrupted Del and Izzy, who seemed to be in full-speed haggle mode.

Engaged in what was apparently a deal to the death, they ignored him.

"What is that?" His voice came out with slight squeak. Trying to cover, he repeated, "What is that hanging in the corner?" He pointed to the small object.

This time Izzy looked over. "That's just Wilbur. He won't hurt you none. He keeps the skeeters down."

"What is he?" As Sam's heart began to beat faster, Del watched him with curiosity. Sam suspected his interest in the mysterious creature was far from masculine, but at the moment, he couldn't have cared less.

"Just a little ole brown bat. He moved in this

summer. I kind of like having him around." Izzy glanced at Wilbur with a fond expression.

Sam felt the blood leave his head. He had to get out of there. "I just remembered something I wanted to look at in the shed. I'll meet you out front." With that, he turned on his heel and made for the bat-free safety of his truck.

As he crossed the threshold into the railroad car, he heard Del ask Izzy, "How about that unique piece you told me about. It around here?"

Nice to know she was wasn't letting concern for him keep her from shopping. Not that he wanted her to comment on his little aversion to bats, but still you'd think she'd want some company besides Izzy's in the dark depths of his shop.

Sam let the door slam behind him with a bang. Hope they had a humdinger of a time rooting through that mess for hogs without him.

Del surfaced from Izzy's House of Antiques an hour later with three hundred fewer dollars and twenty more pigs. How could one man accumulate so much junk, not to mention pigs? And, of course, she'd been forced to buy every last one. Izzy's loyalty didn't come cheap, and his "unique" pig vase was some ugly mottled mess that appeared to have been shaped by an untalented three-year-old.

The overall idea was disturbingly similar to what a pig by Unruh would look like, just out of the wrong clay, with no glaze, and, well, hideous. Del had bought it because she had no choice. She'd probably drop it in a trash bin as quick as she could. The end of her visit with Izzy had made the trip worthwhile though. She had snagged the saloon mini jug for only one hundred dollars. Just thinking about the potential for profit made her smile.

She was glad Sam had left too. A bit surprised, but happy. It would have been tough to wrangle with Izzy in front of Sam without Sam getting wise to her act. She'd kept the horse-trading to a minimum at their earlier stops. She felt evidence of too much talent in that area would raise Sam's suspicions. But if she had taken Izzy at his first price, he would have known something major was up too.

Anyone who knew a Mont knew they didn't take the first price offered, or the second, or the fifth. Hard dealing was a point of pride with her father's family, and one of the few inherited characteristics Del took satisfaction in.

She trotted down the boardwalk, tucking the newspaper-wrapped mini jug more securely into the brown grocery bag as she went. Sam was sitting in his truck with the driver's side door open.

"Thought you were checking out something in the shed," she commented.

"Thought you were lost under a pile of pigs. What took you so long?" He strode to her side, pulled the bag out of her arms, and dropped it into the truck bed. It landed with a muffled thud.

"Hey, be careful with that." Del eyed the small package on top.

"Yeah, wouldn't want to crack a choice cut." He walked to the passenger side and yanked the door open.

Men, what a pain in the patootie. If it was their project you could cool your heels for hours, but take a few minutes for your own interests and they got all snippy. And she was paying this one for the privilege.

"What got your tail in a knot?" Del climbed into the truck and snapped on her seat belt.

"Nothing." He slammed the truck into gear and peeled out of the lot.

They rode in silence back to Allentown. As Sam backed into a space down the hill from the Bunny Hutch, Del gave him a sidelong glance. What had him in such a snit?

"So, what time tomorrow?" she asked.

"You want more?" Sam gave the back of his truck, where her day's accumulation sat, an incredulous look.

"Yeah, but I was thinking it might be good to see some private collectors. Becca at the Hutch said you knew what people around here had in their homes. Today you just took me to shops."

"There something wrong with that?" His tone held a challenge.

"Yeah, since I'm paying you I'd appreciate it if you'd do something to earn your commission. I could've hauled myself into the dirty holes you took me to today."

"Why didn't you?" He unsnapped his seat belt and leaned closer. "Why did you hire me in the first place?"

He wanted to be direct, fine. Del could handle it. She blinked but kept her voice steady. "I hired you to help me find pigs I couldn't find on my own. Based on what Becca said, I thought you knew people around here. I thought you could find me some nice pieces I couldn't find on my own, but all you've done is work as a chauffeur without the fringe benefits." She gestured at the dusty interior of his truck.

His eyes glimmered. Del stared at the mesmerizing blue of them. She felt herself lean forward, pulled toward him as surely as a moth to a bug zapper. The pressure of her seat belt wedging between her breasts stopped her, but Sam, unfettered, moved closer.

"I been wondering about those fringe benefits too," he murmured.

Del knew the instant his hat hit the floor she was in trouble.

Chapter 4

Little pig, little pig, let me in . . .

Del was telling tales again, or at least doing some major evading. Her nose was twitching like a caged rabbit sitting next to a pile of carrots. She must stink at poker.

Course, a little white lie or two didn't bother Sam, especially when the liar was so easy to read and—he glanced at the seat belt slashed between her breasts—so desirable.

He edged closer on the seat, watching her big brown eyes grow round with trepidation. He grasped her seat belt, near where it snapped into the truck's seat.

"This too tight? I don't want you complaining about being uncomfortable." He gave the strap a little tug, allowing it to pull his hand against her hip. "Seems tight to me, but that's safer, isn't it? You like to play safe, Del?" He ran his palm up the length of the nylon strip, the back of his hand skimming her hip, side, stomach. He paused right below her chest.

Del sucked in her breath, like that would put distance between them, but it only made her breasts appear larger. Sam chuckled. "You don't strike me as a woman who only plays safe. I think maybe you've broken a rule or two."

Her eyes narrowed until only a sliver of brown was visible. Seeing his opportunity about to explode in another mercurial moment, Sam slid his hand into her hair, anchoring her head in place, and tilted his face toward hers.

Of all the arrogant, asinine men she'd known, this one took the trophy. Del opened her mouth to say as much, but Sam's lips blocked her words. Her first instinct, to shove him across the truck cab and out the side window, melted under the firm pressure of his lips on hers.

The man could kiss. Del admired good technique wherever she found it. Forgetting the flash of anger at his insinuation she wasn't one hundred percent honest, she wrapped her arms around his body and let her fingers dance down the muscles of his back.

She didn't care what anyone said, there was nothing sexier than a strong, muscular male back, and this one was perfect. Finding the fan of muscle that tapered to his waist, she sighed into his mouth. Apparently taking her reaction as encouragement, Sam unsnapped her seat belt, then slid his arm behind her and under her shirt. Warm fingers massaged sensitive skin. She tensed as they climbed toward her bra, but Sam only skimmed the elastic band. His hand settled above it and began to knead the tension from her upper back. Del groaned. She had never experienced anything so heavenly.

Tilting her back against the window, Sam explored her neck and down into the hollow of her throat with tiny tugging kisses. As he approached her cleavage, she again stiffened, but when he traced the neckline of her Wal-Mart tee with his tongue, she realized her usual hang-up over men diving into what they saw as prime real estate right off the bat wasn't a bad thing at all. In fact, she was beginning to think it was wickedly wise.

Maybe she should do a little drive-by of her own.

Before she could extract her arms from around his back, he shifted his lips to her ear. His tongue flicked forward, followed by a warm breath. Del shivered in response. Her body arched upward in invitation.

With a low, sexy laugh, Sam whispered in her ear, "Why did you hire me in the first place?"

What? Why was he talking? Del reached to pull his face back to hers, when his question registered. Why did she hire him?

He was playing her. Her. *He* was playing *her*.

The blood surging through her veins slowed to an irritated drip. No one played a Mont. She should have stuck with her first instinct. Eager to make up for lost time, she shoved him across the truck.

He grinned at her from the driver's seat. "What? It's a fair question."

She was going to kill him. Better, she'd call up every Mont in southern Missouri and have him hog-tied and prepped for dinner before he'd kicked off his boots and loosened that fancy belt for bed. Her gaze dropped to his horsehair belt, but something lower grabbed her attention.

Wait a minute. All was not quiet on the southern front. A slow smile spread across her face.

Amateur. You should always know your limits or at least do a good job of camouflage.

She crept across the seat. Lightly brushing his five o'clock shadow with her fingers, she put on her best Marilyn Monroe—innocent but full of promise. "Why do you think I hired you?"

She let her hand drift down his chest toward the bulge that revealed his deceit. With her hand touching denim, she leaned closer and slid her tongue lightly over his lips. As the expression in his eyes changed from cocky to carnal, she jerked back and leaped from the truck.

"I told you, to find pigs. You need to start listening," she said.

At his disconcerted stare, she added, "Oh, and you might want to put some ice on that." She pointed to his groin. "We've got a lot of pigs to hunt down tomorrow and you have to keep up." She paused. "But I guess that's your problem right now, isn't it?" With a laugh, she slammed the truck door and headed to her car.

Sam stayed in his truck for a good half hour. She was a ballsy one, Miss Pig-Hunting-Pearl-Wearing Montgomery. Waiting for the throbbing in his groin to subside, he had no choice but to reflect on their latest battle. Beginner's mistake, underestimating the competition. As much as he would have enjoyed winning this particular struggle, he couldn't help but admire a worthy rival. And this rival had plenty to admire.

He picked his favorite hat off the floor and brushed it off. At least she wasn't a stomper. His ego could stand a blow or two, but not his Stetson. In his current financial state, he didn't have sixty bucks to spare on a new one, and a feed hat might keep the sun out of your eyes, but the effect was a little too farm boy for Sam. With his office in a feed store, he was walking a thin line in that regard anyway.

He dusted off the brim of his hat and slipped it on his head. What had he learned today? Nothing much. Since she sashayed into his office, he'd been sure her pig collecting story was, well, hogwash. But she'd bought plenty of pigs. So either she truly wanted the little oinkers or she had cash to burn for her cover.

If it was all a cover, what was it for? Why would a woman like Del hunt him out? What was her motive? Sam tapped his fingers on the steering wheel.

Armstrong? He hadn't booked an auction in Allen County in a year. Had he heard about Sam's plans to expand? Was he taking steps to stop Sam, to maybe even wedge him out of his home county?

The thought that Del might be working for Brewster Armstrong caused Sam's stomach to twist. The man was a phony and a cheat. But even worse than that, he was stupid. Sam had personally seen him sell carnival glass as Tiffany without batting an eye. The thing was, Sam couldn't swear which of Armstrong's faults to attribute the fiasco to. The man was a menace to the business, and

Sam hadn't shed a tear when Armstrong Auctions moved its base of operations out of Allen County.

A few people tsked about tradition giving over to youth and similar misplaced sentiments, but all in all, most of them were tickled Porky Pig pink to have an excuse to bypass Armstrong's sales. He had a bad rep and it finally caught up with him. The fact that Sam's rising popularity might have helped speed Armstrong's journey across the county line by a decade or so was something only the most crass mentioned. Sam grimaced. Of course, around here that meant just about everybody.

But, anyway you looked at it, if somebody was laying a trap for Sam or Samson Auctions, Armstrong had to be at the top of the suspect list.

Sam could deal with traps. He just wished the bait wasn't so tempting, or maybe he didn't. An image of Del strutting around in those impossible heels, like they were normal wear for what was just two steps above Dumpster diving, filled his mind and warmed his groin. Parts might be parts, but all of hers were in the right places. He shook his head and forced himself to move past her perks and back to her treachery.

He didn't have any proof Del was in league with Armstrong, and even if she was, Sam was a long haul from discovering their plan. He needed to play it coy, figure out how to crack her.

He could do it. Hell, he'd charmed eighty-year-old Mrs. Ritter into bidding up a box filled with massage oil and sex manuals. Course, she didn't realize that was what was in the box, but the principle held. He could charm Del into telling him who sent her. He just had to figure out which buttons to push—Sam glanced down at the body part that had betrayed him earlier—and maybe invest in few ice packs.

Sam left the safety of his truck and strolled up the hill to the Bunny Hutch. It was after five. Becca would be cleaning up or taking a few minutes to work on those rabbits she was fixated with. As he reached the diner, he noticed something different. The hutch was empty. Not the restaurant; the light was on in there and he could see Becca bent over a laundry basket of yarn. She was creating more critters for her window, which apparently she needed because the hutch she kept stocked with crocheted rabbits was empty. There were probably thirty of the things in there this morning.

Becca'd been displaying them in the window since she took over the diner three years ago, and he'd never known her to sell more than a couple, and then around Easter. How did she unload thirty of the little carrot thieves in one day? He knocked on the locked door with his knuckles and motioned for her to let him in.

Taking her sweet time, Becca wrapped a length of yarn around what she was working on and dropped it in the basket. She mouthed at him through the glass door, "We're closed, cowboy."

"Just open the door."

With a grin, she turned the lock and the door swung open. "Latch it behind you," she said over her shoulder. Four steps ahead of him, she'd already returned to the basket filled with crochet.

"Where have all the rabbits gone?"

"Isn't that one of those hippie tunes?" Becca

picked up a pink head and began stitching a black hat onto it.

"The rabbits, in the hutch, where'd they go?"

"Oh, those." Becca held the head out to him. "What do you think?"

Sam curled his lip. "It's a pig." Lord, he was getting sick of pigs.

"Yeah, the woman who took the bunnies said I might should branch out, and all this talk of pigs inspired me."

He was thrilled to be part of an "inspiration."

"What woman took the other ones?" he asked.

"Some woman from Daisy Creek. She was in here yesterday, then came back today. I think you know her. She mentioned you, goes to your auctions."

Sam thought for a moment. "Lime-green pantsuit, big hair, lots of makeup?"

Becca grinned again. "That's her. Hard to miss, isn't she?"

Becca was in a good mood. Sam would have to swing a deal to the green pantsuit next auction she attended. "So, she bought all those rabbits?" He gestured to the front window.

"Well, she only bought two, but she took the rest on consignment. She's working with some new Web site and store that specializes in southern Missouri crafts."

Sam wasn't confident that Becca's bunnies were going to be hot commodities. "She think she can sell them?"

Becca gave him a look that said she didn't appreciate his tone. Sam took a step back. Becca *was* a stomper. He knew better than to get in her way.

Besides, what did he know about selling the cute and cuddly?

"Sounds great," he added. A clatter of pans from the kitchen saved him from having to say more.

"Clay Thomas, what are you doing in there?" Becca bellowed to her son.

The skinny six-year-old slunk around the swinging door. "Nothing. It was an accident."

Becca dropped her yarn and jumped up. "Have you been playing in the flour again?"

Sam took a second look at the boy he thought of as his nephew. Clay was covered in white dust. He looked like he'd been mining limestone all day.

"It was an accident." A tear overflowed Clay's lower lashes, making a flesh-colored trail through the flour.

Sam could feel Becca take a calming breath. In an even voice, she said, "I've asked you not to play in the cupboards. The food in there is just like money. It cost money, and it makes money. Without it we . . ." She bit her lip looked from Clay to the floor.

Times must be rough. Sam had never seen Becca unable to finish a sentence. "I bet it's not that bad, right?" Sam grabbed Clay in a one-armed hug and shoved him back through the swinging door into the kitchen. "I'll help him clean up. You just work on your pigs."

Becca looked unsure, but she nodded her head and sat down near the basket of yarn.

Sam took a calming breath of his own when he saw the state of the kitchen. How did one small boy make such a mess? Not only did flour cover

the linoleum, but it had drifted up onto the counters and a stack of previously clean pots.

He grabbed the split bag of flour and dragged it
over to the trash.

"Mom's mad at me." Clay swiped at the flour
with a broom, managing to swirl another cake's
worth into the air.

"She's not mad." Sam gently tugged the broom
from Clay's hand and replaced it with a wet cloth.
"Wipe down the counters, okay?"

While Clay dragged the cloth through the dust,
Sam continued, "She's just busy right now and
wasn't wanting to scour a kitchen she'd just got
done cleaning. Make sense?"

"I guess." Clay rolled little balls of dough out of
the flour and water mixture and flicked them
across the room.

Sam took another deep breath. How did Becca
maintain her sanity? "That's enough helping. Why
don't you just sit over there." Sam pointed to a
chair across the room, well out of the flour zone.
"And have a cookie or something."

"Mom doesn't let me have cookies right before
dinner."

Sam pulled out a giant oatmeal raisin. "Think of
it more as a long time after lunch."

Fifteen minutes later, Sam had contained the ef-
fects of the flour tornado. He escorted Clay out
into the restaurant. Becca had finished the pig's
head and was working on the body. She looked up
as they approached.

"Thanks, Sam. You're a pain in the behind
sometimes, but you always know when I need you."

Grabbing her son, she held him by both arms and stared into his eyes. "You know I love you, right?"

Clay nodded.

"Know there's nothing short of heaven or hell I wouldn't go through for you, even sell Sam to the gypsies if I had to, right?"

Clay grinned and looked at Sam.

"But sometimes I just need you to help out, by not messing things up quite so much. That fair?"

At her son's nod, she pushed him back toward the kitchen. "Go get your lunch box. It's time to go home." She watched him skip away. "And don't open the cupboards," she yelled to his retreating back. She turned to Sam. "Ten bucks says he's in that cupboard three seconds after the door swings closed behind him." She shook her head. "Never mind that. I don't have ten bucks to bet."

"Things not any better?" Sam asked.

"Well, they aren't any worse." She motioned to the bodyless pig. "I've got this now, but I don't think crocheted farm animals are going to buy Clay braces someday, or pay my rent, or even keep us in flour."

"Things will get better. They always do."

"Do they?" Becca cocked a brow at him. "They get better, but not a lot better. I get some little edge, like selling these rabbits, and it's just enough to keep me going, keep me hoping that things will work out, but the big save never comes. I'm twenty-five years old and I feel a hundred. The only thing that reminds me I'm not is Clay and he's also what causes all my stress. If it were just me, I wouldn't care. I'd let my landlord keep my couch, I'd sell this place, not that I'd get anything for it, and I'd move somewhere, take a gamble at getting ahead."

"You could never leave here." Sam squeezed her shoulder.

"I don't have a lot of choices left."

The door to the kitchen swung open and Clay rolled through it like an extra from a bad cop show. Becca laughed. "C'mon, Detective Clay. Get your badge off the ground and let's head home."

Sam left feeling melancholy and helpless. If he had a spare penny, he'd give it to Becca no questions asked, but everything he owned and some he didn't were tied up in a deposit on land for the new Samson's Auction Center. He could back out of the deal, but he'd lose everything he'd invested, which was everything he had. So, no help for Becca there. He'd even double-mortgaged the small one-bedroom house he'd inherited when Dad died.

Times were tough and the Samsons needed a break.

Back at the Ranch, Del kicked her shoes across the room, enjoying the thud as they conked into the wall, then peeled off her jeans. As each inch of denim separated from her body, she sighed in relief. The things were so tight the side seams were impressed into the outer length of her legs. What had she been thinking?

She tilted back on the bed and stared at the closet where her limited wardrobe hung. June Cleaver or Kelly Bundy, what a choice. Del Montgomery or Lilah Mont? Another dandy choice.

Del shoved her hands up into her hair. Why did

she have to come back to southern Missouri? She was content in Chicago, wearing silk shirts and closed-toed shoes, battling with David for the best sales.

She thought of her sterile apartment waiting for her with its thrift-shop furniture and unused stove. Okay, content, but not happy. Not really. Del had never belonged in Chicago. She missed the easy-going pace of the Ozarks, the green hills, and if she was going to be perfectly honest, her family. Hearing Izzy talk about her mama hit her hard. She hadn't spoken to either of her parents for longer than two minutes at a time since she'd left seven years ago.

Not that she regretted leaving. She couldn't. If she'd stayed she'd be living just like her daddy, deal to deal, meal to meal, and that was best-case scenario.

Worst, she'd be sharing a cell with some hooker named Wanda.

She let her body fall flat on the bed and stared up at the stained ceiling. Some things were more important than the almighty deal. Del knew that; her daddy didn't.

Things had never been exactly smooth between them. When he traded off her grandmother's ruby necklace, the only fine thing Del had ever owned, she'd moved out. Momma cried but didn't put up a hand to stop her.

Then when he came to her saying he knew he'd been wrong, could he help her with her new auction business, she believed him, trusted him again. Del rolled over, pressed her face into the bedspread, and inhaled the stale smell. She'd sworn that would be the last mistake she'd ever make in southern Missouri. Now she was one tight black T-shirt from slipping up again.

Sam Samson was everything Del didn't need right now, except in his capacity to lead her to the Unruh Pig. She needed to remember that and not let him get to her again. She needed to be strong, to do something to reassert her feeling of power. Something that would make her feel better about living in her own skin.

She pushed off the bed and yanked out the drawer of the blond bedside table. Reaching for the slim volume of yellow pages, she thought, *Time to let the real Del shine through.* No more playing dress up. She was going to find some clothes that were her, clothes that gave her the confidence to grab what she needed and get out.

No more June Cleaver, but no more torturing her body to fit into pants built for a size ten instead of her more generous proportions. Somewhere there had to be clothing that would make the most of her assets without cutting off her oxygen supply. And if they showed a little attitude, all the better. Del was ready to show a little attitude too.

Sam slouched forward on his polled Hereford desk calendar. He'd spent most of the night wide awake, staring at the ceiling of his soon-to-be-repossessed bedroom, trying to think of some way out of his and Becca's financial problems. Knowing he had another full day of pig hunting planned with Del, he'd spent the rest of the night trying to force himself asleep. Even counting sheep didn't work; maybe he should have tried pigs. He grimaced and checked the celluloid clock on his desk. It was ten minutes past when he expected Del and he could barely keep his eyes open. He would make lively company today.

Kenny tapped on the door. "Wake up, sleeping beauty. You got a visitor."

Sam jerked up, hoping Del hadn't noticed his little snooze and looked directly into the alert eyes of Izzy Malone. Sam glanced back at the door. No Del.

"You expecting someone else?" Izzy clomped in and lowered himself into one of the chairs. He glanced around the room. "Interesting place for an auction office."

Izzy, king of the add-on, could criticize Sam's choice in real estate? "It's temporary," Sam replied.

"That a fact?" Izzy scratched his chin with his hook.

Why was the old coot here? "There something I can help you with?" Sam asked.

"Might be. Might be something I could help you with."

Sam was in no mood for games. "That a fact?" he echoed Izzy's earlier question.

Izzy grinned at him. "Sure enough is."

Sam stared at him from the other side of the desk.

"You're a cool customer, boy. I like that." Izzy chuckled. "Don't know how it'll be enough to help you with that girl, but it won't hurt none."

"You mean Del?" Sam picked up a quarter and ran his thumb over the ridged edge.

"If that's what you're calling her." Izzy tapped on

the desk. "You got something to drink in there? I'm feeling a might parched."

What did he mean, "if that's what you're calling her"? Sam flipped the quarter onto the back of his hand. "There's a Coke machine in back."

"That stuff'll kill you. 'Sides, I was thinking something with a bit of kick to it, if you know what I mean." Izzy slid off his hat and placed it on his lap.

"It's seven in the morning."

"Didn't ask you for the time. Asked you for a drink. You strike me as the type what might have a little something tucked away in them drawers." Another tap on Sam's desk.

How'd he do that? No one, not even Kenny, knew Sam kept a bottle of gin stowed in his right-hand file drawer. Even as bad as things had been looking lately he hadn't cracked it open, but he liked the idea of keeping it there. Very Sam Spade. Sliding the quarter under the thousand-pound beauty on his calendar, he edged open the drawer. The two highball glasses in the back clinked together as he gave the drawer a final jerk.

Twisting the cap off the bottle, Sam stole a glance at Izzy. The man seemed content to lean back in the uncomfortable wooden chair and wait. As Sam pulled out a glass, Izzy nodded to a coffee mug. "In there, if you don't mind." He held up his arms.

Feeling both stupid and insensitive, Sam poured an inch of gin into the mug.

"Don't be stingy now."

Sam added another inch. He kept his face devoid of emotion as he handed it to Izzy.

"So, you said you could help me with something," Sam prompted.

"Might be." Izzy took a delicate sip. "You been taking the girl a lot of places?"

"Enough." Sam got up and filled his own mug with coffee.

"She been buying pigs everywhere?"

"As far as I know." Sam wandered back to his seat.

"Hmmm. She looking for anything special?"

Sam tapped on his cup with his middle finger. What was Izzy digging for? "Doesn't seem to be too choosy."

"No special interest in, say"—Izzy leaned forward—"pottery?"

Pottery. Del had mentioned wanting pottery pigs, and Izzy had said something at his shop about pottery. What did that mean? So she liked pottery pigs; most collectors specialized.

"Not to me," Sam lied, picking up his cup and watching Izzy over the top. "How about you?"

"So, she didn't ask about, say, a vase or somethin'?"

"She ask you for one?"

Izzy grinned at him. "You're quite the two-stepper, ain't you?"

Sam was tired of the dance too. "Why are you here, Izzy? What do you know?"

"I don't know nothing, but I got a hunch, and hunches are what've kept me afloat through many a rough spot." Another swallow of gin slid down Izzy's throat. "If'n I was to share this hunch, what'd be in it for me?"

"Hard to say until I heard it."

Izzy didn't look at him, but Sam could tell he was assessing him all the same. Finally the old trader spoke. "There's a story been going around these parts for purt near thirty years."

Great, a local legend. This was sure to be worth Sam's time. He leaned back in his chair and prepared to issue some amazed nods.

"Myself, I never gave the story too much thought. I mean, there's more fish tales around here than water in the Current after a two-day rain."

More like a weeklong.

"But what with the girl turning up down here after so long and looking for pigs, 'specially pottery pigs, it got me to thinking."

"'After so long'?" Sam interrupted.

Izzy lifted the mug to his lips and said, "This is good. I'd hate to have to leave it half finished."

Fine. Sam would shut up. He could ask questions later.

After watching Sam for a moment, Izzy continued, "As I was saying, this story has to do with a pig, a pottery pig."

Sam opened his mouth, but at a warning glance from Izzy he snapped it shut.

"Way I hear it there was some fancy pottery east of here what made some of the ugliest junk you ever did see, but city folk just gobbled it up. This stuff was all handmade, kind of smooshed looking.

"Anyhow, this collector what was traveling through, looking for more ugly crap, I figure. Got hisself drowned in a gullywasher trying to cross a river when he had no business doing it." Izzy shook his head. "They found the car right off, but it was bad bunged up and there weren't more'n a toothbrush left of his belongings. The old feller didn't have no kin, so nobody with any rights to nothing made a ruckus—

not that it'd done them any good. Once folks squirrel somethin' good away it's hard to smoke 'em out."

Wondering what this had to do with Del and her pig hunt, Sam bit his lip and waited.

"Now the interesting part of this story is that 'parently this old feller had just come up from Arkansas, where he'd bought some pig made by this pottery back east. Way I hear it, collectors had been looking for this thing for forty years then, and this feller was mighty excited when he got it cheap off some hillbilly." Izzy said the last with disgust, leaving no doubt the term was the dead man's. "He'd called a bunch of his fancy friends and bragged it up right. When word got out he was dead, two or three of them were down here off and on for months, beating the weeds along the riverside looking for the thing. Somebody finally convinced the fools a beaver took it away and walled it into his lodge. And you know how mean a big ole beaver can be." Izzy grinned.

Sam waited.

Izzy grunted. "So, what you think, boy? This make sense?"

"You mean, you think Del is looking for this pig?" Sam retrieved his quarter and began rolling it between his fingers again. "Why now, after thirty years, and how would she even know about it? I've lived here my whole life and never heard the story."

"You think it's more likely she came down from Chicago just to stomp around with you and add to some pig collection?" Izzy snorted. "You need to come to my shop more often, boy. I got some good buys for you."

Chapter 5

Crooked as a pig's tail . . .

So, Izzy thought Del was after some rare piece of pottery. Insane as the tale sounded, the old guy was right. It made more sense than the vague story she'd handed Sam.

Sam tilted back in his chair. "So, why you telling me this?"

"Why you think?" Izzy countered.

"Money."

"You're quick as a whip, aren't you?" Izzy lifted the mug to his lips. "Here's what I'm thinkin'. I root around and find as much as I can about the Pig. You keep an eye on the girl. She gets a lead on it, you let me know. If I find something, I let you know. Whoever finds the Pig, we split the profit."

"What about Del?"

"What about her?"

Sam set his chair down on all four legs. "What if she finds the Pig first?"

"She won't if'n you're doing your job. You just stick to her like mud on a sow's side, find out what she knows. If she gets close we'll slip in and get the Pig first. It'll take two of us—one to divert her and one to get the Pig."

Sam was all for out-trading someone to get the better end of a deal, but something about Izzy's proposal seemed a bit more, well, dishonest than Sam liked to operate. Especially the part about deceiving Del. He didn't owe her anything, except his time, but still, the idea of weaseling her completely out of the operation stung a bit.

"I heard a rumor you had some money down on a piece of land." Izzy looked into his mug, then glanced back at Sam. "So, maybe things is going good for you. Maybe you don't need no extra folding money. Course, I been watching the paper and the auction business has seemed a mite slow this year."

Sam studied the lined face in front of him. The old coot wasn't even trying to be sneaky.

Izzy slid the empty coffee mug onto Sam's desk. "I stopped by your cousin's the other day. She's a right pretty little thing, but she was sure wearing a long face.

"That good-for-nothing husband of hers still shorting her checks?" he asked.

Better—of course Sam saw through the mask of concern and innocence Izzy wore. Still, it didn't change the truth of the situation. Sam needed money, and Becca needed money, which meant Clay needed money. He barely knew Del, and she'd even stood him up today without so much as a call. Besides, family came first.

"What kind of split you have in mind?" Sam asked.

"Sixty-forty." Izzy tapped his chest, then pointed his arm toward Sam.

"I think you got that backwards. I'll be the one riding shotgun with the girl." Sam couldn't bring himself to use Del's name.

"Don't see how that's much of a hardship, but I'm a fair man."

And a wet dog didn't stink.

"What say the one of us that gets a bead on the Pig first gets the sixty? Be kind of what you call an incentive to sniff it out."

It was probably as good a deal as Sam could hope for from Izzy. As he nodded his agreement, he swallowed back the bad taste forming in his mouth. He owed Del nothing except what she'd asked for—a tour guide, and she'd been lying to him about that. If Sam and Izzy found the Pig first, it would serve her right for trying to con him.

Izzy stood to leave, and the door to Sam's office swung open. Kenny stood on the other side, a scrap of paper in his hand. "Sorry, forgot to tell you that woman you're working with called this morning. Said she couldn't make it today, but she'd buy you breakfast tomorrow to make up for it. She had some kind of an emergency."

The bad taste swelled forward. "What time'd she call?"

"Must have been around six. You weren't here yet."

Sam looked at Izzy, who flashed him a grin and ambled toward the front. Kenny shoved the paper into Sam's hand and went to help a man choose a salt lick. After shutting the door behind them, Sam returned to his desk and unfolded the note to

stare at the three letters that made up her name.
He didn't owe her anything.

So, why did he suddenly feel lower than a kick to
the balls?

Slumped in his chair, he reached for his file
drawer.

Del let the weight of her purchases pull her down
onto the hotel bed. She'd survived a full day of
shopping, and not for antiques—real shopping, the
kind with fluorescent lights and dressing room cur-
tains that didn't close. Half of southern Missouri
had probably seen her bare butt at some point
today.

She'd called the feed store this morning and left
a message for Sam, claiming an emergency came
up, and it had. She couldn't spend another minute
living in someone else's clothes. That's how she
looked at her entire wardrobe—nothing but a
cheap impersonation of some woman she wasn't
and didn't really want to be. Today somewhere between a rack of red leather jackets and a shelf of
kick-ass studded jeans, she'd finally felt at home.

Yep, she was newly outfitted and every sweater
set, imitation Chanel suit, and pair of tummy-
tucking pantyhose she owned were going straight
to Goodwill, along with the cheap gut-cutting
denims. If she was stuck hunting pigs in southern
Missouri she was going to do it with style.

The only pieces she was keeping from either of
her earlier wardrobes were the man-hunting shoes
and her pearls. Maybe they didn't go together, but
Del wasn't willing to let either go yet. A woman

shouldn't have to choose between sexy and classy. Besides, one symbolized everything she wanted and the other could help her get there.

Exhausted, she leaned back on the bed. Tomorrow she was back on the trail of the Pig, but this time she was going to do it her way. If yesterday was any indicator, Sam Samson had no clue where the Pig was or that it even existed, and Del was beginning to doubt he even had the connections Becca claimed.

No knowledge, no connections, and no clue equaled no reason to keep him around. The only thing he offered was distraction, an unwelcome distraction. It was time to cut Sam loose before the scene in his truck repeated itself. Next round she might not walk away the victor, and with so much at stake, she couldn't afford to let a country con man like Sam Samson get the upper hand. Their partnership had to end now. She'd break it to him first thing tomorrow.

The next morning, Del dug through her bags looking for the perfect dump-the-auctioneer outfit. She set the man-eaters to the side. No reason to hit him too hard. She shook out a hot-pink tee and a pair of low-rise jeans. Pulling them on, she checked her reflection in the mirror. The neckline of the shirt was about an inch short of plunging, but as the salesgirl pointed out, if you had a matched set, you didn't hide them in the stable. The jeans were her favorite though. They hugged her curves without cutting off her blood flow, and the tiny rhinestone music notes—very rock 'n' roll. After finishing the outfit with her pearls and a pair of low-heeled sandals that showed off her new toe ring, she sauntered to her Honda.

She felt great. Sure, she was still packing a few extra pounds, but packaged right that padding could be played to her advantage. Nothing and nobody were getting in her way today.

The diner was full when Del arrived. She snagged a spot at the counter, next to a woman dressed in lime green accented with zebra stripes. With a nod to her flamboyant companion, she flipped over her coffee cup, then studied the pie cabinet that hung on the wall. Looked like jelly doughnuts today. Couldn't beat that for a healthy breakfast. Del hummed Led Zeppelin's "Heartbreaker" under her breath. It was going to be a good day. She could feel it.

The woman next to her nodded and poured a pile of sugar on her grits. "Them doughnuts look good, don't they? The jelly ones were still warm when Becca unpacked them."

Del smiled. "You think it's too early for ice cream?"

The cowbell on the entrance door clanged and Sam walked in the door. He slipped his hat onto a metal rack and scooped a rubber bin of dirty dishes off a table. He strolled into the kitchen without glancing at the counter where Del sat. She couldn't resist taking a peek at his rear as he disappeared through the swinging door.

"Ain't never too early for what you like." The woman cackled and threw Del a wink.

Del could feel a flush working its way up from her bare toes to her mascara-covered lashes.

"No reason to be embarrassed, kid. Be something wrong with you if you didn't take time out to enjoy the sights." The woman cut into her over-easy egg, letting the yellow yolk leak out and mingle with her grits. "I saw you here the other day with that looker." She nodded her head toward the kitchen door. "He a friend of yours?"

In Chicago, Del would have promptly turned her back on a stranger who so boldly delved into her personal business, but this wasn't Chicago. Besides, Del needed every friend she could make. There was no telling who would provide the link she needed to the Pig.

Putting an open smile on her face, she turned to the woman. "I don't know if I'd say friend. We just met."

"Really. Now why'd I get the feeling you knew him a little better than that?" The woman grinned.

Del concentrated on not frowning.

"Maybe it was how he was looking you over. Thought the boy was gonna get out a loupe and check your fillings. Course he's probably got more entertaining ways of doing that." Another cackle from the woman, followed by another blush from Del.

"You are a shy thing, aren't you? Never would have guessed that—just don't fit."

What a strange comment, almost like the woman knew her. A bit nervous that she did, Del asked, "What do you mean it doesn't fit?"

"Hmm? Oh, nothing." The woman stirred her coffee. When she saw Del was still watching her, she continued. "Just you being such a flashy dresser and all." She pointed to Del's shirt. "I wouldn't mind getting me one of them. Course, don't guess it'd look the same without the ammunition you're packing. 'Fraid my holsters ain't got the bang they used to." She patted her chest.

This conversation was going from awkward to awful. Del looked around for Becca. If she was going to survive this chat she needed a jelly glazed—with a triple scoop of ice cream. Becca was in the back waiting on a table full of farmers. She needed more help around here.

Del eyed the cabinet, the mirror mounted above the shelf showed the sugar coating to perfection. And the jelly spilling out one side, it looked like blackberry. She'd never seen anything so purple and luscious. She could slip behind the counter and serve herself. Becca wouldn't mind.

"So what brings you around here?" The woman interrupted Del's lustful thoughts of jelly doughnut à la mode.

With a sigh, Del deserted her dreams and turned to her companion. What the hey, maybe she would be the lead Del was looking for.

"I collect pigs. I'm looking to add to my collection." The words came out in almost a monotone. She really needed to work on her delivery.

"That right? I don't recollect ever meeting someone who collected pigs." The woman picked up her cup.

What a surprise.

"There is that old story though. You know the one I'm talking about?" The woman took a loud slurp of coffee.

Even with senses dulled by lack of sugar, Del perked up.

"An old story?" she asked as casually as she could manage.

"You think that's raspberry or blackberry?" Del's companion nodded to the doughnut display.

"Blackberry." Del didn't spare a glance at the case. "You said something about an old story."

Becca walked up, filled Del's upturned cup with coffee, and wandered off.

"I'm Tilde, by the way." The woman held out a magenta-tipped hand.

Taking a breath of patience, Del slipped her hand into the older woman's and smiled. "Del Montgomery. Now about this story, it was about a pig, you said? I just love old tales."

"Montgomery? You any relation to Harold down near Lebanon?"

Del shook her head. She had to get this woman back on track. "I haven't been collecting pigs for long, but I'm building quite an assortment." That was certainly true. "Pigs are fascinating animals. They're smarter than dogs, you know." Del paused. "I had one when I was a little girl." Her speech slowed. "His name was Toadstool. We took him in when his mother wouldn't feed him. I used to give him a bottle and wrap him up in a little blanket every night before bed. During the day, he'd follow me everywhere." Del stared at a spot behind the counter.

"He sounds like a right nice pet." Concern filled Tilde's eyes.

"He was."

"You have to give him up when he got big?"

Del swallowed. "Yeah, when he got big." And fat and worth more as pork ribs than a pet.

Tilde cleared her throat. "Well, now this story I heard ain't about no real pig. It's about some kind of jug or something."

Still stuck in the past, Del didn't react.

"According to what people say, it was some kind of rare piece of pottery, worth as much as two fools were willing to pay for it. Got lost somewhere around here about thirty years ago; nobody's seen hide nor bristle of it since."

"Pottery?" Del snapped out of her reverie and looked at Tilde with renewed interest. "A pottery pig. Are you sure?"

The door to the kitchen swung open and Sam strode out, a bin filled with clean dishes in his arms. His electric gaze zoomed onto Del.

"Got a line on a pig?" he asked.

Damn his timing. "Just chatting about my collection." Del responded, praying her new friend wouldn't let the piglet out of the bag.

Tilde tapped her spoon against her cup. Looking at Sam she said, "You work around here, son?"

At Sam's confused expression, she nodded to the bin of dishes. He shoved them under the counter and grabbed a dish towel to dry his hands. "I just help out a little every now and then. Looked like Becca needed it today."

"Mighty nice of you." Tilde looked him up and down. "This little gal here's wanting a doughnut. You think you can lend a hand?"

"Sure." Sam gave the women an uneasy look and went to open the cabinet.

Del enjoyed seeing this side of her difficult guide. Sam walked around the world so cocksure, it was entertaining to see him intimidated by the tiny older woman beside her.

Happy to be on the power side of the equation, when Tilde motioned her closer, Del leaned in to listen. "Built for sin and loaded for action. Don't be letting this one get away."

The older woman nudged her in the side. Del felt the flush flood her face again. She hadn't blushed this much since she was twelve and had to explain to her male teacher that the bathroom machine was out of tampons and that she was short the fifty cents to buy one.

Plunking a jelly doughnut down in front of her, Sam's gaze strayed to Del's neckline. "So, you dressed for pig hunting? I thought we could hit another county today."

Now was her chance to dump him. "I was thinking I'd take a break. Maybe just wander around a bit myself."

Beside her, Tilde snapped open a zebra-striped purse and pulled out a compact. Was she leaving?

"Wander around by yourself?" Sam said it like Del'd suggested wading through croc-infested waters in the Amazon. "You think that's a good idea?"

Del pushed her breakfast toward him. "You think I could get some ice cream for this?"

He gave her a suspicious look but picked up the plate and walked to the cooler.

Twisting to face Tilde, she said, "I'd love to hear more about this pottery pig. Would you like to meet for lunch?" Del used her sweetest smile.

Tilde laughed. "Don't be wasting those doe eyes on me. I ain't turned down a free meal yet, but I can't today. I got plans. You give me your number and I'll give you a holler."

Drat. Del had really hoped her colorful new friend would provide her with the lead she needed to snag the pig and head back to Chicago victorious. Keeping an eye on Sam's back, Del dug a pen out of her purse and scribbled her cell number onto a paper napkin. "Call me anytime."

Glancing at the napkin, Tilde asked, "That long distance?"

"Oh." Del took the napkin back and added her hotel number as Sam sauntered up with her breakfast, hidden under five scoops of ice cream.

"Didn't want you complaining you weren't getting your money's worth," he drawled.

"Now, why would I do that?" Del folded the napkin in half and slid it onto the other woman's lap. Tilde picked up the pen Del had dropped and extracted a napkin of her own from the dispenser.

"No reason, but since when did a woman need a reason for anything?" He leaned into the counter, his gaze boring into her. "You gonna eat that before it melts?" He nodded to the ice cream.

"Of course." Del picked up a spoonful and slid it into her mouth. Taking her time, she flipped the utensil over and slowly pulled it back out. With it held in front of her like a lollipop, she gave it one final lick. "Delicious."

The look he gave her sizzled. Laughing to herself, she picked the spoon back up.

She'd teach him.

Before Del could begin the second half of her lesson, Tilde popped up from her seat. Shaking her head, she said, "Don't be too tough on him, kid. 'Member what I said about being loaded for action. I think you might be pulling on his trigger a little too hard." With a grin, she dug some bills out of her purse and flipped them along with the napkin she'd scribbled on earlier onto the counter and left.

Del grabbed the napkin almost before it hit the Formica.

"What was that?" Sam reached out a hand to take the balled paper from her.

"Nothing." Without pausing to think, she tucked the napkin inside her bra.

Smooth, she thought, like he wouldn't notice that. No choice but to brazen it out now. She lifted her gaze and stared him down.

A surprised look flittered across his face but quickly changed to a dangerous smile. "Guess you don't think I'll go in after that?"

She picked up her spoon and scooped another bite of ice cream into her mouth. "No, I don't." Please, God, let her be right.

She could feel his gaze on the V of her shirt. Her traitorous chest rose in response. To make matters worse, the ice cream was causing her to shiver. Her nipples were probably standing up straighter than a drill sergeant at the Pentagon. Maybe he wouldn't notice.

He chuckled. "You cold or just happy to see me?"

She refused to look down. She was going right back to the hotel and changing into a different bra, one with a nice camouflaging layer of fiberfill, right after she finished this doughnut, that was.

"It is a bit chilly in here, don't you think?" she asked.

"Yeah, that's probably it." He gave her a smart-aleck grin.

In return, she gave her spoon a lascivious lick. *Take that.* "Ice cream is so much better when it's hot, don't you think?" *Forget the napkin. Look at me.* She slid the spoon back into the bowl, this time snagging some jelly. "But nothing beats a fresh doughnut with a scoop of vanilla, don't you think?"

He watched the spoon move from her bowl to her mouth with an expression reminiscent of a tomcat outside a hamster cage. When she thought he might be ready to pounce, she dragged her finger through the last drips of cream and, running the digit through her lips, announced, "Thanks for breakfast. I think I'm going to have to take a rain check on the pig hunt today. I feel a headache coming on." Without a backward glance, she tucked the napkin more firmly into her bra and sashayed to the door.

Del was gone five minutes before Sam realized she'd stuck him with her tab. Damn, she was distracting.

As he gathered up the dirty dishes and the bills left behind by the other woman, he remembered the wadded-up napkin. Delicious Del was up to something, and Sam needed to figure out what. He should have dived in and grabbed the note—he was sure that's what she had tucked between her breasts. He would have too, if for no other reason than that he was incapable of backing down from a direct challenge, but then Del had started the X-rated ice cream performance and he had kind of lost track of what he was doing. Hell, he had lost track of who he was.

When he'd walked out of the kitchen he was almost positive he'd heard Del ask the green pantsuit about pottery pigs. Then she'd dismissed him of his guide duties with all the concern a milk-maid showed a horsefly. Nice to know he rated so high in her esteem.

He scraped remnants of grits and egg into the trash with vehemence. Well, she wasn't getting rid of him that easy. After this morning, he was convinced Izzy was right. Del wasn't just hunting pigs. She was hunting one pig in particular, and Sam had every intention of beating her to it.

He glanced around the busy restaurant. He hated to leave Becca shorthanded, but if he let Del get too big a head start there was no telling what holler she'd disappear into. He punched the total for Del's breakfast into the register and turned to leave. Three steps from the door, twenty ladies from the Sophisticate Society twittered through the door. *Great.*

Becca spied them from the back and almost split a seam sprinting through the tables to greet them. "Ladies, I'm so glad you decided to give the Bunny Hutch a try. Just give us a second to pull some tables together and we'll get you all set up." She gave Sam an urgent look.

"I can't stay, Becca." Might as well let her know right from the get-go.

Yanking a four-top into position, Becca just nodded. "I understand. You got your own problems to worry about, I'm sure. You've done enough for me and Clay already." She glanced up at the waiting women. "It's not like they won't understand if the service is a little slow. They're all nice, upstanding ladies. They won't go around bad-mouthing the Hutch or nothing and they'll probably give me another chance next month"—she whacked the table into place with her hip—"maybe."

Sam looked at the middle-aged clique. Evelyn Snider, reigning queen bee of the group, flicked a stray crumb of doughnut off the stool Del had recently vacated. Her second in command, Mary Leonard, pointed to an unbused table and made a comment behind her hand to the woman next to her.

Oh yeah, this group would be understanding. With a snap he shoved another table into the one Becca held.

Help his family or chase his dreams? Life was filled with dandy choices. Exhaling through his teeth, he said, "I'll stay, but anyone touches my butt and I'm out of here."

Waving the women over, Becca murmured, "I can't make any promises. I hear Evelyn Snider's pretty fast on the pinch."

Great, just great.

Chapter 6

Bring home the bacon . . .

Del smoothed the napkin out on her dashboard. "Hollywell Hogs." What was that? Didn't sound like any kind of shop. Could it actually be a hog farm? Just what Del didn't want to do—visit a hog farm.

She shoved her keys into the ignition and started the engine. If only she'd had a chance to talk more to Tilde. Maybe this note was nothing, maybe it was completely unrelated to her conversation with Del, and maybe it was where the Unruh Pig called home. There was only one way to find out. She'd have to track down the Hollywells. How hard could that be?

Two gas stations later, Del gave up on searching for a phone book and headed back to her room. What was this obsession people had with stealing white pages? There should be a law.

Annoyed with the phone book–stealing public, she peeled into the hotel lot and jogged to her room. Inside she dug out the white pages and flipped to *H*. Hollywell, unusual name. How many could there be? Her finger ran down the lines of print and back up. *These people must bop like bunnies.* She slammed the book shut.

She'd wasted enough time. Sam was already suspicious. He could be hot on her trail right now. She needed to find someone who'd know not only which Hollywell had hogs, but also how to get there. If the Unruh Pig was at the farm, she needed to talk to the owner in person. A phone call would just tip him off that he had something of value. Del tapped her finger against her chin.

The obvious answer was the feed store, except Sam would most certainly learn of any questions she asked there.

Izzy might know, but she'd trust him as far as she could toss a ten-ton tater.

She could head to the square and stop every man in a feed hat that passed by. That wouldn't take long—ha.

There was no help for it. She would have to visit the feed store. She'd just have to hope she had enough of a lead on Sam to get the Pig before he tracked her down.

The music notes on her jeans glimmered in the light from the bedside lamp. Hundred-dollar jeans—her Visa had squealed in outrage when she made the purchase—and a thirty-dollar toe ring— not the best outfit for a hog farm, but it was pretty good for getting information—as long as she was dealing with a man, anyway.

Del hadn't met a female hog farmer yet and Kenny, the blond cutie she'd seen at the feed store, was most definitely packing a Y chromosome. Satisfied with her choice, she hitched up her bra straps and stalked out to her Insight.

Parked in the feed store lot, Del checked her makeup in the visor mirror. After applying a fresh coat of lipstick, she strolled up the ramp. Her prey was bent over a pallet loaded with dog chow. Del took a moment to enjoy the view. He had a nice rear, no doubt about it, but for some reason the sight didn't give her much of a thrill today. Must be too stressed over her pig endeavor.

Clearing her throat, she alerted him he wasn't alone.

"Sam isn't here," he announced.

"Actually, I was hoping you could help me." She sashayed forward and leaned against a stack of chicken feed.

"That a fact?" Kenny mimicked her posture, leaning against the dog chow.

Wasn't there a trusting soul left in this town? Course with a friend like Sam, who could blame him? He'd probably been witness to every play in the book. Deciding games were just going to prolong the process, Del cut to the chase. "I need directions."

"Don't people usually get a map or go to a gas station?"

At least she was right about avoiding the games. She pushed away from the feed bags. "Who poked a hole in your bag?"

"Nobody." He began stacking dog food again. "You gonna help me?"

A bag of chow plopped onto the stack. The

accompanying smell of chicken by-product almost caused Del to gag.

"You think you could take a break or something?" she asked.

He dropped another bag onto the pile. "What are you doing here, anyhow?"

"I told you I need directions."

He reached for a bag of kibble.

"Stop." She held out a once—nicely manicured hand. "You have some problem with me?"

Looking her up and down, he replied, "Yeah, I think I do."

She waited.

"There's something about you that doesn't ring true. I think you're up to something. I think most people don't see past your"—he motioned with his hands, forming the shape of an hourglass—"but I do."

Just her luck. Del wished she could kick the woman who'd put the bag of chips on his shoulder. "Look, you don't even know me. Besides, all I want is directions. The sooner you give them to me, the sooner I'm gone."

"For today or for good?"

What a pain. "Both."

After another assessing gaze, he pulled off his hat and ran his hand his hair. "What do you want to know?"

With a map scratched onto the back of a flyer featuring the latest in measuring bull sperm density, Del tromped out of the store. It was a sad world when a tight shirt and a good bra didn't equal quick information. She might as well have been dealing with a woman. It was downright disheartening.

Somebody ought to give that boy an attitude adjustment, or hunt down the woman who'd screwed him up in the first place and kick her sorry butt to Purina Farms and back.

Today, Del had other problems, though. According to Mr. Charisma, Hollywell Hogs was a small family-run operation about thirty miles from town, a good ten of that down a rutted dirt road. Kenny acted like driving the trek in a car would be like fording the Mississippi in ballet slippers—not only impossible, but just plain ignorant. Del didn't figure he was exactly the most trustworthy source of information though, so she wasn't sweating it.

Besides, she'd been down plenty of dirt roads, most of them with the distinct purpose of getting sweaty. If her oversexed male companions of the past could maneuver the loose gravel and washboard surfaces of Missouri's back roads, she certainly could.

Even in a low-bottomed coupe.

She had to. She had more than a hormonal itch to scratch this time. She had a pig to buy.

Sam escaped the Hutch feeling like a dishrag that'd been dragged over one too many crumb-covered tables. At least he'd made it through the torment with bruise-free buns. He'd danced around the Sophisticates' table like it was surrounded by flames, flinching every time a hand stroked his arm or tapped his backside. One bawdy breakfaster even insisted on studying his belt buckle 'cause she'd "never seen anything quite like it."

If Sam was attached to it, she wouldn't again, either.

But he'd flirted and cajoled and pretty much used every empty compliment he could think up—until he was one wink from begging Becca for mercy.

When Evelyn Snider signaled the end by slipping him a dollar for "his extra-attentive service," he almost fell to his knees in relief. For the first time in weeks, he was glad he didn't have an auction coming up. A bug-eyed tree frog had more charm than was left in Sam. No one better cross him today, especially no one female. There wasn't a schmooze left in him.

To add to his annoyance, he realized Del now had a two-hour head start on him. The odds of catching her were about the same as Elvis showing up in his blue suede shoes. Sam spun through The Ranch's parking lot on the off chance Del had completed her mission and was busy packing her pigs to head north, but the lot was empty. He wasn't sure if that was a good thing, but the girl working the desk assured him Del hadn't checked out, so he hoped for the best.

Nothing much to do now but go back to the office and wait, maybe call Izzy and see if he'd learned anything. Sam parked his truck in back and entered through the loading door. Kenny was doing the two-fingered peck on the computer up front. Sam swung a right into his office, slipped off his hat, and plopped into his chair. Interlacing his fingers, he swung them behind his head. He could feel his chances of rescuing his business and helping Becca fade with each tick of his desk clock.

There had to be something he could do. What would Sam Spade do?

Nothing, that's what. About now shady characters and sultry sirens would be parading into his office like he had hundred-dollar bills stapled to his forehead, free for the taking. Course somebody'd probably be shooting at him or maybe have the cops threatening him with time in the pokey, but that's what the bottle of gin was for.

Sam had the gin, but no excuse to drink it. Life as an overextended auctioneer lacked the thrills of life as a hard-boiled private eye.

He dropped his arms onto the desk in front of him. He needed a break. Kenny stalked past the open door.

"Hey, what bur's under your saddle?" Sam yelled. Kenny was out of sight, but Sam could hear his Red Wing boots clomping back toward the office.

"I was wondering when you were gonna drag in here." Kenny leaned in the door, looking around as if he expected to see someone besides Sam.

"Why, were you looking for me? I told you I'd be out most of the day."

"Yeah, you did, but then your little tootsie came swinging in and figured you wouldn't be far behind."

"You mean Del?"

"You got another tootsie you're following around?"

Sam scowled at Kenny's tone. "I'm working for her."

Seemingly unconcerned that he was treading on Sam's one good nerve, Kenny replied, "Sure, that's why your head's as empty as your wallet when she's around."

Sam eyed the chalk horse bookends that sat on his desk. Deciding it would take way too much effort to chuck them at his friend, he retorted, "You're one to talk."

Kenny snapped his shoulder blades together. "I learn from my mistakes."

"Right." Sure, he could dish it, but he couldn't take it back. Sam studied Kenny for a moment and decided to let it go. His friend obviously knew something about Del, and Sam needed to know too. Getting Kenny more riled than he was wasn't going to help Sam's cause any. He took a deep breath, then let it out in one loud puff. "So, Del stopped by? She mention where she was headed?"

Kenny leaned against the door. "You know what you're getting into with that one?"

Not as much as he would like. "I'm not getting into anything. Let's just say I think the lady has a few secrets and it may be to my benefit to track her down."

Kenny mulled this over for a minute. "She's not as brainless as she acts, you know?"

Sam lifted one hand in agreement.

"A body like that and smarts, that can be a deadly combination." Pain flickered through Kenny's eyes.

Guess he wasn't over Charlie yet.

Glad he hadn't smacked Kenny with a ten-pound bookend, Sam tried to lighten the gloom that hung around his friend. "She's not exactly Mata Hari, and I'm not carrying state secrets."

Kenny grunted. "Yeah, well, it's your business, not mine." He turned to leave.

"Hey, where was she going?" Sam yelled after him.

Kenny paused to study him from the doorway. "If I were you I'd leave off chasing after her, but like I said, I figure it's your business." His gaze drilled into Sam like he was willing him to come to his senses. Shaking his head, Kenny replied, "Hollywell's, the hog farm. Don't know why, but that's where she's going. 'Bout now she's probably collecting gravel in those fancy shoes of hers. That foreign make'll never get down that road. I told her so, but she won't have listened." With a final rap on the door frame with his fist, he tramped off.

Now why would Del be headed to Hollywell's? They sure enough had pigs, but none that weren't destined for bacon.

Del stared at the low-water bridge in front of her. Curse her luck, again. The water streaming over the cement looked harmless enough, but Del knew better. Every spring in the Ozarks, some fool got himself washed downstream trying to cross just this kind of bridge.

Ozark humor, even calling it a bridge. It was really nothing more than some concrete poured right at creek level. So, even when there wasn't a big storm, water flowed over it. The weather had been fairly nice since she'd arrived in Allentown, but just the week before there'd been days of pouring rain. The creek still told the tale. If she tried to cross the thing in her Insight, she'd be washed down to Arkansas.

She didn't have anything against the state, but she'd prefer to stay nice and dry right where she was, thank you very little.

Darn her luck. The pig was so close, but she couldn't see how drowning would help her career any. She slipped off her sandals, rolled up her rock 'n' roll jeans, and eyed the rippling water. The car didn't have the clearance to make it, but how about her? Was it worth the risk?

Sam slowed his 4 x 4 as he approached the low-water bridge and Del's car. Glad to see she had enough sense not to try making it across in that thing. Even if the current wasn't strong enough to wash the car off the bridge, the low-slung vehicle would certainly have stalled halfway across.

Sam shivered at the thought. The water looked damn cold and he was in no mood to play hero, getting soaked trying to tow some fool's car out, even if the fool was worth a pretty penny to him. He pushed away a sudden disturbing notion that Del was becoming something more than just a possible monetary payoff, that if she wound up two states downstream, he'd actually miss her, not just the hope of some greenbacks to dig him and Becca out of the hole they'd fallen into.

Crunching to a stop behind Del's coupe, he flung open his door. Where was she? Sam swaggered toward the car, expecting his bodacious little pig hunter to be slumped behind the wheel in full pout mode. The car was empty.

Sam pulled his hat low over his eyes and surveyed the area. Waist-high weeds covered in red dust grew along both sides of the road. A gully separated the grass from a ramshackle barbwire fence. A path dotted with cow manure led from the road to a particularly large hole in the fence, obviously a well-used escape route for some bored bovine. Not able to think of any reason Del would have wandered into the field, Sam turned to study the water rushing over the bridge.

If he wanted something bad and nothing but some fast-running water was between him and his prize, what would he do? A frown creased his forehead. Surely Del wouldn't be stupid enough to try fording the bridge on foot. Even a strong man could lose his footing in the current and get washed downstream. A top-heavy woman like Del would tumble quicker than interest in a flash glass butter dish once the lid was busted.

No, she wouldn't wade out there, would she? Sam stepped toward the water. About four feet from the other side something glinted in the midday light. He angled his neck but couldn't make out what the object was. Another pace closer and the water swirled over the tops of his best boots.

Dangling from a briar bush that overhung the bridge was a rhinestone-bedecked sandal. Without pausing to think, Sam strode into the frigid water. He yanked the sandal off the bush, willing it to be different than the one he had noticed this morning slipped over a rebellious toe ring. Recognition hit him like a bowling ball to the groin. It was Del's, which could mean only one thing—she'd tried to make it across and failed. If her shoe was here, she could only be one place—downstream.

Apprehension filled his chest. Brushing the

brambles to the side with his bare hand, he stepped off the bridge and into the creek. He ignored the pull of the icy water as it encircled his waist. Shoving tree branches and trash out of his way, he searched the water for a glimpse of blond hair.

Nothing but minnows and frogs struggled against the current. Sam stumbled over a sunken log but kept pushing forward, fighting to keep the rushing water from dragging him down.

Where was she? Could she hear him? He yelled her name. Only the roar of water replied.

Panic welled up in his throat, bringing the acidic burn of bile with it. Could she have dragged herself onto shore somewhere? She had to be here. Praying, he ignored the numbness in his legs and floundered forward, heading toward a thick growth of pokeberry bushes.

"What the hell are you doing in there? Have you taken leave of your senses?" Del's voice kicked through the wall of desperation that had built around him.

Thrashing through the current, he could see her standing by her car, slapping the heel of one sandal against her palm. "Did you find my other shoe? I dropped one upstream. It must have washed down."

Relief swept over Sam, but faster than the water he stood in, irritation followed. He clenched the flashy footwear in his fist. A sandal. He had ruined a pair of Tony Lama boots for two straps of leather covered in rhinestones. Not to mention freezing his balls off and risking drowning in the swollen creek. He slogged toward the bank, using a misshapen oak to pull himself out of the water.

On dry land he felt wetter, colder, and madder than a barn cat after a January bath. He narrowed his eyes and stalked toward his quarry.

Del couldn't suppress a grin as she watched Sam slog toward her. What had the fool been doing in the stream? As soon as her big toe hit the frigid water, she'd decided against it. Instead, she'd gone to look for an alternate route. She'd lost a shoe in the process but still had enough sense not to step into the creek.

She dropped her gaze from his glowering expression to his white-knuckled hands. One fist was clenched around her missing sandal.

Surely he hadn't gone in over that. She liked the shoes, but $29.99 wasn't worth wading into that ice floe of a creek. As she looked from the shoe almost folded in two by the pressure of his hand, to the steely look in his eyes, it dawned on her—he thought she'd been washed downstream. He had been playing knight to her damsel in distress.

Something warm flickered in her chest. To cover any soft feelings that threatened to leak out, she pressed one hand over her heart and the back of the other to her forehead. Eyes closed and head tipped back, she exclaimed, "My fair prince, didst thou save my slipper?"

Silence followed. Del squeezed open one eye to peek at him. He had ground to a halt and now stood staring at the shoe clutched in his hand. A dangerous smile lit his face. Quicker than Del could say "mirror, mirror," he pulled back his arm and flung her new shoe into the creek.

Striding past an openmouthed Del, he said, "Sorry, princess, wrong friggin' fairy tale."

What Del's act didn't accomplish, his did. All warm thoughts of Sam Samson evaporated. She slapped the sole of her remaining shoe against her palm and considered the consequences of walloping him in the back of the head. Arrogant son of a bitch would probably leave her stranded on the wrong side of the creek, the side without the Pig.

From the driver's seat of his truck, Sam assessed her. "You getting in, or you waiting for a pumpkin?"

Mumbling what he could do with his pumpkin, she hobbled to the passenger door and climbed in.

"What are you doing here, anyway?" she asked, arms folded under her chest.

"Funny, I was going to ask you the same thing. When Kenny said you were headed to a hog farm, I thought for sure he was yanking my chain. You expanding your collection?" He looked cross as a treed coon.

Double darn, if it hadn't been for the swollen creek she'd have the Unruh Pig and be headed back to Chicago. Instead she was at the mercy of an uptight auctioneer. She cursed her luck for the hundredth time in the past three hours.

Taking a deep breath, she evaluated her situation. There was no way she could get across that sorry excuse for a bridge without Sam's help, but how to get him to drive her without revealing the truth?

"I'm just sightseeing," she blurted.

"At a hog farm?" He didn't sound exactly believing.

Once the pitch is on the table you can't pull it back. Del stuck to the Mont rules and blustered forward, trying to sound as exasperated with his ignorance as possible. "Yes, at a hog farm. I collect pigs, you know. I thought it would be nice to see how they're raised."

"Yeah, nice." Del thought she detected a slight snort before he continued. "You want to see them hung up and butchered too? That's always a pretty sight." He dropped his hat onto the seat between them.

If the deal isn't going your way, change direction. "So, why are you here?" she countered.

"Me, I'm just sightseeing, had a hankering to see a fancy city girl stranded ten miles from nowhere."

Funny. "I wasn't stranded." And she wasn't a city girl, but she stopped herself from retorting the latter. "I could leave whenever I wanted to."

"Can't get where you want to go though, can you?"

God, he was a pain. Del ran her hand over the smooth leather sole of her shoe. Just one good whack, that's all she asked.

Oblivious to the threat, Sam gunned up the truck. "You gonna tell me your real reason for heading to Hollywell's?"

Del bit her lower lip and stared out the windshield.

"Okey dokey, then, guess we'll find out the hard way." Sam put the truck into four-wheel drive and rolled it forward. As the dually churned through the water, Del's lone sandal bobbed to the surface but then, caught by a current, it disappeared over the edge of the bridge.

Del tossed its mate onto the floorboard; $29.99 down the creek. The worst part was, she had a

sneaking suspicion it wouldn't be the last thing she
lost to this man.

The truck bounced over the rutted ground. Del
suspected Sam was purposely hitting every pothole
and ripple in the road he could locate. When he
whammed into a chasm big enough to swallow a
fleet of 4 x 4s, she counted to ten, then said, "It's
such a nice day for a drive in the country, don't you
think?"

When he only grunted in reply, she knew she'd
guessed right.

She was back on track. It would take more than
his amateur efforts to get her to lose her cool
again.

She spent the rest of the trip concocting her plan
and sneaking peeks at her unsuspecting chauffeur.
By the time he hopped out of the truck to swing
open the aluminum gate that stood between them
and her Pig, she was relaxed enough to appraise the
difference between the view of his backside when
he bent to unloop the chain that held the gate and
her earlier look at Kenny's. It wasn't that the two
were that different; both had been graced with a
properly padded but firm posterior, but with her
guard down something about Sam caused her in-
sides to tighten and her heart to speed up. Maybe
analyzing the situation would weaken the attraction.

Could be that he insisted on wearing simple but
snug T-shirts that emphasized every bulge and
bundle of muscle. Or that his Levi's clung to
strong thighs while still accentuating that tempting
backside. Could be the way he carried himself,
with the confidence and innate sexuality of a
tomcat after a successful turf fight.

Could be that she was a sick, twisted, pig-befuddled mess. Really, that was the only answer. He was arrogant, listened to the countriest of country music, and refused to be led astray by even her best efforts. Basically, he was a complete pain in the behind and very likely the only thing standing between her and the Unruh Pig. She cursed the muse who had guided her to him in the first place.

The chain swung free and Sam pushed the gate open with one water-stained boot. They looked expensive, must have cost him four hundred dollars.

They'd dry out. Besides, it wasn't like she had asked him to jump into the creek to save her Shoe Barn specials.

Okay, so maybe he had thought he was saving her, but still, that was insulting. Like she didn't have enough sense to keep out of a flooded creek. Del folded her arms over her chest and tried to work up a good head of steam.

Sam finished propping the gate open with a rock and trotted back to the truck. His T-shirt stretched across his stomach, showing every line of his six-pack abs.

Del's mouth went dry.

He yanked open the truck door and winged himself into the driver's seat on a breeze filled with the smell of sunshine and cow manure, a combination she found bizarrely alluring. She truly was sick.

The jaunt seemed to have improved Sam's mood. Maybe cow manure had the same effect on him. He flashed her a cocky grin and her already racing heart gunned its engine. Before she could do something idiotic like fling herself across the cab and rip the T-shirt off his chest, she heaved open her door and threw herself from the cab. "I'll close the gate behind us," she yelled from the wholesome surface of the rutted dirt.

He gave her a curious look but put the truck in gear and rolled through the opening. Del practiced counting again. This time she got to thirty before she felt safe to reenter the dually.

"What were you counting?" Sam greeted her.

"My torments," she murmured.

"Don't you mean your blessings?" He flashed her another grin.

Noticing how white his teeth appeared against the tan of his skin, Del shook her head. "No, definitely torments."

Sam ran his finger alongside his nose, using his hand to hide his glance at Del. She hadn't said more than two words since they'd passed onto Hollywell's property.

His annoyance with her had dissipated. There was nothing like fresh air, sunshine, and being on the trail of a rare find to promote forgiveness and tolerance of others. Besides, his boots would dry. The caiman that gave up his hide for them spent most his reptilian existence in the water; a few minutes in a creek would be nothing. On the other hand, Del's shoe was gone. Its mate lay on the floor near her feet. He was glad it was hidden from view.

He'd been angry at the creek, but he'd had no call to toss out her shoe. In his calmer, more giving state of mind, he resolved to make it up to her. Course she probably wouldn't be too worried about a lost pair of shoes once he snagged this rare Pig out from under her cute little turned-up nose.

Why couldn't she have had a big old honker? Sam had always been a sucker for a sexy little nose—maybe he had watched too many reruns of *Bewitched* as a kid. Then, too, Del had that habit of twitching her nose when she was getting ready to tell a whopper. Sexy and a giveaway, it was more than a man could hope for.

Despite his soaked jeans, he felt movement in his groin. Not over a nose. He moved in his seat, attempting to suppress the errant body part. It was one thing to get a hard-on when Del was bouncing around in that tight-fitting pink shirt. The ruffle at the neck practically screamed "look at what I'm decorating," and the way her nipples stood at attention at the slightest cool breeze begged him to come unwrap the package. But an erection over a nose? That was past demented.

He glanced at her to prove his control. Lost in thought, she skimmed her hand across the V of her shirt and twitched her pert nose. The pressure in his pants responded in turn.

He groaned, and Del shot him a curious glance.

Think of something else. Noticing a pile of manure in their path, he started counting cow patties.

At around ten, Del interrupted him. "What you counting?"

She'd rolled down her window, and the ruffle flapped him an invitation. Rubbing his forehead, he focused on his task. "Cow patties."

"Oh." Her tone said this was a perfectly normal activity, but he didn't risk looking at her again to check for sarcasm. She'd asked and he'd answered. That was good enough.

Eleven. Twelve. He guided the dually over number thirteen, feeling an odd sense of victory when it squished under the tire.

Chapter 7

Happy as a pig in mud . . .

The clack of tires rolling over a white wooden cattle guard alerted Del they were almost at their destination. Ahead stood a faded gray farmhouse with a sloping, red rock porch and peeling white pillars. She waited for the dually to come to a stop under a massive maple before unsnapping her seat belt and swinging to the ground.

Her bare toes sunk into sandy earth. Way to make an impression. Every barefoot hillbilly joke she'd ever heard reverberated through her head.

At least she wasn't pregnant.

She couldn't suppress a snort. No risk of that; she hadn't even had a date for almost a year. Life in the big city of Chicago seemed to leave Del behind. Not that there weren't men interested, but none of them appealed to her. Fancy restaurants with waiters waving corks under her nose, or yuppie sports bars with blaring TVs, or, worst of all, glitzy dance clubs with music mixed to order were not her idea of a fun evening.

Del missed the more basic dates of her youth, a cold beer, old-fashioned rock and roll, and a man who knew how to fill out a pair of Levi's. That's what she needed.

Sam sauntered up. Damp denim clung to his thighs and a dribble of water leaked out of his boots as he came to a halt. Refusing to admit he fulfilled any part of her needs, Del turned and stomped toward the cracked cement walk that led to the house. He was country. She was rock and roll. There were some things a great body didn't overcome. She rolled her eyes at the weakness of her argument. Wonder how he felt about beer?

Lost in her thoughts, she got another six feet before she heard the droning of a bee. She froze.

"What's wrong?" Sam squished up behind her.

Afraid to move more than a hair, Del gritted out through clenched teeth, "A bee. I'm allergic."

"How allergic?" Sam asked.

"Enough." Idiot—couldn't he see she was busy here? He could get her medical history later. "Why?"

"'Cause a honeybee's hunting nectar about an inch from your cleavage."

Del jerked her gaze down. Sure enough, the little black and yellow demon was hotfooting it across her neckline. "Flick him. Flick him off." It took every bit of her control to not hop up and down, but she knew that would just aggravate the insect.

"Flick him?" Sam seemed to be analyzing the bee's position way too closely.

"Quit ogling my breasts and flick the damn bee."

He raised a brow. "What language. And I thought you were a lady."

If Del hadn't been paralyzed with panic, she would have snorted.

Grinning, Sam made an *O* with his thumb and middle finger and sent the bee flying. Safe, Del filled her lungs with air.

"You know, if you're allergic you shouldn't be walking around barefoot. There's more clover in this lawn than freckles on a turkey egg."

She did not need his advice on bee avoidance. She'd spent the last twenty years of her life dodging the little killers. "Not like I have a lot of choices, now is there?" Not waiting for his answer, she took another step toward the house.

"Sam, what you doing out here?" A man dressed in overalls and the obligatory feed hat dusted dried mud off his knees as he walked around the corner of the house.

Must be Hollywell. Del tucked a lock of hair behind her ear and smoothed the wrinkled jeans down her thighs. She was glad she couldn't see herself. Sometimes believing in yourself was all you had. If she looked as ragtag as she suspected, her conning confidence might be shot to smithereens. Wetting her lips, she slid on a sultry smile and prepared to charm.

"Daddy, who's that lady? She looks just like Dolly Parton." A grubby urchin wrapped her arms around the man's leg and peeked around him at Del. Apparently deciding Del was safe, the child skipped forward. Squeezing one eye shut, she looked Del up one side and down the other.

"You know Dolly Parton? We went to Dollywood

last year. They had pictures of her everywhere. You look just like her, except your hair ain't as big. Hers is a wig, you know. Leastways that's what my grandma says, and she knows. She can spot a fake from a mile away. Is yours real?" The girl didn't wait for Del's response. "Grandma says other parts of her ain't too real either, but I don't rightly know what she means. You got an idea?"

Del did, but she didn't feel like discussing those particular parts with the child or the men, for that matter. She hunched her shoulders over her one hundred percent natural assets and looked at Sam for rescue. He grinned back at her.

"This's Del Montgomery, Bill. She's interested in hog raising."

The man in overalls walked over and placed a hand on his daughter's shoulder. Looking at Del, he said, "That right?"

The girl abandoned her analysis of Del's rhinestones and asked, "You here to see Eloise? She's a mite grumpy today. Won't let hardly none of her babies grab a teat. Daddy's afraid some are gonna starve to death." She made the announcement in the matter-of-fact tone the weatherman used to predict rain. "We been feeding the little one with a bottle, but Daddy won't let me name him. Says one named hog is enough. The rest gotta be sold, no reason to be getting attached." Del thought she detected a quiver this time in the girl's voice.

"Eloise a sow?" she asked.

The child nodded. "She just had seven babies. The runt's no bigger than a minute. Daddy had to pull him out of the pen before she rolled on top of him. Pigs ain't the best mamas, you know."

Del knew more about the perils of pig farming than she wanted to admit, especially with Sam tapping his toe mere inches away, but she couldn't resist the girl's charm. She knelt down next to her. "You like pigs?"

At the child's solemn nod, Del continued, "You know, I like pigs too. I collect them." Thinking of a garish flowered piggy bank she'd picked up the first day out with Sam, she said, "I may have one you'd like. It's a bank. You could start collecting pigs too. What do you think?"

The girl's eyes lit up. "You collect pigs?"

"I sure do."

"I got a pig planter. I keep rocks in it."

The vein at the base of Del's throat jumped. She shot a glance at Sam to see if he'd heard the child's announcement, but he seemed engrossed in a conversation with Hollywell.

"If you come with me I can show you." A tiny hand streaked with dirt reached for Del's.

"Where you taking her, Jenny?" Hollywell broke off his conversation with Sam to address his daughter.

Not wanting to alert Sam what she was up to, Del answered. "She's just going to show me the pigs." Let the men think she meant the ham hock variety. She hopped off the walk onto a large patch of clover.

"Del, remember the bees," Sam called after her.

She turned to wave off his warning. As her hand fluttered in disdain, she felt a piercing pain shoot from the arch of her foot up her leg. Her less than perfect day had just taken distinct turn for the worse. Of course, the same could be said for the worker bee just smashed by her size eight. At this absurd thought, her knees gave way and she sunk to the ground. The last thing she saw before giving way to unconsciousness were two electric blue eyes blazing with anxiety.

Sam leaped from the walkway and grabbed Del before her head collided with the cement. Damn fool. Why was she stomping through clover without any shoes? The image of her sandal floating over the bridge and down the creek popped into his brain. As he looked at her pale face, guilt knifed into him.

There was no time for that now. He had to help her. Yanking off his belt, he fashioned it into a makeshift tourniquet and tightened it around her ankle. As he yelled at Hollywell to find antihistamines, he moved to Del's feet and, careful to not release more venom into her bloodstream, scraped the stinger out of her foot. That done, he switched back to her head and checked to make sure she was breathing. Assured there was no sign of swelling anywhere but her foot, he waited for Hollywell to return.

In town he could have called 911, but here there was little use. If the antihistamines didn't work he'd rush her to the hospital himself. The seconds ticked by. Sam brushed blond hair away from Del's face and ran the back of his fingers down her cheek. She looked so innocent and vulnerable like this. People died from bee stings. Sam knew it was rare, but it wasn't unheard of. How allergic was she? She hadn't answered that. Could she be carrying adrenaline?

He started to yell for Jenny to run to the truck and search Del's purse, when he remembered she had climbed into the vehicle carrying nothing but her lone shoe. After the scene by the creek she must have forgotten her purse in her car. If she did have a prescription, she didn't have it with her.

He glanced at her wrist. No MedicAlert bracelet. That was a good sign, wasn't it?

By the time Hollywell came jogging back, a woman running behind him carrying a portable phone and some water, Sam had worked himself into a frenzy. Del had to be okay. She had to be.

"Here." Hollywell shoved two pills and the glass into Sam's hand. "Sharon has the doctor on the phone. He said if she doesn't come to soon, we need to start heading to town."

Sam sprinkled a few drops on Del's face and murmured a prayer. He was afraid to shove the pills down her throat while she was out, for fear of choking her. Another baptismal and her eyelids fluttered. Sam's heart jumped with them. When he saw a slit of sweet-tea brown he tilted her upward and poked the pills through her lips. "Take these."

For the first time since he'd met her, she took his advice without argument. Long after she'd swallowed the pills and the water, he sat there with her cradled in his arms. Nothing had ever felt so right.

Del was embarrassed. She knew she'd overreacted. She'd passed out, for God's sake—over a bee sting. She'd been allergic all her life and the fear built a little more each time she was stung. She'd never had a severe enough reaction to warrant an EpiPen, but there was always that threat, the knowledge that each time could be worse than the last. When she'd realized she'd stepped on the bee, she'd panicked, plain and simple. Now Sam sat holding her in his arms like she was made of spun sugar and she was too embarrassed to open her eyes fully and apologize.

She hated showing weakness, but stupidity—that was unforgivable. Sinking into a mire of self-castigation, she dropped lower in Sam's arms and let her head slump against his chest. His fingers brushed across her forehead. Snuggled close, it was impossible to ignore his warm male scent, accented by his lemony cologne. She rubbed her nose against the smooth cloth of his T-shirt and inhaled.

"Del, you coming to? You okay?" The concern in his voice made her stomach flip. She was afraid to open her eyes, afraid the worry in his would send her into a fit of ashamed tears or, worse, drive her to lock her lips on his and not come up for air.

"Del?" He gave her a little shake.

With a sigh, she admitted defeat.

It was worse than she'd feared. Anxiety traced his face, his brow was lowered, his gaze intent. The soft, scary feeling she'd avoided at the low-water bridge smacked into her again, leaving her breathless and vulnerable. Their eyes met and everything else faded away.

Del had never felt truly cared for, worried about. Sure, her parents loved her in their own way, but her entire life had been a make-it-on-your-own kind of existence. To have someone so obviously moved with concern for her unleashed emotions she'd never felt before. It was terrifying—and exhilarating.

A bead of sweat clung to Sam's upper lip; without thinking Del swept it aside with her thumb. He grabbed her hand and pressed a kiss to her palm.

"She all right?" Jenny poked her head between them. "You still want to see Mama's pigs?"

"Child, don't be bothering her now." A woman Del assumed was Jenny's mother tapped the child on the shoulder and waved her onto the porch. Addressing Sam she asked, "You want I should call the doctor back? Tell him you're bringing her in?"

Go to the doctor? Admit she fainted like a no-brain ninny? Del shoved her hands against Sam's chest and teetered to a stand. Sam's belt was twisted around her ankle. Geez, the man was thorough. She freed her leg with a jerk. "I'm fine." The momentum from pulling the belt loose sent her staggering into Sam, who leaped to his feet to support her.

"You're always fine." Sam flashed her a seductive smile and Del's heart jumped. "But it still wouldn't hurt to have the doctor look you over."

"No, no, I'm fine, really." Her voice sounded pleading, and for once it wasn't a ploy.

Sam looked uncertain, but he didn't argue. "Well, why don't you sit down for a while anyway?"

Jenny hopped off the porch. "Great, you can see the pig and meet the runt." With a grin as irresistible as sin, she skipped around the side of the house.

The Pig. Jenny was going to come dancing back with the Unruh Pig tucked under her arm, and at the moment, Del couldn't think of one decent lie to get Sam out of the way. To be honest, at the moment she didn't want Sam out of the way. She wanted everyone else out of the way so she could snuggle back up against his chest and see where it took them.

Sam seemed to have moved past the moment faster than her, however. "Pig?" He turned to Holly-well. "Does she mean a real pig or something else?"

"Hard to know with Jenny. There's no telling what she's all fired up about."

Thirty seconds later, Jenny came whirling back around the corner a piece of pottery under one arm and a squirming pig in the other. From ten feet away, Del could identify the pottery, a pig in blue jeans and a green shirt leaning against a box. It was a known maker, but Shawnee, not Unruh. And worth maybe thirty dollars, not the take-the-top-off amount the Unruh Pig would bring. She dropped to a sit on the red stone porch. At least she didn't have to worry about conning Sam so soon after he had held her with concern.

Jenny sidled up to Del and slipped the Shawnee planter into her lap. "You like it?"

"It's very nice," Del murmured, hoping she looked properly impressed.

The child whispered in Del's ear, "You can have it, if you get my daddy to sell you Runt."

"Runt?"

"Yeah, Runt." Jenny released the piglet onto the porch. "I told you Daddy won't let me name him, seeing as how he's destined for bacon."

The little black and white pig snuffled and snorted his way to Del's lap, nudging the planter with his dirt-covered nose. "Destined for bacon," Del repeated.

"Yeah." Jenny ran her tiny hand down the piglet's back. "Momma told me not to get attached, but it's right hard, feeding him by hand and all. I just don't know what I'd do if he got sold for bacon."

Del knew. Her heart would break and her trust in the world would change forever. Then, as time went on, more betrayals would follow until she couldn't stand the sight of a farm, her family, or southern Missouri.

"How much you want for the pig?" Del directed a steady gaze at Hollywell.

He looked from her to his daughter with confusion. "That planter's Jenny's."

"Not the planter, the pig. How much do you want for him?"

The look of confusion changed to downright amazement. "You want to buy that runt? You got some place to raise a hog?"

Did she? Del briefly thought of her tidy and tiny apartment in Chicago. She didn't think they even took cats, much less a two hundred–pound hog. It didn't matter. She'd move.

"Yes, I want to buy him. How much?"

Based on the determined glint in Del's eyes, Sam guessed he was going to be hauling a pig home in his dually—a squealing, mud-loving pig, not a nice clean piece of art pottery worth six figures. What in the blazes did she want with a pig?

Women, just when you thought you had them figured out, they did something unfathomable— like buy livestock.

Sam wandered to the porch and leaned against a column. What did he care if she saddled herself with the little beast? Wasn't like it was going to be spending any more time with him than it took to get back across the low-water bridge where they had left her car.

He tipped his hat over his eyes and relaxed. Ten minutes later the haggling was over, and the piglet had a new owner, except for one minor detail.

"Sam . . ." At the coy tone, Sam pushed back his hat. Sweet Tea was back to her sexy, manipulative ways. He was glad to see it.

She lowered the piglet to the ground and leaned toward Sam, offering him a glimpse of the most perfect breasts this side of creation. She added an eyelash flutter before continuing. "Sam, would you mind loaning me a little cash? Just until we get to my car. In all the commotion, I seem to have forgotten my purse."

All this for a football wannabe. He couldn't wait to see her act when they found the art pottery he was sure she was hunting.

"Sam . . ." She hopped off the porch. As her bee-stung foot hit the ground, she yelped and slid back to a sit. Sam strode over and cupped it in his hands. She wouldn't miss her shoes. Her foot was now three times its normal size.

"Shit," he exclaimed. "We need to get you to the doctor."

"It's fine," she argued, but a glimmer of tears shone in her eyes.

Sam practiced mumbling every four-letter word he knew, repeating the mouth-wash-worthy ones twice. Not giving her a chance to quarrel more, he scooped her into his arms and headed to his truck.

"What about Toadstool?"

She was obviously delirious. He kept walking.

"Stop." She thumped him on the chest with balled fists.

He gained another three feet before she smacked him again.

With a sigh he looked down at her. Better humor her; if she was addled he didn't want her getting too upset.

"We can't leave without Toadstool." She gazed at him with strained patience.

Why was she looking at him like that? She was the one being hardheaded. He started to snap out a response, but one glance at her swollen foot stopped him. In what he hoped was a calming voice, he said, "We can get you some mushrooms in town if you like, right after you see the doctor."

"Don't talk to me like I'm bidding without a number. I don't need a doctor. I need my pig." She looked crosser than the business end of a copperhead.

Her pig? Glancing back toward the porch where the piglet snuffled in the clover, Sam said, "You mean that pork rind reject?"

She pulled back her fist and punched him in the shoulder—hard. "Don't talk about my pig that way."

Well, hell, he was trying to make sure she was safe, and all she cared about was that damn piglet. He thought about dropping her butt-first onto the grass. Envisioning her outraged scream when she hit the ground, he checked to make sure she wasn't reading his thoughts and preparing to sock him again.

She seemed to have forgotten him. She was

fixated on her hand, opening and closing it with obvious difficulty.

"What's wrong with your hand?"

She dropped her fist behind her back. "Nothing, just happens sometimes when I get a bee sting."

"But you were stung on your foot."

"Yeah, well, other parts swell too."

A river of cuss words began to flow again. He turned toward his truck.

"Sam, please . . ." She wasn't playing him this time; he could see it in her eyes. She wanted that pig. For some reason he couldn't fathom, that piglet was important to her.

Suddenly, it was important to Sam too.

"I'll put you in the truck, then come back and pay for him."

"Toadstool."

"What?"

"Toadstool, his name is Toadstool." Her voice was low and earnest.

Sam wrenched open the truck door and placed her on the seat. With more tenderness than he meant to show, he said, "Yeah, Toadstool."

The smile she gave him was worth hauling a barn full of muddy pigs in his truck. He reached across her to grab his checkbook.

"And, Sam?"

Stretched across her, he could smell the sweet flowery scent of her cologne. He drew in the deepest breath he could and still stay under control.

She leaned forward and pressed a light kiss to his lips. "Thanks."

Sam nodded and withdrew like she'd loosed a

herd of porcupines on him. Something was cooking between them, something scary. Neither of them trusted the other, for good reason, but somehow they seemed to be getting closer and closer. Or was he just getting closer? Maybe the whole thing was an act for Del.

Shaking his head to clear the fog, he went to buy a pig.

Chapter 8

Hog heaven . . .

Del hugged the tiny pig to her chest, giggling when his damp nose nuzzled her exposed skin.

She'd sent Sam back to the porch to return Jenny's planter. The girl had insisted he bring the Shawnee piece along with Toadstool, but Del told him to take it back. She was taking the girl's pig. She wouldn't take her keepsake too.

The little creature climbed up her chest, his tiny hooves digging into her skin. Inches from her face, he grunted and sniffed. After checking to make sure Sam was still out of hearing distance, Del cooed in return.

Bacon? How could anyone eat pork again after holding such a cutie?

"You got a grip on Pork Chop?" Sam asked with a grin as he winged into the driver's seat and dropped his hat onto the floor by her feet.

The bristly hairs on the piglet's back pricked Del's fingers. Without sparing Sam a glance, she said, "Toadstool."

Silence descended around them. Only Toadstool's snuffles broke through. Del ran her palms down the runt's back. He settled in, stretching his front legs in front of him and falling asleep.

Keeping one hand on the steering wheel, Sam scratched the little pig between the eyes with the other. "You know much about raising a pig?"

Del shrugged. "Enough. What I don't know I can figure out, but it can't be too tough. You couldn't ask for a better pet. They're smart and they're clean." After stopping to roll her eyes at Sam's raised eyebrow, she explained, "They just wallow in mud to keep cool."

Toadstool pushed his hind hooves against Del's leg as he edged closer to Sam.

"So, how long you planning on keeping him?" Sam asked.

Del twisted the piglet's curly tail around her index finger. "Forever. When something little and helpless is counting on you, you don't let it down— no matter what the cost. Besides, I don't make the same mistake twice." Tears threatened to form in her eyes. She turned her face away so Sam wouldn't see them. When she had her emotions under control, she turned back.

"So, do you have a pet?" she asked.

He shook his head. "Never have."

"Not even as a child?"

"No." He slowed down as they approached the gate.

"Why not? I never knew a kid who didn't have something, dog, cat, or at least a turtle."

As the truck slowed to a stop, Toadstool stood up and trotted across Del to look out the window.

"Just didn't." His voice was tense and Del could tell he wanted to drop the subject, but that just made her want to hear the answer more.

As he opened the door to exit the truck, she placed a hand on his arm. "Why not?"

Masculine eyes tinged with melancholy flicked from Toadstool to her face. For a second she thought he wasn't going to answer. When he did, his voice was devoid of emotion. "My dad didn't believe in pets. Said animals were dirty and spread germs. I snuck home a rabbit once, but he found it and set it loose."

"A wild rabbit?"

"No, tame—white with pink eyes."

"But a tame rabbit wouldn't survive in the wild."

Sam pushed open the truck door. "Yeah, I know."

Del gathered Toadstool to her chest as she watched Sam stride across the rocky ground. Guess she wasn't the only one with parent issues. How could people supposedly love someone and still screw them up so royally? Not that Sam seemed screwed up. If anything he seemed to have everything under control. A bit oddball maybe, having his office in a feed store, but now that she'd heard his pet story, maybe that made some kind of twisted sense too. Wasn't allowed around animals as a child so as an adult worked somewhere animals were the bread and butter.

Sam walked toward the truck, stretching his arm across his chest as he came. The motion caused the short sleeve of his T-shirt to roll above his bicep. Sensitive and sizzling with sin, the man was a dangerous combination.

Del chucked Toadstool under the chin and said,

"You'll have to be extra nice to Sam." Then softer, "'Cause good Lord knows I can't trust myself to do it."

Sam climbed into the truck.

Damn Del for reminding him of that rabbit. He'd forgotten him long ago. At eight it had been pretty traumatizing, though. He could still see the old man standing by the screen door, holding it open with one hand, pointing to the woods behind their house with the other. Even then Sam knew there was no way that rabbit would survive the night, but he'd trudged out the door with the little beastie tucked under his arm. He'd stayed with the rabbit till midnight, when his father started screaming from the back porch and Sam knew if he didn't hightail it back he'd have to endure a thrashing with the old man's belt. He'd still considered staying, making his dad come after him, but he knew it would be no use. The rabbit wasn't coming home with him. So, he placed some stones around the opening to the log and prayed for the best.

The next morning he rushed back to the woods, but there was no sign of the rabbit. That was the only thing that kept him from sobbing like a toddler, convincing himself that if something had gotten to his pet there'd have been some sign— tufts of hair or spots of blood. He'd looked for the animal all summer, but it never showed up again.

Twenty-four years later and the memory of some brainless bunny could still tie his stomach into knots. What would the old man think of that?

He glanced at Del. She and her pig appeared to have dozed off. After shoving the truck into gear, he turned back onto the gravel road and headed in the direction of her car. He suspected Del might be playing possum, but his well of conversation was about dried up too. With one eye on his companion, he slid a Hank Williams Sr. CD into the player. As "Hey, Good Lookin'" filled the cab, Del flinched. Suppressing a grin, he twisted the volume up a few notches and hummed along.

Hank had barely made it to the second chorus of "what you got cooking" when a distressing hacking sound reverberated through the truck. Del was immediately alert.

"Oh, my God, it's Toadstool. What's wrong?"

She jerked the piglet up and stared into his snout. The tiny critter was beginning to look a bit green, in Sam's opinion.

"You might want to point him another direction." He motioned with his hand toward the window.

With Toadstool gagging louder than a frat boy after a weekend of keggers, Del fumbled with the electric window button.

"Get the damn thing open," Sam yelled.

"It won't come down, there's something wrong." Del alternated between punching the window button and stroking the increasingly distressed pig.

"Well, hell, it ain't rocket science." Sam slammed the truck into park and leaned across to open the window. Toadstool gave him one last pleading look before twisting his head to the side and urping down Sam's arm and onto the floor.

Great, just great.

The piglet looked happier, Del looked horrified, and Sam felt like punting both of them out the door. Only two things stopped him—number one, by some miracle his cowboy hat had survived the gush of pig puke unscathed, nary a drop on it, and number two, Sam'd had the child safety latch flipped. Del couldn't have gotten the window open without a crow bar. He didn't bother mentioning this last discovery to her, but it made him reconsider the boot scoot onto the gravel road.

After scraping up the worst of the mess with an old rag he found in the glove box, he moved his hat to safety on the high ground of the seat and ordered Del to relocate Toadstool to the floor.

"But he's sick. He might need me."

"It's not like I'm making him ride in back, which isn't a bad idea, by the way."

Del's eyes practically crossed in warning.

"But I guess the damage's done, not like he can make it stink any worse in here." Sam rolled down his window and Del's.

Appearing somewhat mollified, she tucked the pig in between her bare feet, stroking him under the chin with her toe. Sam would have sworn the lucky little porker winked at him.

Cunning critter. He got a free ride with Del fawning all over him, and Sam got a stench-filled truck.

When they arrived at the low-water bridge, Del opened the door and hopped out. Toadstool rose on four legs, wavered for a minute, then collapsed back onto the floor.

"What's wrong with him? Do you think I need to call the vet?" Del's hand shook as she ran it down the pig's back.

Sam sighed. "He's probably just carsick. I doubt he's been on a lot of road trips."

"You don't know. Besides, you're still mad he spewed in your dually." She made it sound like the whole mess was Sam's fault.

"Of course, I don't know, but it stands to reason, and yeah, since you asked, I am less than thrilled that my only mode of transportation reeks of re-gurgitated pig formula. Call me uncaring, but there it is." He slammed out of the truck and strode around to the side where she stood.

Her hand flew to her neck and those damn pearls. Sam was starting to hate them more than a high-reserve auction. He prepared for a lambast-ing, but after twisting the beads for a second she dropped her hand and placed it on his chest.

"I'm worried about him. You know a vet I can call?"

Heat from each of her fingertips seared into Sam's chest. How did she do that? Ignoring the urge to yank her against him, he replied, "Their of-fices will be closed by now, but Kenny will know someone. When we get to town, I can ask him."

Sucking her lower lip between her teeth, she nodded. Sam zeroed in on the gesture, so inno-cent, but so suggestive. He curled his fingers into his palms. He had to get her into her car, away from him, before he pressed her against the side of his truck and showed her she had more to worry about than a carsick pig.

"I'll take him," he blurted.

"What?"

"I'll take him. There's no reason to take the risk he'll get sick in your car too. He's already chris-tened mine, might as well leave him. I can run by the store, get the doctor's name, and take him for a checkup."

She shook her head. "No, I can't leave him."

"Fine, you follow us."

She peered into the truck at the piglet. When she looked back at Sam, she still seemed unsure.

"He'll be fine. It's not like I'm going to shove an apple in his mouth and drop him off at a luau."

As her eyes narrowed, he softened his tone. "He'll be fine, trust me."

After another thirty-second stare down, she walked to her car. "I'll be right behind you. If he gets worse, pull over."

Sam stalked to the driver's side. Now he was a sick pig's nursemaid. Couldn't get much worse than that.

He wrenched opened the door. His patient was stretched out in apparent contentment—right on top of Sam's now crushed Resistol hat.

Four hours later, Sam kicked back in his oak chair and yanked open his gin drawer. He was never serving as chauffeur to a hog again. It took two hours to hunt down the vet and get Toadstool a clean bill of health and another two to de-stink the dually. To be honest he wasn't sure it was one hundred percent stink free, but he was past caring. There was only so much one man could do.

He sloshed a couple fingers of gin in a glass and held it up to the light. He'd never understood why people did that. What were they looking for—bugs?

With a shrug, he took a sip. The liquid burned a

trail down to his belly, and Sam stifled a cough. He was an embarrassment to Dashiell Hammett fans everywhere. He set the glass to the side, covering his bovine calendar beauty's rump roast.

As he was digging in his desk drawer for coins for the Coke machine, his phone rang.

"Sam, you doing okay?" Del's voice was sweet as syrup, but this fly knew better than to get too close. That's how you got stuck, and then eaten.

"I been better." He kept his tone cool and noncommittal.

"I feel really bad about your truck," drawled the spider. "I just don't know what Toadstool and I would have done without you."

Sam grunted.

"Toadstool's doing a lot better. I think the vet was right, he just got excited with all the change and everything. I'm sure it won't happen again."

Sam's B.S.-ometer started ticking.

"You should see him. He's so cute. I put him in that little red harness the vet gave me and took him for a walk. He just trotted all around the parking lot."

Tick. Tick. Tick.

The spider paused. He could almost hear her moistening her lips, getting ready for the final drop.

"But, well, the thing is, the woman who owns this hotel, she saw us out there."

Another pause. The ticking elevated to a tock.

"And, well, she thought Toadstool was as cute as a rabbit's rump, but, well, she has a strict no-pets policy. I guess some floaters smuggled a snake in last summer and it got loose, and, well, you can imagine."

"Did he puke up pig parts?"

The spider took a second to refocus. "I know this is a lot to ask, but I was wondering if it would be at all possible for you to watch Toadstool for me—just for a couple days until I can find someplace that will let me keep him."

The fly opened his mouth. He had to draw the line somewhere and this was it—no more. Rare art pottery or no rare art pottery, he wasn't living with an animal that had ruined his truck and his hat. Bad enough the pig's owner had ruined Sam's boots and seemed to be working on his life.

"Oh, the swelling's gone down in my hand too. My foot's still puffed up, but it doesn't hurt too bad."

And there it was. He fell, floundering. Stuck in the syrup, all ready for the spider's snack.

"I'll be here for the next hour." Sam heard himself mutter.

"I'll be right there."

A dial tone hummed in his ear. Sam picked up his glass and slammed the gin to the back of his throat. His life had been animal free for twenty-four years and what does he start up with? A pig. Envisioning himself in a year lifting two hundred pounds of pampered pig into his truck, he grabbed the gin bottle and threw another swallow to the back of his throat.

Gagging almost as bad as Toadstool had earlier, he placed his crushed hat over his eyes and waited for his guests.

When Del arrived at the feed store, Sam was passed out at his desk, a squashed cowboy hat over his face.

"I think you need a new hat," she announced as she tugged the piglet in behind her. Toadstool had shown quite a bit of interest in a bag of goat chow. Del wasn't sure how having a pet pig trotting around the feed store was going to work, but she was desperate. Allentown wasn't exactly lousy with hotel choices—well, the choices were lousy, and there weren't a lot of them.

Sam made some kind of grumphing noise and shoved his hat back far enough to glare at her with one eye.

"This here is my best hat."

"You don't have to be surly. It's not my fault you're too cheap to buy a new hat." Del scooped up Toadstool and perched herself on the edge of a chair. "You know anything about feeding a piglet?"

Sam mumbled something Del suspected was a curse and sat up. His hat fell to the floor. He left it there.

"I thought that was your specialty."

Man, he was crabby. She opened her mouth to reply, but he waved her to silence.

"I talked to Kenny"—he gave Toadstool an appraising look—"before I knew the half-pint hog was moving in with me." He ran his hand over his face and took a deep breath. "Anyway, Kenny has everything you, or I guess *we*, need to feed him. Right now the runt needs a bottle and in a couple weeks we can start him on creep feed."

Del was impressed. He'd researched Toadstool's needs even before she'd asked for help. This was going to work out better than she'd hoped.

"So Kenny is okay with Toadstool being here?" She tried to sound casual. No reason to alert Sam

that she thought his friend would rather open a
nest of yellow jackets than help her.

"Haven't talked to him about it yet. He was gone
by the time you dropped your bacon bomb on me."

"Oh." Del lowered Toadstool, who had started to
wriggle, to the floor.

"But what problem could he have with it? I mean,
who wouldn't want a hog rooting around a store
filled with highly edible stock feed?"

Sam's mood didn't seem to have improved
much in the past few hours.

She snapped the lead off Toadstool's harness,
wishing she didn't need Sam on her side right now.
The man was more cantankerous than a new bride
with a missing groom.

While Toadstool toddled around Sam's desk and
out of view, Del twisted the leash around her wrist.

Sam picked up an empty highball glass and held
it to the light. What was he doing? Suppressing an
eye roll, she wet her lips and pushed her shoulders
back. Obviously some charm was called for.

Again, he held up a hand. "Don't get yourself all
geared up for nothing. I'll talk to Kenny. He'll be
fine."

Del twisted her head in annoyance. Was he insinuating that she was manipulating him? Okay, so she
was, but it was still rude for him to point it out. She
unwound the leash and plopped it down on his desk.

"Well, then, here."

He glanced at the lead, then back at his glass.
"Dandy. I'll see you tomorrow. I assume we're still pig
hunting?" He spared her a glance. "Meet me at the
Hutch at seven. Hauling Hogzilla in there'll proba-

bly break a book's worth of health codes, but I don't figure he's the worst customer Becca's ever served."

After giving Toadstool a good-bye scratch and Sam an exasperated look, Del strode to her car.

This had certainly changed her plans. Like it or not, she was stuck with Sam for a while, at least until she could find somewhere else to house Toadstool.

Fact was, if she wanted to have her pig and hunt one too, she needed Sam Samson. Talk about being trapped between a rock and a hardhead.

The bold bundle of temptation and torment gone, Sam turned to look for his new companion. Little pig, little pig . . . Sam shook his head; maybe he needed to lay off the gin. After screwing the cap back on, he stored the bottle in his drawer.

Now, where was Toadstool? A snoring grunt answered his question. The runt was stretched out in his favorite position, front feet straight ahead, on what Sam suspected was now his favorite bed— Sam's Resistol hat.

With a resigned sigh, Sam scooped up the tiny animal, hat and all.

"Might as well keep it. Don't think I'll be wearing it anytime soon."

Flipping off the lights, he headed for home.

The next morning Sam rolled over in his bed and came face to belly with his houseguest. How did the tiny critter get up here? Sam had left him in an open cardboard box on the floor the night before. He didn't think the animal could get out of the carton, much less scramble up on the bed, but there he was—feet stretched out and his little mouth opening and closing with each snore. At least he wasn't sleeping on Sam's hat. Instead he had countermanded a pillow, covered in a pillowcase hand-embroidered by Sam's deceased grandmother. One tiny black hoof scratched against the center of a blue forget-me-not.

The old man would've had a cow if he were alive to see a pig curled up on his mother's linens.

A second hoof joined in the movement, giving the impression the little guy was running from something. After a quick glance around the empty bedroom, Sam ran his hand lightly down the runt's side.

"Shush, you're okay," he whispered. The hooves calmed, and after another stroke from Sam, Toadstool settled into a deeper sleep.

One last soothing murmur and Sam went to fix breakfast. He stood staring at an unopened packet of bacon for five minutes. With a glance at the bedroom door, he dumped it in the trash and whipped a box of cereal out of the cabinet.

He was polishing off his second helping of Life when the phone rang.

"Is this Samson?" The male voice was loud and grating so early in the morning.

Not in the mood to be bullied, Sam replied, "Who's asking?"

There was a moment of silence on the other end of the line, followed by, "A business associate of Del Montgomery's. Is this Samson? Is my information correct, that you're working with her?"

Sam hesitated. A business associate? "What kind of business?"

"Are you working with Del Montgomery?" the other man countered.

Filling his coffeemaker with water, Sam grunted, then, "Yeah, I'm working with her. Now, who is this, and what do you want?"

Chapter 9

Save your bacon . . .

Six A.M. and Del was wide awake. It was unnatural. If God had meant for her to be up this early, he'd have sent someone dark, dangerous, and undeniably sexy to her door with a steaming cup of Starbucks. She rolled over and shoved her face into her pillow. Hell, she'd settle for just undeniably sexy and a tepid cup of QuikTrip brew. Maybe just the undeniably sexy part would be okay. She groaned.

Sam was starting to grow on her. She'd been up most of the night alternating between worrying over Toadstool and fantasizing about Sam. She'd spent exactly zero time on what she needed to be concentrating on—the Unruh Pig. Now more than ever she needed a plan. Because of Toadstool, she needed Sam, and because of her fast-awakening libido, she needed to avoid him.

Dark and dangerous. Sam fit the bill. Tight T-shirts and snug jeans—her mouth went dry just thinking about how they hugged his body. Plus, he had an edge to him, a "don't tread on me" thing going.

That had always been Del's favorite U.S. flag, "Don't Tread on Me" with a big picture of a hissing rattlesnake. As annoying as she found Sam, his take-no-flack attitude was sexy as hell.

She rolled over again, this time pulling the pillow over her face. What to do at this ungodly hour? Sam had ordered her to meet him at seven sharp at the Bunny Hutch, which, of course, meant she couldn't be there before seven-thirty at the earliest. Eight would be even better.

But then again she wanted to see Toadstool so bad she could hardly stand it. She screamed into the hard foam pillow. Why couldn't the man have been the easy target she'd prepared for? Why did everything have to be so difficult?

The last was a rhetorical question. She knew exactly why everything had to be difficult. Because she was a Mont and nothing came easy, never had, never would.

Maybe she could call him, wake him up to check on Toadstool, then still show up an hour late. That would work, satisfy her need for information on her pig and show a complete disregard for his imagined authority. Energized by the solution, she bounced off the bed and into the bathroom to take care of a few more basic needs before implementing her plan.

She was washing her hands when the phone rang. Terrified Toadstool had relapsed, she flung her body across the bed and yanked up the receiver.

"Is he okay? Did he puke?" she yelled into the phone.

"Kid, what you talking about? Sounds like you need to be hanging around with a different crowd."

Surprised to hear a female voice instead of Sam's, Del had a hard time placing it. The woman continued, "I hope I'm not calling you too early, but I gotta get down to Mountain View before noon, and them roads are crookeder than a room full of aldermen looking to line their pockets. Plus, there's sure to be some farmer blocking all the good passing zones." She paused for a breath. "Least it's too early for hauling hay. You get behind a trailer full of that and you might as well throw out seeds and wait for harvest."

Del spun through her mental Rolodex. Considering hardly anyone knew she was here, it took her way too long to place the voice. Maybe she need the Starbucks more than the sexy.

"Tilde." She hesitated, to give the woman a chance to correct her. When she didn't, Del continued, "No, it's not too early. I was already up and getting ready to start my day." She strived to sound perky and way more awake than she was.

"Good to hear. Listen"—there was a muffled sound as if Tilde was talking to someone in the background—"I was just calling"—her voice rose in volume for a second like she was drowning someone else out—"to see if you still wanted to get together for that lunch. I found something the other day I think may interest you."

Del's heart skipped a few beats. "Really. What exactly did you find?"

"Nothing I can describe over the phone. You need to see it in person. So, you want to have that lunch?"

Did Sam Samson have a tight butt? "Sure, how about today?"

"Told you, I'm heading down to Mountain View today. How about Friday? I've got another appoint up your way then."

Del didn't bother to act unavailable—that was for men and hoity-toity women with one too many Lalique vases to sell.

"Sure, name the place."

"How 'bout the Bunny Hutch? I surely do like helping that little Becca out with some extra business."

Del liked helping Becca out too, but she didn't want Becca's kissable cousin horning in on any information Del learned about the Unruh Pig.

"Name another place," she replied.

"You got a problem with the Hutch?" Tilde asked.

Del twitched her nose back and forth. "No, I love the Hutch, love Becca. I just seem to eat there about every meal. With you knowing the area so much better than me, I thought maybe you could introduce me to something new. Price doesn't matter—my treat."

"You think I know the area better than you, do you? Well, that might be up for argument." Tilde paused long enough for Del to wonder about her comment. "But I'm not one to turn down a free trip to the hay trough," Tilde continued. "There's a new place down 72, catfish and hush puppies. Slim thing like you, you eat that?"

Del decided Tilde might just be her new best friend. After agreeing to meet her at the catfish place at one on Friday, she hung up.

She immediately picked up the phone and

dialed Sam's. The line was busy. Del checked the
digital clock on the bedside table, six twenty. Who
could he be talking to at this hour?

Coffee had already started to drip out of Sam's
Bunn by the time the rude SOB on the other end
of the line chose to answer his question.

"What I want isn't as important as how I can help
you."

Sam shoved a chipped ironstone mug under the
stream of java. "You planning on helping me?"
God save him from the arrogance.

He could tell by the man's accent he wasn't from
around here. Probably some college boy, city dweller
thinking he could hoodwink the uneducated hillbilly. Sam was tempted to slam down the receiver
and go feed his pig.

He took a loud sip of coffee. Course, the man
obviously knew something about Del, something
Sam didn't.

The easiest man to con was one who underesti-
mated you.

Putting an extra twang in his voice, Sam repeated, "You planning on helping me?"

There was a second of silence, making Sam
wonder if he'd overplayed the hillbilly card, but
then the man continued. "I'm hoping we can help
each other. What exactly has Del told you about
the Pig?"

So Izzy was right. Del was after the legendary Pig.
Sam pulled open the screen door that led to his
front porch and slid into one of the white metal

chairs that sat there. With his feet up on the wooden railing, he took another sip of coffee.

"The Pig? Well, no more'n she told you, I reckon."

The man paused again. "Did she tell you what's she's authorized to pay for it?"

Authorized to pay? Sounded like Del was working for someone else. Sam waved at old Mrs. Blackwell as she tottered out her front door and started yanking weeds from her flower bed.

"I can't say she mentioned it. I guess I figured she'd pay what she had to. You got a firmer number?"

The man cleared his throat. "Let's just say my resources are a bit more varied than Del's. If you have a lead on the Unruh Pig, you'd be best served to work with me."

Unruh. Sam had heard the name before. Some fancy pottery company. He'd never sold a piece, but he knew a couple people who were always hunting it.

"Well, from what I hear, Unruh don't go cheap." Sam put more twang in his voice than a *Hee Haw* regular. "You know money's like manure. You got enough to spread around?"

Sam could feel his caller's nose curl in disgust. "As I said, I have resources," he replied.

"We talking folding money or gum ball money?" Sam asked.

An edge of irritation crept into the other man's voice. "As much as it takes. I can locate a buyer tomorrow willing to offer six figures. If I find another one, at auction who knows what the Pig will bring, but we have to get it to auction first." He paused. "You, of course, would be eligible for the finder's fee."

"What kind of fee we talking?"

"The standard ten percent, I'd imagine."

Sam tapped a finger against his cup. "Twenty's a bit more standard here."

He could almost hear the other man's teeth grinding. "That can probably be arranged."

Swirling the coffee in his cup, Sam asked, "Where you planning on having this auction?"

The man sounded suspicious. "You did say you were working with Del, didn't you?"

Sam chided himself. Apparently he should already know the answer to the question. Now he had to cover his mistake. "I'm working with her, but you still haven't made it real clear who you are and who you're working for."

Mrs. Blackwell tossed a handful of weeds into the gutter and hobbled back up her walk. As the screen door swung shut behind her, the man answered.

"The name's David Curtis."

Sam flicked a bit of white paint off the chair arm. His coffee was getting cold and his patience was running out. "And you know Del how, exactly?"

David Curtis sounded like his tolerance was on the thin side too. "I told you. I'm a business associate of Del's. I'm another auctioneer at Porter Auctions."

Surprise made Sam forget his hillbilly act. "Another?"

"Yes, another. Didn't Del tell you she was an auctioneer?"

Somewhere in Sam's yard a cricket called for a mate. For the insect's sake, Sam hoped no female was around to chirp back. She'd just suck him in with lies and deceit—probably eat him for his trouble.

Okay, that was a praying mantis, but it was still a good lesson to remember.

Refocusing on his current conversation, Sam replied, "Course she told me. I just didn't understand that you meant you and her. Thought you were saying there was another auctioneer gonna show up."

The man laughed. "No, just me. So, you have a lead on the Pig yet?"

Sam had a lot of thinking to do. He seemed to be attracting business offers like a picnic attracted ants. "Not yet, but I'm working on it. Why don't you give me your number? I learn something and I'll give you a call."

The man seemed less than happy with Sam's put-off, but he complied. After walking inside to get a pencil and piece of paper, Sam jotted down the number.

"You have any idea how long it'll take you to get more information?" Curtis asked.

"No, but I'll be in touch. You can count on that." Right after he talked to a certain conniving female auctioneer.

As Sam was pulling the phone from his ear, Curtis's voice halted him. "Oh, and Samson? I think it would be in our mutual best interest if you didn't alert Del that we spoke. There's nothing she could do to stop us, but why make trouble, right?"

Yeah, why make trouble? Sam hung up the phone and went to feed the pig.

Del had called Sam at least twenty times. Who could the man be talking to? She punched "end" on her cell phone and swung her car into his drive. She didn't even grimace when the bottom of her vehicle scraped the cement of the steep drive. Cell phone gripped in one hand, she slammed her car door shut with the other.

Her man-eater shoes tapped up the sidewalk. With her new sandal drifting down to Arkansas, she hadn't had any other choices; besides, they were appropriate. She wanted to look good when she kicked Sam's butt into next week.

He should have known she'd be worried about Toadstool. He had no business jawing on the phone for the past half hour, and if there was something wrong with the pig, Sam should have called her before doing anything else. Plus, it was almost seven and his truck was still in his drive. There was no way he would make it to the Hutch in time for their appointment. Was he just going to stand her up? With indignation spurred by this last thought buzzing through her veins, she pushed the doorbell button and held on.

Cussing sounded from inside the house. Del released her hold for a few seconds, then punched the bell again.

The front door jerked open and a scowling Sam glared back at her. "You got glue on your finger or are you just trying to send me round the bend?"

Del shoved him out of her way. The interior was scarcely furnished but neat. A vintage cabinet radio with an oversized round dial sat against one wall. An art deco metal magazine rack filled with *Auctioneering Today* and *Antiques Weekly* leaned against an olive streamlined couch. It was like stepping onto the set of some old movie—the kind

Del's mother talked about whenever Del tried to beg a few dollars off her to go to the theatre. In her mother's opinion there was never going to be another Bogart. Del'd heard the lament over and over. It was a wonder the woman hadn't erected a shrine. Who knew—by now maybe she had.

Lost in her thoughts, Del jumped when something wet and sticky dripped between her bare toes.

"You interrupted his meal." Sam bent to rub Toadstool's milk-covered chin with a tea towel. The pig burped his thanks.

"Is he okay?" Del pulled the towel from Sam's hand and patted the piglet's face.

"Fat, sassy, and not on his way to market, at least not today. That's more than any pig can hope for."

"He hasn't thrown up any more?"

"Not unless your love affair with my doorbell sent him into some kind of frenzy I haven't discovered yet." Sam took the towel back and picked up the pig.

Del crossed her arms under her breasts and frowned at Sam's retreating back. "Where you going with him? He's my pig, you know."

Sam turned and raised one eyebrow. "I know all kinds of things, but right now I know he needs to finish his breakfast and he isn't doing it on my couch." Scratching Toadstool under the chin, Sam continued to the kitchen. Annoyed that she didn't have a response, Del trudged after him.

The kitchen was just as retro, but more country— farm chairs and a battered oak table. Sam nodded to an open cabinet. "Grab yourself a mug. There's coffee in the pot." Settling into one of the chairs, he picked up a baby bottle and nudged the nipple into Toadstool's mouth.

Del froze at the sight.

Sam looked so nurturing and caring. He stroked the little pig under the chin while the animal grunted and slurped his way through the bottle. A half smile warmed Sam's face. A clump of dark hair fell across his forehead.

Del fought the urge the brush it away from his face. She jerked open the refrigerator. "You have any cream?"

"In the door." Sam didn't look up from his task.

Del poured the mug half full with cream before topping it off with coffee.

"I thought we were meeting at the Hutch." Sam pulled the nipple out of the pig's mouth long enough to wipe the animal's chin again.

"We were, but it's past seven now. Were you going to stand me up?" Del tried to sound indignant, but watching the tenderness with which Sam eased the bottle back into Toadstool's mouth took the edge off.

"Is it? I guess I lost track of time. Had a lot on my mind."

Toadstool finished his breakfast and, still balanced in Sam's lap, lolled onto his back.

Del gave the pig's belly a scratch.

"Like what?" she asked.

Sam looked up in surprise.

"What's been going on around here at six in the morning that you have a lot on your mind?" she asked.

Sam flipped the pig over and set him on the ground. "I think you need to go outside." With

Toadstool inches from his heels, Sam strode to the back door.

What had put him in a huff? She had a right to ask what was more important than meeting her on time.

Del took a sip from her mug—a perfect coffee-to-cream ratio. Walking past an oak rolltop desk shoved in one corner of the kitchen, she noticed a yellow legal pad with a number scrawled on it.

After checking to make sure Sam wasn't peering in the back door at her, she picked up the pad. The writing was close to illegible, but there was no mistaking the number—Porter Auctions and, worst of all, David's extension. How had Sam gotten this?

At the creak of the back door being pulled open, Del dropped the paper and jumped toward the coffeemaker.

Sam raised one brow. "You sure you need more of that?"

Del ignored him as she slopped more coffee into her cup. David must have tracked her down somehow. Did Porter rat her out? He was the only person who knew not only where she was but also why. If he was tired of waiting on her to produce the Pig, why didn't he just call her and tell her? Why sic David the weasel on her?

Del snorted. Because Porter was a weasel too. He could dress himself up and act the mink all he liked, but he was a weasel through and through, right down to his beady little eyes.

She hated playing Porter's games, hated being played by anyone. She shouldn't give Porter the satisfaction of seeing her and David battle it out over the Pig and the prestige that would go along with hauling it back to Chicago. She should wash her hands of the whole thing, pack her bags, and go back to coddling rich widows out of their Tiffany punch bowls.

Sam bent down to wipe Toadstool's hooves with the towel he'd used earlier to clean the pig's chin. Sam lifted each foot with a delicacy that made Del's heart contract. He was so gentle with the little creature, treated him with a care Del had never witnessed a man exhibit before.

She glanced at the desk where the legal pad lay.

Screw Porter. She wasn't going anywhere—at least not until she had the Unruh Pig firmly in her grasp and could return to Chicago victorious, leaving David sniveling in her wake.

Now she had to find out what Sam knew and twist it to her advantage. She had the upper hand this time. Sam thought he had information on her, but she was ready. She just needed to buy some time until she could formulate a plan.

Sam wadded up the dirty towel and threw it onto his desk. The cloth landed on the pad he'd used earlier to write down his caller's number.

Sam glanced at Del. She'd jumped when he came in the back door. Had she seen the number?

Del took a sip of her coffee and smiled at him with a benign ease. She didn't look like a woman whose secret had just been revealed. Course, she didn't look like the devious trickster he knew her to be either.

She twirled her finger into her coffee, then

popped the digit into her mouth. With it still between her teeth, she smiled at him.

Damn.

He grabbed the towel back up and strode to the laundry room. After tossing it into the washer, he leaned against the cool metal and refocused.

Del was an auctioneer. His head was still spinning from this. Sure, Sam knew some female auctioneers, but not many, and most of them just filled in for their fathers or husbands. He couldn't imagine what caused someone young and attractive like Del to go into the auction business.

Course, her auction business wasn't his. No, she worked in some fancy-schmancy air-conditioned building where the bidders politely waved little round paddles when they wanted to bid.

At Sam's last auction, Earl Dent had gotten ahold of an old automotive bulb horn and squeezed the thing every time he upped a bid. If Earl hadn't been increasing Sam's commission with each blare, Sam would have been tempted to shove it . . . well, somewhere only Mrs. Dent and Earl's proctologist could have found it.

"What you doing?" Del called from the kitchen.

"Starting a load. It'll just be a minute." Sam twisted the knob on the washer. As water flowed into the tub, he slammed the lid on the lone tea towel.

Del was an auctioneer and she was after a pig made by Unruh, a pig worth six figures, minimum. Sam was an auctioneer and he needed every dime he could scrape up to get his business out of hock and his cousin out of the fire.

There was no choice in the matter. He had to

get Del to talk, to let loose of some kind of information that would lead him to the Pig first. And he had to do it without letting her get to him, without falling for her and her siren ways.

The sound of Del's heels tapping across his wood floors announced her arrival in the laundry room. She cocked one hip and leaned against the washer. Her pink shirt emphasized the rose tint of her cheeks and her eyes glistened in the dim light.

Sam brushed past her, back into the kitchen. Kenny was right. This one might be his downfall.

Chapter 10

Like getting milk from a boar's teat . . .

Sam had a plan. He would weaken Del one notch at a time.

First, he needed her to admit her real purpose for being in Allen County. Then he'd get her to reveal more—like what she knew about the Pig.

Should be a simple enough matter. He just had to gain her trust. To do that he had to show some vulnerability—not something Sam liked to do, but this was a serious situation.

After they were settled into his truck, including Toadstool, who Sam insisted ride in an easy-rinse Rubbermaid container, Sam announced their agenda for the day.

"You ever been to an auction?" he asked.

Del's nose started twitching. "One or two."

"Well, I heard a rumor an auction a few miles from here might have some pigs in it. Thought we should check it out." He watched Del from the corner of his eye. She seemed undisturbed by his plan.

"What kind of pigs?" she asked, bending over to adjust the rolled-up towel she'd put in Toadstool's box.

"Not that kind." Sam nodded to the runt. "I still can't believe you bought him. What possessed you?"

She turned an amused gaze on him. "You don't fool me. I saw how you treated him back at your house. He's gotten to you. When he and I move on, you'll probably trot right out and get a pig of your own."

Sam snorted and returned his gaze to the road.

When she moved on. He'd been so caught up in his quest to beat her out of the Pig, he'd forgotten that once the rare piece of pottery was found, she and Toadstool would be scurrying back to her life elsewhere.

She was right. He would miss the piglet. It was nice having something that needed you, that appreciated being cared for, that cared for you in return. But Del, that's who he would really miss. He was growing very used to their battles. Even when he knew she was working him, he appreciated her technique.

There were other pigs to be had and other women too, but he was afraid there was no one else like Del.

He risked another sideways glance at her. No one built like her either. He felt a wide smile slip onto his face.

"Why are you grinning like a possum?" Del looked at him through narrowed eyes.

"No reason. Just eager to get to the sale." He turned on his blinker and bumped into the field beside a hand-painted sign that read AUCTION TODAY.

Del eyed him for a second, but the lines of people wandering from their cars toward the area

where the sale would be held diverted her attention. She seemed to tense as she studied the crowd.

Strange reaction. Maybe there was even more to
learn about Miss Fancy-Pants Auctioneer than Sam
already suspected.

Del scanned the crowd for any sign of old
acquaintances—or worse, family. The auction Sam
had delivered her to was a good sixty miles from her
father's normal haunts, but it was still very possible
he'd venture this far for a promising sale. When she
saw no familiar faces in the sea of feed caps and
cowboy hats, she allowed herself to relax a smidge.

She hadn't been to a country auction since
she'd left Missouri. Waist-high grass rustled as she
struggled to make her way through it, Toadstool
cradled in her arms. When a long bunch tangled
around her ankle and refused to let go, she stumbled. Sam wrapped his arms around her and her
pig, saving both of them from a tumble.

"Those shoes aren't meant for walking through
weeds. You're gonna break your neck." Though
his words were gruff, his tone was soft. He gave her
a squeeze, then rescued Toadstool from his precar-
ious position. Sam snapped the leash on the piglet
and handed the looped end to Del.

"You can think I'm soft on him all you like, but
I'll be damned if I'm going to be seen trotting
around a sale with a pig on a leash."

Grinning, Del took the lead with one hand and
slipped her shoes off with the other. "How about
these?" She shook the strappy sandals at him. "Can
I trust you not to pitch them in the closest river?"

With a huff, Sam grabbed the shoes and tossed them back into his truck.

"Let's go. The sale'll be starting soon, and you'll want to get a number."

The sun was warm, the air filled with the smell of new grass, and Del hadn't been happier in years. She was at an auction—a real auction, with dirty boxes and piles of moth-eaten linens. No fancy pretensions here. No one looking for something special for their summer home in Aspen. Just plain folks looking for the best deal they could finagle.

As they approached the flat area between an old green house and a dilapidated barn, Del picked up her pace.

God, she loved an auction. You never knew what you would find—might not be the Unruh Pig, but today she didn't care.

She wanted to forget the Pig, forget David, and forget that Sam was watching her like a rat watched a rattler. She just wanted to be like everyone else—drink some thick coffee, eat some cold sandwiches, and snap up a deal from right under the auctioneer's nose. And maybe pretend, just for a while, that she and Sam were here because they enjoyed the same things and liked spending a day digging through dusty treasures together.

She turned a broad grin Sam's direction and looped her arm through his. Ignoring his surprised expression, she said, "Well, come on. We don't want to miss out on anything good."

Sam watched as Del picked up every piece of cracked pottery and worn-out dish on the makeshift table. So far he'd seen no signs of anything suspicious on her part.

He hadn't had an opportunity to sing his sob story yet, either. Armstrong had kept himself scarce—almost like the old bastard knew for once Sam needed him to come out and try to one-up him.

As Del ran her fingers around the inside edge of a pig-shaped cookie jar, Armstrong waddled over to the back of a truck and, using the tire as a step, pulled himself up. Sam grinned as the truck bed sank a good three inches under the extra weight.

Man kept eating, Sam wouldn't have to worry about his tricks—he'd be tricking Satan out of ice cubes.

Sam pulled his hat down so it would look like he was trying to blend. Shouldn't be long now.

Armstrong pulled his red suspenders away from his chest and surveyed his kingdom. Sam muttered an oath.

"You say something?" Del sauntered over, the cookie jar in her hand.

Sam tipped his hat lower and shook his head. Shrugging, Del asked, "What do you think? Some of the paint's worn off, but there's no chips or cracks."

What did he care about a cookie jar? And more important, what did she care? She was supposed to be feeling as uncomfortable as a church marm at a beer brawl about now; instead she was shopping and humming like she didn't have a thing to hide.

Sam muttered again.

Misinterpreting his mood, Del responded, "What's wrong with it? It's marked Shawnee." She held the pig up. "I like him."

Sam had seen the light that gleamed from her

eyes before. She was hooked. If somebody else wanted that pig, it would be a battle to the rind.

Del set down the jar and moved to the next box. As soon as her hand touched a Depression glass candy dish, another woman in a Mickey Mouse T-shirt and red high-tops picked the piece of Shawnee up. Del's eyes narrowed and she reached for her pearls. Sam grabbed her by the forearm and tugged her close.

"Don't be hurting anybody now," he drawled. "There's plenty of pigs for everybody. I should know, I've seen you buy a barnyard full."

Del shot him a haughty look. "I wasn't going to hurt anybody. Why would you say such a thing?"

Sam laughed. "You touched your pearls."

Del blinked.

"It's your tell. You touch your pearls when you're thinking of clobbering somebody."

With another laugh he smacked her on the rear and walked toward the woman in the Mickey shirt.

"Sam," Del called after him. When she was sure he was watching she reached up and caressed her necklace. "You want to come back over here?" Her smile was sweeter than sorghum.

With a chuckle, he replied, "No, Sweet Tea, I don't think I do."

Del tugged Toadstool away from a beagle who was chewing on what looked to be a ham hock and gave the dog's owner her most disgusted stare. What was wrong with people, letting their flea-bitten hounds chaw away right in front of her pig? She'd move except it was almost time for the

cookie jar to go up for sale and she couldn't hope
to grab another spot with such good viewing.

Instead she picked Toadstool up and set him on
the now half-empty flatbed trailer. Earlier the
thing had been full of boxes, but after three hours
of solid selling, it was down to just a few—one of
them holding the Shawnee cookie jar, a cookie jar
she knew from her brief Internet search the other
evening had to be worth at least twelve hundred
dollars.

Her heart skipped a few beats and her fist tightened on Toadstool's leash. She wanted that cookie
jar. She couldn't be getting distracted by taking
care of her runt, even if she did love him more
than a box of Entenmann's.

She looked around. She could pass Toadstool
off to Sam, if he was anywhere to be seen, but he'd
disappeared twenty minutes ago. Part of her was
concerned he might be after an Unruh lead, but
the antiquer in her wouldn't allow her to walk
away this close to nabbing something she had her
eye on. Besides, it was good for her cover. She still
wasn't sure what Sam knew.

He hadn't made a single crack all day to indicate
he'd learned anything from David. Maybe Sam
hadn't learned anything about her after all. Maybe
David had called him on his own. Of course that
would still alert Sam that something was ripe, but
it wouldn't be as bad as David out and out blowing
her story.

As she was contemplating the likelihood that
Sam still thought she was in Allentown to add to a
pig collection, the bull of an auctioneer pulled
on his suspenders and looked right at her.

"You planning on bidding on something, darling? You been holding down that plot of ground all morning."

Now this was the type of auctioneer she'd envisioned when she'd first heard of Sam.

She gave him a flicker of a smile. She didn't need to charm this one. She just needed him to shut up and sell her the cookie jar before someone with half a brain looked at it and realized what it was worth.

"Now where'd the man what brought you go?" He craned his tree trunk of a neck as if searching the grounds. Turning back to the front, he tapped his hand against the mike and addressed the crowd. "You all know my fellow auctioneer, Sam Samson, don't you?"

A low rumble echoed through the bidders.

Del was beginning to get a distinctly uncomfortable feeling.

"Now, I don't mean to put you on the spot none, miss, but seeings as how you came with Samson, I feel it's only fair to warn you. I don't hold with none of that funny business that you might have seen at sales in Allentown." He dragged his fleshy paw over his equally fleshy chin and shook his head. "No, I keep my sales on the up-and-up."

Del blinked back at him. Was he insinuating that Sam used shills? And that she might be involved too? Her blood pressure dropped to her bare feet.

"So, if you plan on bidding on something, it better be with a plan to buy it, 'cause we don't up bids just to make an extra buck or two around here. Ain't that right, folks?" He waved his arms in the air like a Baptist preacher calling for sinners.

A few of the loyal called their "hallelujahs" and "amens," but most shifted from foot to foot or muttered under their breath.

Del barely took notice of any of them. The fat son of a bitch was calling her and Sam crooks, and here she was all primed to bid up some of his merchandise.

She trembled with hidden rage.

Satisfied with his performance, the auctioneer motioned for one of his helpers to hold up the Shawnee jar.

Del stared at the painted pottery pig, all twelve hundred dollars of him. He probably wouldn't go for a quarter of that here. She clinched her fists around Toadstool's leash. Problem was, thirty percent of anything she paid would go directly in the pompous ass of an auctioneer's pocket.

Why couldn't he have waited until after she bought the cookie jar to mouth off?

She looked at the woman in the Mickey Mouse shirt, clutching her bid card close. Hopefully, the woman knew her stuff, 'cause if Del wasn't going to get the jar, she'd do what she could to keep Armstrong from getting anywhere near the jar's worth.

She motioned Armstrong's helper closer and tapped one fingernail against the pig's snout.

"Not bad for a fake, is it?" She announced with as much volume as her well-developed lungs could muster, then stared directly into the auctioneer's eyes.

At his startled look, she continued, "Oh, I'm sorry, weren't you going to mention that?" Then she picked up Toadstool and strode to the truck.

* * *

Standing in line for lunch, Sam saw Del stomp away from the bidding area like she had a crawdaddy clamped on her tail. Behind her, one of Armstrong's minions held the cookie jar she'd been eyeing since they arrived, and Armstrong begged for an opening bid.

Sam didn't know what had happened to make her walk away from that jar, but he knew it wasn't good.

He glanced at Armstrong. The jackass was looking a few shades paler than his normal ruby skin tone. Whatever had ticked Del off, she hadn't left without shooting a parting blow.

Sam grinned. You had to love a girl with spunk.

He froze at his wayward thought. Love. Sam didn't love. Sam was too busy to love. He worked and helped out Becca when he could. He didn't get involved, especially not with someone like Del. She was too much like him, which meant he couldn't trust her. Hell, he couldn't trust himself around her.

"You want mustard?" The preteen boy at the 4-H booth held out a naked burger and a bottle of French's high-grade yellow.

Sam shook his head to dislodge his disturbing thoughts. "No, just ketchup." He grabbed a handful of packets from a plastic bowl.

"How 'bout to drink? You want a Coke?" The boy held up a soda can.

Sam motioned to a yellow drink cooler. "No, tea." He paused. "Sweet tea, that's my drink." He stared at the retreating figure heading to his truck. "There's nothing better."

* * *

Del was stewing. She wasn't sure who she was more angry at—the fat bastard who called her a cheat in front of fifty people she'd never met, or Sam for leaving her alone to face the fat bastard on her own.

She slammed the passenger door of the truck closed and focused on Sam. He had to have known what Armstrong thought of him. He could have warned her—or better yet, not left her to face the corpulent clod by herself.

She reopened the door and kicked the Rubbermaid box into the grass, then with Toadstool nestled beside her waited for Sam.

He approached almost instantly, a sappy smile on his face and a paper tray of food in his hands. Her fingers drifted to her pearls, then froze.

She did have a tell. She bit her lip and shoved her hand under her leg.

Sam paused as he passed Toadstool's box, now almost hidden in the weeds. Glancing at Del, his smile faltered, but he recovered quickly, weaving around the box to get to the truck.

"You hungry?" Sam leaned in the driver's door, extending the paper tray of food.

The smell of burgers and greasy fries filled the truck. Del's stomach rumbled in response. Without batting an eye, she took the tray and chomped into a hamburger. After climbing into his seat, Sam watched her with a raised brow.

"You hungry?" This time his tone was less friendly and more smart-assy.

Del responded by picking up the second burger and biting off a huge chunk.

"Don't worry about me," Sam said.

Del dove into the fries.

"You shouldn't eat so fast. You'll wind up like your pig did yesterday."

She popped the last bite of hamburger into her mouth and purposely licked her fingers.

He took off his hat and dropped it next to Toadstool. "What has you in such a fizz?"

"Nothing," she mumbled around another handful of fries.

"Is this about me pointing out your little issue with the pearls?"

She grunted.

"Or did something happen at the sale? I saw you stomp off right before that jar went up. I didn't figure you were going to back off that pig without a knockdown drag-out."

The burgers were gone, and the last fry followed, but she hadn't touched her necklace once. How dare he say she had a tell. She'd hidden the fact that she was mad enough to chew pig iron just fine, thank you very little.

She shoved the empty burger wrappers into the cardboard box and flung it onto his chest.

"Well, hell." He stared at a damp blot of ketchup that now adorned his black tee.

A grin broke over Del's face. She hoped Toadstool spewed on his new hat too.

Seeing Del's expression, Sam's changed too. His eyebrows moved together and his jaw tightened. "You think you might at least let me know what

I've done? Whatever happened at the sale, I was fifty feet away, for God's sake."

"Exactly." Del cocked her head.

Sam flung the lunch trash onto the floor where Toadstool's box had been, then leaned forward. "'Exactly' what? What happened over there?"

After shifting Toadstool from the seat to her lap, Del stroked the pig's head for comfort and replied, "I was humiliated. That's what. That ignoramus of an auctioneer accused me of working as your shill."

Sam laughed. "Is that all? You spend more than twenty minutes in the auction business and somebody thinks you're using shills. That's like accusing a dog of having fleas. It's not always true, but it's an easy insult."

"Not to me, nobody's accused me of that, not since . . ." She bit her lip.

"Since when?"

"Ever, no one's ever accused me of cheating like that." That part was true, no one had ever made an announcement over a loudspeaker singling her out.

"Well, and why would they? This was your first auction, right?" Sam leaned against the door and folded his arms over his chest.

Del stared at the ketchup stain right above his forearm. She walked into that one. For some reason that seemed to keep happening around this man.

"You got an itch?" Sam interrupted her thoughts.

"What?"

"Your nose, it seems to be twitching a lot. I wondered if you had an itch." He smiled.

What was that about? "No, you're seeing things."

Sam shrugged, but his smile grew. "Maybe."

Man, that I-know-something-you-don't smirk was annoying. Del plunged ahead. "And in answer to your first question, yes, this was my first auction, but that doesn't make being called a cheat any more pleasant."

"A shill, you mean."

"A shill, a cheat—whatever. They're the same thing and not something I want people calling me."

"Yep, they're the same thing, all right." He grinned again.

He was supposed to be begging her forgiveness or at least offering some comfort. What was wrong with this man? Annoyed, she snapped, "You have a point?"

"Nothing major. Just that a shill is a pretty specific term for somebody who ups bids for the auctioneer without the other bidders knowing." He paused and Del tensed. This wasn't going in a good direction.

"Now, a cheat, that's a whole lot broader, don't you think?" Sam scratched his chin.

Just get to the point, Del screamed mentally.

"Yep, seems to me that only someone familiar with auctions would use the term *shill* and know exactly what it means."

He looked so pleased with himself. Del considered tossing his hat out the window after the Rubbermaid.

"I read," she mumbled.

"What, *Auctioneer Today*?" The smirk grew wider.

"Maybe I do." Del mimicked his posture, folding her own arms over her chest.

"Maybe there's something you should be telling me." He relaxed his arms, laying one along the back of the seat. As his fingers brushed Del's shoulders, she jumped.

A good offense always made the best defense. "Maybe there's something you should be telling me," she replied.

His fingers rubbed a light circle on her shoulder. She stiffened but refused to move away. She wouldn't give him the satisfaction of knowing he was getting to her, and he was getting to her. Scenes of their last encounter in his truck cab floated through her mind.

Her life was so darn complicated. For once it would be nice if she could just take what she wanted, and she wanted Sam. He was arrogant and annoying as all get out; that was true. But he was also smart, sneaky, and sexy. It was a sorry thing to admit, but the sneaky part probably had as much to do with her undeniable attraction to him as the smart or sexy part.

She was a sucker for a man who could work a deal, and a horse trader like Sam who liked antiques and could cuddle her pig . . . well, that was a web she couldn't seem to escape.

"Del?" Sam's fingers stilled. "There something you should be telling me?"

Looking him straight in the eye, Del leaned across Toadstool, shoved her hands around Sam's neck, and said, "Not a damn thing."

Chapter 11

Hog-tied . . .

Sam had all of two seconds to register what Del was doing before his head was yanked down and his lips met the sweetest-tasting mouth in Missouri.

He'd heard of your evasive moves, but this one won the prize. And what a prize. Del's lips parted and her tongue darted against his lips. Not being a man who missed an opportunity, he opened his mouth and welcomed the invasion.

Her hands were locked into his hair. Through the fog filling his brain it registered that he couldn't escape even if he wanted to—so, why fight it?

Del made a little purr-like sound in the back of her throat and Sam made a growl in return. He felt her grin against his lips. Not wanting her to get sidetracked from her purpose, he nudged her with his lips, then traced her lower lip with his tongue. She purred again, but this time he kept all comments to himself.

Placing his hands on her shoulders, he prepared to pull her to him. As they grappled to close the space between their bodies, a sharp, yelping oink rang through the truck.

"Oh, my God, are you hurt?" Del twisted away to examine an outraged Toadstool.

Sam was hurting, but it wasn't anything that was going to be helped by stopping. He reached for Del again.

"Watch out. You're going to crush him." Del smacked Sam against the chest and snuggled Toadstool next to her breasts.

Sam glared at the lucky little porker. The pig waggled his hooves and snuffled deeper into Del's cleavage.

Sam was seriously rethinking his stance on bacon.

Gripping the steering wheel, he practiced deep breathing. Worked for women in labor, ought to take care of his problem.

When the urge to toss Toadstool out the window and jerk Del back into his arms had passed, he placed an understanding smile on his face and prepared to play nice, or at least civilized.

Sam swiveled in his seat, just as Toadstool emptied his gullet into Sam's second-best hat.

Sam blinked.

Tomorrow, BLTs were on the menu.

Del scooped the pig up and cooed her concern. A dollop of pig puke rolled off the seat and splattered onto Sam's boots.

BLTs, and a side of ham.

"So, why didn't you tell me you were an auctioneer?" Sam spit out.

Engrossed in Toadstool's problems, it took Del a few minutes for the question to register and for her to realize he'd quit pussyfooting around the issue and thrown down the gauntlet.

"You mind if we clean this"—she gestured to the smelly mess beside her—"before we get in a big ole battle?"

Sam glanced at the sick pig and the surrounding goo. "Maybe the stink'll make you answer quicker."

Yuck. "You can't be serious. Get out of the truck and get us something to clean this up." She gave him her best "don't argue with me" look.

It worked. He grabbed his ruined hat and slammed open his door. She watched as he stomped across the grass carrying his Stetson at arm's length in front of him.

After depositing it in a trash bin near the food booth, he stepped out of her view for a few minutes. Sitting in the closed-in space of the cab, Del began to feel a little sick herself. She pushed open her door.

It wasn't just the smell, which would send a weaker woman running. It was everything. Her cover was good and blown and she was no closer to finding the Pig. A week in southern Missouri and all she had to show for it was a cheap motel room full of pig collectibles and a pet who couldn't handle his formula.

She ran her hand over Toadstool's head. Of course, he made everything else worthwhile. She didn't care if he urped on her daily, as long as he was there for her to take care of.

Sam reappeared, a spray bottle and a roll of paper towels under his arm. As he trotted back across the field, Del couldn't help but admire the athletic sway of his body. He moved like a panther—looked like one too, always outfitted in black. She sighed.

She'd gained Sam too. Well, not him, but their relationship, whatever it was. But now that was over. He'd caught on to her act. She didn't think he would be willing to help her any longer, not for the measly fee they'd agreed to. No, if he knew what she was looking for, he'd be wanting a much bigger cut.

She didn't think Pamela Anderson had enough sex appeal to divert a man from a six-figure deal. Especially a man who lived for deal-making.

Sam approached her side of the truck and, standing outside, shoved the bottle and roll of towels through the open door. "I'm not getting back in until the smell is gone."

"But . . ." Del began.

"Your pig, your mess." He furrowed his brow, but his tone didn't fool her. His anger was already dissipating.

With a small smile, she first wiped down Toadstool, then held him up, looking for a safe and clean place to set him.

"Give him here." Sam held out his hands, his mouth in a straight line, but a warmth in his eyes.

Knowing now was not the time to again point out his feelings for the pig, Del kept her face serious as she placed the little runt in his arms.

She made quick work of the mess. After spraying and rubbing until she thought she would pass out from the combination of fumes and effort, she gathered up the waste and pushed her leg out the open door.

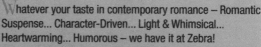
Zebra Contemporary

Whatever your taste in contemporary romance – Romantic Suspense... Character-Driven... Light & Whimsical... Heartwarming... Humorous – we have it at Zebra!

And now Zebra has created a Book Club for readers like yourself who enjoy fine Contemporary Romance written by today's best-selling authors.

Authors like Fern Michaels... Lori Foster... Janet Dailey... Lisa Jackson...Janelle Taylor... Kasey Michaels... Shannon Drake... Kat Martin... to name but a few!

These are the finest
contemporary romances available
anywhere today!

But don't take our word for it! Accept our gift of FREE Zebra Contemporary Romances – and see for yourself. You only pay $1.99 for shipping and handling.

Once you've read them, we're sure you'll want to continue receiving the newest Zebra Contemporaries as soon as they're published each month! And you can by becoming a member of the Zebra Contemporary Romance Book Club!

As a member of Zebra Contemporary Romance Book Club,

- You'll receive four books every month. Each book will be by one of Zebra's best-selling authors.

- You'll have variety – you'll never receive two of the same kind of story in one month.

- You'll get your books hot off the press, usually before they appear in bookstores.

- You'll ALWAYS save up to 30% off the cover price.

SEND FOR YOUR FREE BOOKS TODAY!

To start your membership, simply complete and return the Free Book Certificate. You'll receive your Introductory Shipment of FREE Zebra Contemporary Romances, you only pay $1.99 for shipping and handling. Then, each month you will receive the 4 newest Zebra Contemporary Romances. Each shipment will be yours to examine FREE for 10 days. If you decide to keep the books, you'll pay the preferred subscriber price (a savings of up to 30% off the cover price), plus shipping and handling. If you want us to stop sending books, just say the word... it's that simple.

FREE BOOK CERTIFICATE

Yes! Please send me FREE Zebra Contemporary romance novels. I only pay $1.99 for shipping and handling. I understand that each month thereafter I will be able to preview 4 brand-new Contemporary Romances FREE for 10 days. Then, if I should decide to keep them, I will pay the money-saving preferred subscriber's price (that's a savings of up to 30% off the retail price), plus shipping and handling. I understand I am under no obligation to purchase any books, as explained on this card.

NAME _____

ADDRESS _____ APT. _____

CITY _____ STATE _____ ZIP _____

TELEPHONE (_____) _____

E-MAIL _____

SIGNATURE _____

(If under 18, parent or guardian must sign)

Offer limited to one per household and not to current subscribers. Terms, offer and prices subject to change.
Orders subject to acceptance by Zebra Contemporary Book Club. Offer Valid in the U.S. only.

Thank You!

CN056A

THE BENEFITS
OF BOOK CLUB
MEMBERSHIP

• You'll get your books
hot off the press, usually
before they appear in
bookstores.

• You'll ALWAYS save
up to 30% off the cover
price.

• You'll get our FREE
monthly newsletter filled
with author interviews,
book previews, special
offers and MORE!

• There's no obligation
— you can cancel at any
time and you have no
minimum number of
books to buy.

• And — if you decide you
don't like the books you
receive, you can return
them. (You always have
ten days to decide.)

Be sure to visit our website at www.kensingtonbooks.com.

Zebra Contemporary Romance Book Club
Zebra Home Subscription Service, Inc.
P.O. Box 5214
Clifton NJ 07015-5214

PLACE
STAMP
HERE

"I can take it." Sam moved as if to set Toadstool back in the cab.

Del shook her head. "No, you were right; it's my mess. Can't sit around waiting for somebody else to clean up after you, can you?"

At Sam's concerned look, she laughed. "Besides, I need to find somewhere to wash up. You think they'll let me in the house?"

With a quick wave, she pushed past him and headed toward the sale.

What she'd said was true. A mess didn't go away on its own and it was only right that the person responsible should clean it up. Too bad life didn't work like that.

During the drive back to town, neither of them mentioned Del's career, or why she was in Allentown, or why Sam had David's number. Del wanted to know the latter, but she didn't want to discuss the first two, and all the day's activities had completely drained her B.S. capabilities. She figured Sam was feeling the same way.

They drove in silence until Del saw Sam's hand reach for his Hank Williams Sr. CD. Nothing could be worse than that.

"So, Becca's your cousin?" She kept her eye on the CD player as she jostled Toadstool's front end onto her lap.

Sam dropped his hand onto the steering wheel. "Yeah, we pretty much grew up together." He thumped his palm against the wheel. "Her mom died when she was two and her dad was more interested in seeing the bottom of a whiskey bottle than looking after a little girl. She wound up spending most days at our house. Just went home to sleep."

"Sounds like she was lucky to have you and your family."

Sam grunted. "The other way around, really. My mom left when I was a baby. I guess she couldn't handle being a mother at eighteen. My dad raised me by himself, until Becca came along. Probably sounds strange to say someone four years younger than me helped raise me, but Becca did. She always had a confidence about her. She was like one of those blow-up punching bags; no matter what knocked her down or how often, she popped right back up smiling."

A soft snore escaped from Toadstool's mouth. Del stroked the side of his snout.

"She sounds special." Del wished she'd known someone like that. Her mother always seemed worn-out and her father just didn't pay a lot of attention to her. He was always preoccupied with his latest scam, or as he called them, opportunities.

"She was special and she made you feel that way too. My dad wasn't what you would exactly call warm and fuzzy. Becca made up for it."

"What happened?" The Becca Del knew reminded her a whole lot more of her own mother than the child Sam was describing.

"She got married, just like my mama at eighteen. Got pregnant within a month, but she lost the baby. Then, a few years later she had Clay. One week after that her husband skipped out. He hung around town for a while, but he wasn't much help to her, and last year he moved north. She hasn't seen a check since." Sam's hands tightened on the wheel.

"Both Becca and my mother might have married young, but no matter how bad things get Becca'll never run away. Somewhere under all her worry there's still that old bounce—it takes longer for her to rebound and the smile isn't as frequent, but it's in there."

Del wasn't sure if he believed this or just said it to convince her.

"You ever see your mother?" she asked.

He shook his head. "No."

The still sleeping Toadstool shuffled his legs. Sam glanced at him and smiled. Looking back at the road, he continued, "My mom came back once when I was five. My dad wouldn't let her in the house. She could've fought him, got the sheriff or something, but I guess it wasn't worth it to her."

Del winced. She could imagine the five-year-old Sam watching the mother he'd never met walk away, thinking he wasn't worth fighting over.

"You don't know what was going on. Things can look a lot different to a five-year-old than to an adult. If you met her now everything might make sense, not be as bad as you thought."

"No chance of that happening." He swerved the truck onto the street that led to his house. "She died of lung cancer last year. Guess she found giving up cigarettes harder than giving up her son."

Del watched as he changed gears. His movements were quick and controlled. He could act like his mother's desertion didn't bother him, but he wasn't fooling Del. She had graduated magna cum laude from the school of "what my parents do have nothing to do with me." As much as you denied it publicly, all that stupid childhood garbage was hard to forget.

She rubbed the bridge of her nose. She was getting a headache. Too much time spent thinking about family, even someone else's, and a migraine the size of four counties was sure to follow.

She glanced back at Sam. He still sat as unbending as a Griswold griddle. Wanting to ease his pain somehow, she touched his arm. He looked at the fingers resting on his tan skin, then let his gaze travel up her arm until his eyes found hers.

The initial look was pure curiosity, with a touch of sadness, but something else soon followed—a heat that seemed to vibrate between them. Del needed to look away, to break the bond, but she couldn't. She wanted the moment to last forever.

A blaring horn jerked her gaze from Sam's and onto the road. Sam wrenched the dually back onto the right side of the street just as a beat-up white pickup brushed by.

"Crazy driver. How fast you think he was going?" Sam asked, irritation in his voice.

Del released the breath she'd been holding. "Fast enough, especially since he wasn't nice enough to get up on the sidewalk and let us by." She grinned.

With a quick glance her way, Sam laughed. "You saying you don't like my driving? 'Cause I don't have to be hauling your pig-hunting behind all over kingdom come."

Del grinned again. "If my butt wasn't here you'd be sitting on that guy's front seat right now."

Both of Sam's eyebrows shot up. "How you figure?"

"I yelled at you. That's what saved you."

"Ha, you're living in a dream world, Sweet Tea." Hitting the brake, Sam turned the truck into his drive.

He reached over and scooped the sleeping pig from her lap. A dream world, yeah, maybe she was.

The next day the sound of even breathing and the feel of warm breath on Sam's neck woke him up. It had been a long time since he'd awoken to someone in his bed—too long. Still in the fog of sleep, he sighed and reached to caress his companion's cheek. Instead of the smooth skin he anticipated, he touched five o'clock shadow.

His hand frozen, one eye popped open. Two brown orbs stared back at him, and a short wet nose nuzzled his ear. With a groan, Sam sat up and wiped pig breath off his neck.

"You have to find another bed, buddy. This is getting uncomfortable."

Toadstool, lolled back on the pillows, seemed unconcerned. Grabbing yesterday's jeans, Sam tugged them on and padded barefoot into his kitchen.

For the second time in two days, his breakfast was interrupted by the phone.

"David Curtis here. Is this Samson?" a voice spit out in clipped tones.

Well, good morning to you too, you pompous pain in the ass. "Last time I checked." Back to his *Hee Haw* voice.

"You locate the Pig yet?"

Sam sauntered to the refrigerator and began mixing Toadstool's breakfast. Nursemaid to a pig and errand boy to Fancy Pants here. The first job rocketed skyward in Sam's estimation.

"There's a lot of pigs down here. You want to be more specific?" His day hadn't started out exactly how he'd dreamed it; might as well share the joy with someone else—especially someone annoying.

"Don't play games with me, Samson. You know what Pig I'm talking about."

Sam twisted a nipple onto Toadstool's bottle and shook it. Holding it up to the light he checked to see if the contents were mixed.

"You there?"

Man, the guy needed to knock back a whiskey or two. "Yeah, I'm here. It's been less than a day since I talked to you. You expecting miracles?"

"Maybe it will make you move a little faster when I let you know I have another contact down there. Someone who's already given me twice the information you have." Curtis paused. "More than that actually, since you haven't given me shit."

Oooo, Mr. Fancy Pants cussed. Now Sam was shaking.

"This other contact seems pretty confident he can turn up the Pig within the week. You think you can beat that?"

Sam leaned against the refrigerator. "You mind telling me who this other contact is?"

Curtis laughed. "What, so you can hunt him down and make a deal behind my back? I don't think so. Just consider this a courtesy call, since I talked with you first. If you don't get moving you're going to miss out."

Sam dropped the receiver onto the cradle. He smelled a rat, a big ole antique-selling pack rat.

Well, it solved his problem of facing Del today. The more he saw her, the more he wanted to see her, and the more he knew he was getting too close to finish the deal in a way that wouldn't leave him holding an empty poke. He needed some time away to clear his brain and focus on the task of saving his business and his cousin. He couldn't let some inconvenience like whatever was going on between him and Del get in his way.

He strode to the bedroom to feed his guest and call Kenny. Del wouldn't be looking for Sam and Toadstool for a couple hours. He could use the time to get to Izzy's and bargain some information out of the old trader.

By the time Del showed up at the feed store, Sam would already have the information he needed and be halfway to finding the Pig.

He slipped the bottle into Toadstool's waiting mouth. The Unruh Pig, that is.

"What do you mean Sam's not coming in? He has to come in, he has my pig." Del glared at Sam's message boy.

"Just what I told you. He's not coming in and he's not at home, so just save yourself the trip." Kenny turned his back on her and dusted corn-meal off a bag of Iams.

"He can't just run off with my pig," she insisted.

Over his shoulder, Kenny replied, "Tell him that."

Son of a bitch. Del kicked Sam's door as she walked past. He had a lead on the Pig, she knew it, and he was exposing her piglet to his backstabbing business. That was beyond rude.

She needed to find out where the pig-napper was. She glanced at Kenny's stiff back. Not going to get much there. She kicked the door again, then stomped past Sam's misogynistic minion and out to her car.

Tapping her fingers on the dash, she checked the time. Eight-thirty A.M. She'd done the late thing today to show Sam who was working for whom. See where it had gotten her? Gave Sam an extra half hour to get to wherever he was going. Without a good lead or a pack of bloodhounds, she'd never catch him now.

At least it solved her problem of ditching him before her lunch appointment with Tilde. She'd just have to hope the colorful older woman had something worthwhile to show her.

Del gunned up the engine and slipped a Zeppelin CD into the player. Yeah, she needed something worthwhile, like a map with a big ole *X* marked "find Pig here." That wasn't too much to ask, was it?

Sam stared at the zebra-striped leash in his hand. Where had Del found this embarrassment? It was bad enough a black and white pig outfitted in a red harness was trotting around with him. He'd be

damned if he'd use this lead. Izzy would have a
heyday with that.

Sam grabbed the piglet under the front legs and
lowered him to the ground. Toadstool immediately
began sniffing and rooting like the place was covered in acorns, which, come to think of it, it was.

"That your hog?" Izzy sat perched on an old
stump next to the train car. In the shadow of the
trees, Sam hadn't noticed him.

"What's that in your hand?" Izzy spit in a Coke
can as he nodded at the leash Sam held. Always
startled by Izzy's dexterity with nothing but a bent
piece of metal and a stump, Sam forced his gaze
away from the makeshift spittoon.

"Nothing." Sam tossed the zebra fur into the
truck.

"You ain't gonna let that critter ruin my yard,
now are ya? I spent a lotta time getting it just
right." There was no trace of a smile on Izzy's face.

Sam glanced at the molehills, rocks, and various
bits of discarded old metal that decorated Izzy's
"yard." "Don't think he'll do it much harm," he
drawled.

"Hmm." The sound of tobacco juice pinging
against the inside of the can accented Izzy's grunt.
"You here for a reason, or just taking in the sights?"

"That any way to greet your business partner?"
Sam shut the truck door and leaned against an
oak tree where Toadstool was busy searching for
snacks.

Izzy lowered the can to his thigh. "You gotta
lead?"

"I heard maybe you did."

"Me? Naw, I've just been gathering dust."

Sam eyed the old man. He was putting on yet another act. "Way I hear it, you have a big lead."

Izzy relaxed against the wall of the train car and crossed his arms over his chest. "Who you been talking to, son?"

"Nobody I care to talk to again."

Izzy laughed, revealing a flash of white in his grizzled face. "Ain't that the truth?"

"So, you been talking to the same pain in the behind I have?" Sam used his foot to clear away the acorns from the ground surrounding Toadstool. Last thing he needed was another trip with a carsick pig.

"Let him eat 'em. They won't hurt him none." Izzy gestured with his can.

"They won't help my truck interior any, either, not after he pukes them back up."

Izzy treated him to a grin that was a perfect illustration of "ear-to-ear." "That girl got you all tied up, don't she? Hog-tied, you might even say." Bent over with laughter, Izzy thumped his leg.

Sam hoped the old coot wet himself. As he waited for Izzy to get under control, something occurred to him. "How'd you know Toadstool was Del's?"

Wiping tears from his eyes, Izzy reached down for his Coke can. "She named him Toadstool, did she? That's interesting. Now, about this fellow what called you . . ."

There was something not right here. "How'd you know the piglet was Del's?"

Izzy used his hook to scrape the remains of tobacco out of his cheek. "I reckon you told me."

Sam kept his gaze steady. "I reckon, I didn't."

"You got a sore spot, son?" Izzy peered at him with one brow raised.

Sam sighed. "Quit the act, Izzy. There's something going on here, and as much as it pains me to say it, I just don't think you've been on the up-and-up with me."

"That last sounded a bit on the smart-aleck side to me. Don't you be getting an attitude. Won't help you learn nothing, that's for sure."

"So, you do know something?"

"Son, I got thirty years on you. I better know something."

This was like dancing with a cobra—no way to win.

Sam gave up. Izzy knew more about Del than he would let on, but once again he wasn't letting go of it. Sam could banter with him all day, or settle for the information the old man seemed more willing to part with.

"So'd some snooty auctioneer from Chicago call you?" Sam asked.

"I talked with him some." Back on firm ground, Izzy's Red Man pouch appeared.

"What'd you talk about? You holding out on me?"

Izzy adjusted his chaw in his cheek while he studied Sam. "What you want more, to find that Pig or to find out about the girl?"

Sam froze. Izzy did know something, and he was offering to share. At least as close to an offer as Izzy would make. "Well, I want to find the Pig, but I might be a bit curious about the other."

"A bit, eh?" Izzy cocked his head at Toadstool,

who had wandered over and was sniffing the old man's shoe.

Irritation prickled Sam. "You going to tell me or not?"

Izzy, busy rubbing Toadstool's head, murmured, "Hog-tied, and can't admit it."

Sam clenched and unclenched his fists.

Grinning, Izzy looked up. "Well, if'n you're interested in the girl, I'd take a little trip down to Docia. You might learn yourself something there, but if it's the Pig you're interested in, I'd stick right where you are. I got a feeling it's gonna turn up around here real soon, and if you ain't here, you just might miss out."

Chapter 12

Pig tales . . .

Del stared up at the smirking-catfish sign. If someone was serving her up for dinner, she didn't think she'd have a big ole grin slapped on her face. Flinging her purse strap onto her shoulder, she strode up the wooden boardwalk.

Inside, the place was outfitted with picnic tables and red-checked tablecloths. The scent of fried breading filled the air. Del inhaled deeply. Fried catfish and hush puppies—it was almost enough to make her forget Sam Samson and his pig-thieving ways.

Almost, but not quite. Right after lunch she was hunting down Samson and taking her pig back, and there had better not be a bristle out of place.

Busy planning her revenge, she stood tapping her foot.

A balled-up piece of paper smacked her in the forehead. "Hey, kid, you planning on joining me, or you just gonna stand there stomping a hole in the floor?" Tilde yelled at her from a table in the back.

The woman had quite an arm on her.

Del rubbed her forehead and weaved her way toward her assailant.

"Grab another menu as you go by." Tilde gestured to an empty table where two greasy paper menus lay. "I used mine to get your attention."

That she did. Del snagged a menu and slid onto the bench across from Tilde.

"So, what bur's under your saddle?" Tilde moved a pitcher of tea to peer at Del.

Del put on her sweetest smile as she replied, "Oh, nothing's bothering me. I was just afraid I was late, didn't want you thinking I was standing you up."

"It's just ten to." Tilde tapped on the glass of her rhinestone and leopard-print watch.

"Nice watch." Del ran a finger over the faux fur. "I just got a zebra-print lead for my pig."

"You gotta pig?"

"Hmm?" Del hadn't really meant to mention Toadstool, but she reflected, what did it matter? "Yeah, he's a cutie too. Black and white. A Hampshire."

"Well, that's just dandy." Tilde patted Del's hand with a look of genuine pleasure on her face.

Del briefly wondered why the other woman would care about Del's new pet, but let it pass. Tilde was just that kind of person, interested in others.

"So, you said you had something on that pottery pig that disappeared around here," Del said.

"I guess I did, but we can't talk now, kid. Lunch is here."

Del turned to see a woman approaching, weighed down with a steaming platter of fried fish and an even bigger bowl of hush puppies. Thumping them down on the table, she said, "I'll be right back with the slaw and beans."

Del stared at the food with round eyes. "I was thinking I'd have a nice salad."

Already smacking the bottom of an upturned ketchup bottle, Tilde laughed. "Not here, you ain't. You can have greens anywhere. You don't want to miss out on this catfish, do you?" She waved a golden fillet under Del's nose.

No, Del decided, she didn't. "Are you done with the ketchup?" she asked.

Thirty minutes later, Del popped one last hush puppy into her mouth. "I'm stuffed to the gills." She chuckled at her own joke.

Tilde took a sip of tea and shoved the menu across the table. "You sure you don't want some pie?"

Del groaned. Of course she wanted pie, but for once she could truly say there was no way she could eat another bite. "I'm going to have to pass," she replied, with regret.

Tilde grinned. "Well, at least you seem more relaxed than when you got here. You ready to tell me what had you all riled up?"

Her anger hidden under three servings of catfish, Del had a hard time remembering. Oh, yeah, Sam, pig thief.

No reason to be mad about that. He'd take good care of Toadstool, and he wasn't going to beat her to the Unruh Pig, either, 'cause Tilde was about to tell her exactly where she could find it.

"Oh, nothing." Del waved the other woman's

frown away. "Really, I've never been better. Now tell me about the Pig."

Tilde eyed her for another couple of seconds, then reached for her handbag, green leather with trim to match her watch. Del couldn't suppress a tiny speck of jealousy.

"It's not so much a telling thing as a showing thing." Pinched between two scarlet nails Tilde held a scrap of newspaper. "When I was down in Mountain View t'other day I found this shoved in an old book. Thought it might interest you."

Del grabbed the paper and spread it out flat on the table in front of her. It was a yellowed picture from a newspaper dated July 1975. The photo showed a half-submerged car with a group of men milling around it. The caption read, "Car washed down creek. Man drowns."

"Is this the . . . ?"

Tilde nodded. "Must be, don't you think? See the plates." She pointed at the photo. "I can't read them, but they ain't Missouri plates. Back then our plates was red and those are white. Couldn't have been too many foreigners washed down a creek back then."

Del studied the picture. One man in the background caught her eye. She dropped the picture on the table. She should have known it. If there was a dime to be made selling donkey dung, her daddy'd sniff it out. She should have realized he, or one of his buddies, was involved in the disappearance of the Pig.

"Where'd you say this happened?" she asked.

"Don't recollect I did say, but it was near Docia. You know where that is? Purt near the Arkansas line." Tilde pulled out a gold compact and flipped it open.

Did she know Docia? Better than a butcher knew bacon. Problem was, Docia knew her too and not as sophisticated Del Montgomery.

She'd be hard-pressed to get within sixty miles of the place without somebody sighting her and ratting her out to her mama, daddy—or the sheriff. Del tapped her foot against the wood floor.

"You signaling for ships?" Tilde peered at her over the compact.

How many tells did she have? Del forced her foot to a standstill.

Del picked the picture back up to study it. Now knowing it was near Docia, she thought she recognized the site. "You know if this is near the old Howe place?" she asked.

In the middle of applying lipstick, Tilde stopped midlip. "You been to Docia?"

Crap. Del was really slipping. "No, I'm thinking of somewhere else. I forgot you said Docia."

Tilde finished her touch-up and smacked a bright red lip print onto a paper napkin. "You see anybody what looks familiar in that photo?"

Del kept her gaze on the newsprint. "Can't say that I do."

Tilde leaned forward so she could look at the picture too. "You sure? 'Cause that would be the best source of information, somebody who was there when this all happened."

Del looked the other woman straight in the eye. "No. There's not a soul there I recognize."

Fifteen minutes later, Del had paid the bill and waved good-bye to Tilde. The scrap of newsprint was safely tucked away in her wallet. She still couldn't believe her rotten luck. The Pig would have had to disappear near Docia and, by the looks of it, within a few miles of her house. Del had spent more than one spring day wandering through the woods around that creek. Had waded across that same low-water bridge too.

The Mont luck again. It had hit her daddy too, all those years ago. He was probably standing within a hundred yards of the find of the century and never knew it.

After thinking it over, Del was confident her daddy'd had no part in the Pig's disappearance. If he had, he'd have sold it faster than spit, and Del sure didn't remember any sudden influxes of cash in the family coffers.

So, now Del knew where the Pig had disappeared from. The problem was, it was the last place she wanted to be, or certainly to be seen. There was no way she could go traipsing into town and start asking questions. That was completely out, but she might be able to sneak close enough to check out the area around the bridge. It was the long shot of all long shots, but right now it was all she had.

Maybe once she crossed into Ozark County, inspiration would hit.

"Hang on to your hog chow, Toadstool, we're going for a ride." Sam tucked an old blanket he'd bought off Izzy around the pig. If he was driving all the way to Docia, he wasn't doing it with unprotected seats.

He wasn't going to Docia because he had an interest in Del personally, he told himself. No, he was going to Docia first because Izzy had acted like he'd be better off staying here. If Izzy said he'd have better luck finding the Pig by staying in Allen County, then Sam figured doing the opposite had to be his best bet. His second rationale for heading south was that, while he had no personal need to learn more about Del, professionally speaking, it was always good to know about the competition, and it sounded like Docia was where he could pick up some needed information.

Realizing the incongruity of his reasoning— don't trust Izzy on the first point, trust him on the second—Sam faltered for a minute. Glancing at his four-legged passenger, Sam mumbled, "Doesn't matter. Going to Docia's the right choice."

He flipped on his blinker and turned south on Highway 5.

Two hours later, Sam pulled into the impressive burg of Docia. Most of the town seemed to hug the main road, with a few signs pointing off toward various places of note—Docia High, Docia Elementary, National Guard armory.

Must be a big help for all the tourists searching for an education or a gently used tank.

What he needed was a DEL MONTGOMERY SLEPT HERE sign. He settled for ANTIQUES. If there was information on Del here, somehow it would be connected to antiques. There was no missing the fact that it was in her blood. She was not new to the collecting business. No, Del probably started at the ripe old age of two, charming marbles out of the pockets of preschoolers.

As he pulled off the road and stopped in front of the building, he noticed a second sign, TOURIST INFORMATION. Even better; he was a tourist, and he needed information. He was swinging his leg out of the truck when a snort stopped him.

He'd forgotten his traveling companion.

Toadstool stood with his front hooves pressing into the seat, his snout wiggling in anticipation.

"I think you'd better stay in the truck for this one. I'm wanting to make a good impression, and no offense, but seeing you wouldn't exactly be a help."

Toadstool burped—loudly.

Damn Izzy and his acorns. Sam grabbed the zebra lead and snapped it on the pig. If you were going to go prancing into a place with a pig, you might as well go whole hog.

Sam grinned. Least he hadn't lost his ability to laugh. All sense of male pride, sure, but at least his sense of humor was intact.

A 50% OFF EVERYTHING sign greeted him inside the shop. Sam was no expert, but based on the faded colors of the once-red ink, he suspected this particular sale had been going on since Sam Spade traded his baby bottle for gin.

"What can I do you for?" A large man in overalls and a Civil War cap sauntered toward him. By the color of the wool cap, Sam guessed the man was a rebel.

The man pointed to one of the signs. "Got a real good sale going on today. Don't see prices like this around Branson."

Sam looked down at his black T-shirt and jeans, wondering what about him made the man assume he was a tourist. Then he saw the man staring at the fur lead in Sam's hand. Well, that explained that.

"I'm pet sitting," he explained.

"Is that one of those fancy foreign pigs?" The shop owner squatted down and studied Toadstool. "He looks just like a Hampshire."

Sam sighed. "He is a Hampshire. Don't ask me to explain it. Like I said, I'm pet sitting."

"Must be a woman involved." The man grinned and gouged Sam in the side with an elbow. "Can't see no other reason a fellow like yourself'd be walking a pig around on a sissy leash like that." He grinned again.

Sam lived to be the source of entertainment for the masses.

"Yeah, well, you know how it is." Sam attempted to smile.

"Married man myself, but I still got some memories." The man gouged him again.

Enough already. "Sam Samson."

A huge paw engulfed Sam's outstretched hand. "Jed, Jed Mont."

Sam froze for a minute, but when Jed stopped at "Mont," he relaxed. Close. For a minute he thought he'd completed his search at his first stop.

"So what you looking for, son?" Jed leaned against a glass-fronted lawyer's bookcase.

Sam's mind whirled. He couldn't just ask about Del. He needed to look around a bit first, maybe buy something. "You have any pigs?"

Jed glanced at Toadstool, who had sat down right at Sam's feet. "You need more than one?"

"Not this kind of . . ." Sam began.

Laughing, Jed straightened. "I know, son. I was

just yanking your chain a bit. This wouldn't be for the pig-owning lady, now would it?"

Sam nodded. It didn't really seem like a response was necessary. When you came into a place with a pig tied to you, it was best to just play along and, hopefully, avoid as much humiliation as possible.

"I got a sweet little pair of salt and pepper shakers back here somewheres." Yanking on his overall straps, Jed lumbered between laden tables and overfilled shelves.

"You have a cookie jar?" Del yanked Toadstool to a stand.

After blowing cobwebs off a dozen boxes and inhaling a dirt road's worth of dust, Sam returned to the front with the set of salt and peppers and an oversized piggy bank with pink and green flowers on one side.

While Jed wrapped up his purchases, Sam pondered what to do next. He loved junking as much as the next guy, but he was here on an information-gathering mission. He needed to approach Jed on either Del or the Pig. The Pig seemed more natural.

"Speaking of pig collecting, I heard a tale the other day."

Jed looked up from tying a length of twine around Sam's package. Seeing the spark of interest in his hazel eyes, Sam continued.

"The way I heard it, some rich city collector came through here with a rare pottery pig. Was on his way home with it, had even called and bragged about it to all his pals, but somewhere in Missouri he tried to cross a low-water bridge during a high-water time and got washed downstream. He drowned and the Pig was never seen again."

Jed handed Sam the package. "That ain't no tale, son. That's the truth. Happened right here in Docia going on thirty years ago. I was there when they pulled the car out." He shook his head. "That feller had no business trying to make it across that bridge, the water that high."

Sam almost dropped the salt and peppers. He'd stumbled onto the spot where the Pig was last thought to be. Had Izzy known that when he'd pointed Sam toward Docia? But he'd said the Pig was sure to turn up in Allentown. Sam resisted the urge to knock his palm against his head. Wasn't going to help make any sense of the mess and Jed here would just think Sam was stranger than he already did.

Making an effort to keep his tone casual, Sam asked, "So you think the story's true?"

"I know it. I took three of those fancy pottery collectors out to the place myself. They strapped on waders and walked up and down that creek. Didn't find nothing any more interesting than a couple arrowheads though."

"You think someone else found it first?"

"Hard telling. The thing could have broke into pieces and sunk to the bottom, be hard pressed to tell pottery bits from rocks once they were on the bottom of a creek bed."

Sam had had similar thoughts himself, but he refused to believe them. There was some reason Del was after this Pig and it had to be something more solid than a thirty-year-old legend. Somebody somewhere knew where that Pig was.

"Was the place far from here?" Sam asked.

"Not too. Why? You ain't thinking of hunting for it, are you?"

"Just interested." And Sam had no other leads; might as well take a little drive in the country. A little peace migh. help him think better.

The closer Del got to home, the tighter her chest got. Too bad Toadstool wasn't there; they could have puked together.

She'd taken a back road to the bridge. The main road went right by her childhood home. She was afraid if she saw the mailbox, the black-eyed Susans that surrounded it, and the bullet-riddled NO TRES- PASSING signs that lined the roadway, she'd weaken and turn down the drive. If she got as far as that, it'd be just a quarter mile to the house, and her mama would sense her like a box turtle sensed rain. She was probably already roaming around, watching for her daughter.

Del didn't believe in all that old folk garbage, but she couldn't deny that as far as her mama was concerned she'd never been able to get much past her. Even now when they talked on the phone, Del got that prickly feeling on the back of her neck, like her mama was in the room watching her, knowing Del was lying about where she lived and what she did.

Up close and personal, there'd be no hope for it. All Del's years of building her own life away from her family would be lost.

Spotting a place where the road bled into a pas- ture, Del pulled off. Both hands on the wheel, she took a deep breath. She could do this. She could be back here without returning permanently. She was not the girl who ran away seven years ago. She had her own identity. No one was going to judge her based on what her father did, if for no other reason than no one in her new life was going to know who her father was.

This might hurt her momma, maybe even her daddy too, but it couldn't be helped. Del was done sacrificing her life to her father's addiction to getting the best end of a deal. She was done having people respect her one day and paint her with that big ole Mont paintbrush full of shame the next. She'd taken her chance and lost it all.

She wasn't going through that again. Not for anyone.

Dressed in camouflage and hiking boots, compliments of yet another trip to Wal-Mart, she opened her door and took off down the road. She'd start at the bridge and work her way south.

Sam gathered up Izzy's blanket and made Toadstool a bed in the floorboard. This looked like rough country, no place for someone with four-inch legs. With the pig fast asleep and the windows rolled down a few inches, Sam grabbed a flashlight from his roadside emergency kit and strode toward the creek.

It was already getting dusky out; in another hour it would be dark. He should have waited until tomorrow to mount his search, but once he left Docia, Sam wasn't planning on returning. It was a nice enough town and all, but you'd seen one wide space in the road and you'd seen them all.

There was nothing of note at the bridge. He hadn't expected there to be. Couldn't even say why he was here. Just seemed like the thing to do. Switching on the light, he ran the beam over the bank. A startled frog sounded an alarm and leapt into the water.

Directing the beam farther down the creek, Sam noticed a large mass of deserted metal about ten yards away. Couldn't be the car. They'd have hauled that off years ago, surely.

Intrigued, he picked his way through the brambles that grew along the bank. The mass he had seen was lodged on a sandbank. He skipped over a fallen tree and strode toward it. Definitely a car, but unless the rich collector was driving a circa 1972 Gremlin, this wasn't the vehicle.

Sam wondered if another driver had met the same fate in the same spot as the Unruh collector. On further inspection, he decided no. The Gremlin was just dumped. He'd never understood the mentality that said it was all right to dump your worn-out machinery in the nearest gulley. Not that he could blame anyone for dumping a Gremlin, but have the decency to haul it to an actual dump, not some creek.

Disgusted with whoever had left the rusty mess behind, he kicked the back end. The movement caused the front bumper to detach and plop into the water. With a guilty look around, Sam tramped over the sand and reached for the bumper. He could haul this much off himself.

As he was dragging the bumper out of the weeds, the sound of a gun firing exploded somewhere in the woods in front of him, followed by a feminine shriek.

Del.

He didn't pause to think why his first instinct was that the squeal had come from Del. He dropped the bumper and scrambled toward the sound. Back on the bank, he saw an overgrown path leading from the creek, into the woods. Another explosion, but no cry. Cursing, he jogged down the path.

The trees and underbrush grew thicker as he moved along. Sweat streamed down his neck, and in the woods it was darker than by the stream.

Hell. He'd dropped his flashlight to pull the bumper free. As he stood cursing his own stupidity, another blast sounded. This time he was close enough to hear pattering through the leaves above him. Shotgun. Someone was shooting at Del with a shotgun.

Or were they? Maybe it was just kids shooting at cans, not realizing there were people in the woods.

"Hold your fire. There are people out here," he yelled.

Silence answered him.

"Del? Are you out there?"

He thought he heard muffled movement somewhere to his left. Turning, he scanned the woods. Someone was there. He could feel them. Desperate, he yelled again. "Del. Answer me. I know—"

A shotgun blast cut him off. As shot spattered the tree closest to him, he dropped to the ground. Shit. Now they were shooting at him.

At least he'd drawn the fire from Del.

Scrambling forward, he sighted an outcropping of rock. With a burst of adrenaline, he reached the first boulder. Crouched behind it, he paused to take a breath.

He had to find Del or whoever had made that first shriek. She could be hit, bleeding in the woods. But it was almost dark, he had no light, and some idiot or worse was peppering the hillside with buckshot.

Both palms pressed against the stone, he peered around the side. Once it was dark, the shooter wouldn't be able to see him at all. Of course Sam wouldn't be able to see the shooter or find Del either, but he wasn't going to dwell on that right now. He just had to wait.

As he prepared to sit, two hands reached from behind him and grabbed hold of his belt. One strong tug and he was down.

Chapter 13

Pig headed . . .

Sam fell like a dead deer, with a thump, right on top of Del. His stunned stillness didn't last long. With a quick flip he had her pinned to the ground.

"Get off me, you idiot," she whispered through clenched teeth.

He didn't.

A thick covering of last fall's leaves had softened her fall, but dampness was leaking through the seat of her pants and something was crawling through her hair. She tried to slap it away and met Sam's hand.

"I was looking for you," he murmured.

"Yeah, I heard. You think you could have been a little louder?"

He pulled back, giving Del's lungs a little room for oxygen. "Hey, I thought you might be hurt. I was worried."

"So what? You wanted to make sure whoever's shooting at me had a chance to finish me off by broadcasting my location?"

"They stopped shooting at you and were aiming at me. I'd say I was saving you." Even cowering in the dirt he managed to sound cocky.

"Well, next time, don't." Del was ticked. First, she was pretty sure her daddy was shooting at her. Maybe he knew it was her, maybe he didn't, but she was sure it was him. He always used a shotgun to scare off trespassers, and even though she wasn't on his land, she was close enough. It was just like him to pull out the shotgun.

The only plus side to this was that she was also pretty confident he was only using rock salt—his preferred ammunition for ridding his land of interlopers. Rock salt wouldn't kill you, but it sure would sting like the dickens. Could leave a nasty bruise too.

Then, just as she was about to start firing back with a nice hunk of limestone and a few choice words, Sam came tramping onto the scene. Put her at a distinct disadvantage so far as confronting her father, and if it wasn't her daddy hiding behind the shotgun, what Sam did was just plain stupid.

Okay, maybe a little brave.

For some reason the admittance annoyed her more. She frowned up at him. In the growing darkness she could barely make out his grin.

"You planning on getting off me?" she asked.

"I don't know. Seems to me you're a lot safer down here. All the shots seem to be hitting the leaves. On the ground you should be safe and snug." On the "snug," he leaned back down, sniffing the length of her neck. "How do you smell so good after tromping around these woods?"

Del wasn't feeling safe. What she was feeling was

a distinct edge of panic surfacing. Sam was heavy and solid on top of her, too solid, and it felt way too good to be safe.

"I think you should get off me." She kept her voice cold, with as much authority as she could muster with a wet seat and bugs in her hair.

To her surprise, it worked. After a long gaze, he pushed himself up, then reached down for her. "Thought you wanted to get up," he said.

Ignoring his hand and his grin, she scrambled to a stand. "I'm leaving." She brushed dried leaves off her pants and turned to weave back through the boulders where she'd left the path.

Sam's hand stopped her. "I don't think so." All tone of banter was gone. "Someone was shooting at you. You can't just go trotting out there."

She tried to shake off his hand, but it wouldn't budge. "It's dark now. They can't see me, and unlike you I can walk quietly through the woods."

"No."

Del couldn't remember anyone ever just telling her no, not like that. Not in a no-argument, this-is-for-your-own-good voice. Fact was, when she had been told no, it was always for someone else's good, not hers. A warmth filled her chest.

She looked at Sam again. He was protecting her, worrying about her. Del prided herself on being self-sufficient; maybe that's why his concern felt so good. It was tiring never depending on anyone. Tiring and lonely. Del was tired of being tired, and even more tired of being lonely.

She laid her hand on his arm. "Thank you."

"For what?" It was too dark now to see his face,

but she could tell by his voice he was surprised and maybe a tad suspicious.

"For caring. No one ever has before."

She sensed he was going to say something or do something, the air around them held the promise, like the silence before a tornado hits. Something big was about to happen and when it did, Del would never be the same.

Sam's nose grazed her hair. "Del—"

Another explosion of rock salt—at least she prayed it was rock salt—tore through the leaves above their heads.

She grabbed Sam's horsehair belt and yanked him toward the rocks. "Come on. There's a cave back here. We can wait him out in there."

"A cave?" Sam stopped and Del jerked to a halt in front of him.

"What are you doing? Let's get inside before he shoots again." More and more Del wondered if it was her father shooting. She'd never known him to hunt someone down like this. A few potshots to scare them good and then he was off. This was something else, almost calculated. Like someone knew they would be here and was sending them some message Del couldn't quite interpret.

And if it wasn't her father, then there was no reason to think whoever was shooting was packing anything other than one hundred percent turkey-tried and true buckshot.

She gave Sam's belt another yank. She might as well have been tugging on his dually.

"There bats in this cave?" he asked.

"Bats?" Who cared about bats? What was this, a field

trip? "Sure, bats. Bats live in caves." She dug in her heels and gripped the horsehair with both hands.

No movement.

"One of us should stand watch. You get inside." He took a step backward.

She was not losing ground. With her entire weight dangling from his belt, she said, "We don't need a guard. We just need to get away from the spray. I don't think he'll follow us into the cave, and if he does we can jump him inside. There's, like an overlook."

He clasped her hands. "You go inside. I'll wait here."

A burst of shot pinged against the rocks behind them. She was getting him inside one way or another. Without pausing to think, she shoved one hand up his neck into his hair and kept the other tight on his belt. Yanking his face to hers, she followed the motion with her lips.

After a start of surprise, his tongue danced forward to meet hers. Reeling from the unexpected swoosh of emotion that engulfed her, she tugged him step by step toward the cave.

At the opening, Sam braced his outstretched arms on the rocks.

She wasn't losing him now. With a surge of resolve, Del grabbed a handful of black T-shirt and pulled it out of his jeans. At the same moment, she wrapped one leg around his thigh. Sam tensed, then pushed her backward into the gloom of the cave.

It was darker than the inside of a whiskey jug inside. Sam paused long enough in his exploration

of Del's tonsils to think about the bats. It was now
dark outside. Bats flew out at dusk. The cave should
be bat free for a good seven hours. Plenty of time
to fulfill a fantasy or two. What with the adrenaline
pumping through him, maybe even three.

"Where's the overlook?" he murmured against
Del's lips.

"Hmmm?"

"The overlook. You said there was somewhere
we could watch out for the shooter."

"You want to watch out for the shooter?" Her
pant was indignant.

Sam smiled. "C'mon, I can see now." Making out
the outline of a low ledge, he grabbed Del by the
waist and heaved her up. "You see this in the day-
light?" he asked.

"Why?" she replied.

"Just wondering how much weight it can hold."
He patted the ledge.

"Hey." Her hiking boot swung out to meet him
in the chest.

"What was that for?" *Women.*

"Like you don't know." He could feel her glare.

Great. He'd gone into the bowels of batdom for
her, and she chose now to claim an attitude.

"Move over." He scaled the rock ledge beside
her.

"You sure it's safe? Don't want you tipping the
weight limit here."

So that was it. She thought he was making a
crack about her weight.

"Move over," he ordered.

When she crossed her arms and refused to
budge, he said, "Fine, have it your way." He contin-

ued to crawl up, covering her body with his. "This what you had in mind?" he asked.

"Not exactly." The words were soft, making Sam want to discover exactly what she did have in mind.

"How about this?" He placed a hand on each side of her head, then lowered his mouth to her neck. With each soft, nibbling kiss he felt her body tremble.

"Or maybe this?" He shifted his lips to her ear, blowing softly first into one, then the other.

She groaned.

He'd found another tell.

"I just don't seem to be getting it. How about one more try?" His tongue darted into her ear. He followed the motion with another warm breath.

She moaned, then grabbed his head in both hands and pulled his lips to hers. She ran her tongue along the seam of his mouth, urging him to open his. Not one to balk at a challenge, he complied.

This was the way to wage a war.

He placed one hand under her head to protect her from the hard rock. The other he skimmed down her body.

Ah, the stuff that dreams were made of.

He could feel the lace edge of her bra through the form-fitting tee. He traced the dainty material with his finger until he lost it in the plunge of her cleavage. Cupping as much of her breast as would fit in his hand, he massaged her flesh through the cloth.

It wasn't enough. With the same hand, he found the bottom of her shirt and, much like she had done to him earlier, jerked it out of her pants.

Sighing, he ran his hand up her bare skin and prayed she wore a front hook. When his hand met solid lace instead of the metal he'd hoped for, he bit back a curse. A two-foot-wide rock ledge was not the best place to be searching for a bra hook. Of course, it wasn't the best place to be doing any of this, and he sure wasn't going to let that stop him.

While he pondered the safest way to relieve Del of her brassiere without tossing her onto the dirt below, Del let out an impatient huff.

"You waiting for something I should know about? It's not exactly nice to prime the pump, then stop short of using the handle."

He chuckled. "Oh, I plan on using the handle. Don't worry about that."

Another woman would have been embarrassed, but not Del. "So?"

Still laughing, he levered her body up enough to run his hand behind her. With an expert snap, her bra fell loose.

"Guess I better make up for lost time," he whispered against her chest. He lifted her shirt off and settled his mouth on her breast.

Someone groaned, but with his face snuggled into her cleavage, Sam couldn't tell if it was him or Del. He was in the most perfect place on earth. Better than an auction full of money-heavy bidders. Better than a yard sale full of underpriced Redwing. Better than anywhere he'd ever been or ever hoped to be. The crazed shooter outside could come in and blow him away, and Sam wouldn't move a speck.

Except Del would be left alone and unprotected. Through the fog of desire, he remembered what had brought them to the cave. He lifted his head.

Del yanked it back down.

"We need to watch out for the shooter," he stammered out between breaths.

"Let him find his own friend." Del jiggled her shoulders, causing her breasts to brush against his face.

"Really, we need to—"

She shifted her hips, causing her groin to collide with his. "We need to what?" she asked.

With a growl, Sam dropped his mouth back to her breasts. They were perfect, full, round, and soft. Just the way God meant them to be. No need for Sam to go to church; he could worship right here.

He pulled her bra down farther, exposing her nipple to the night air. Finding it with his mouth, he traced the puckered skin around it with his tongue. Del responded by grabbing his belt buckle and jerking it free. Without bothering to unzip his jeans, she shoved her hand down his pants and wrapped her fingers around his penis. Sam froze.

His opponent had just one-upped him, and if he didn't want this fantasy to end right now, he was going to have to practice some major deep breathing.

Del ran her fingers along the shaft of his erection. As the skin slid against the hard flesh within, Sam groaned. Her thumb wandered to the tip, circling until a few drops of moisture broke free.

Sam reached for his fly.

About time.

Sam's boot hit the dirt floor beneath them with a thump. While he kicked off his second, Del wriggled out of her own pants, at least as much as she could.

Sex in a cave wasn't all it was cracked up to be.

When Sam lowered himself back down, she realized he'd removed his shirt too. He was completely naked—just the way she wanted him. Running her hands over the muscles of his back, Del decided a little inconvenience was well worth the rewards.

Sam smoothed his hand down her bare leg until he hit denim. He tugged on the material, but her pants refused to budge past the barrier of her hiking boots.

"Shoes," she panted against his bare chest.

In a quick succession of moves he yanked off her boots and pulled her legs free of her cammies.

"Thanks." Del turned her attention to his neck, in particular the spot where it met his shoulders. The scent of his cologne was strongest there and she breathed it in. Lemony. She nibbled lightly on the muscle. Salty.

Eager to sample other sensations, she ran her hand down his back, tracing his spine with her thumb. As she reached his tailbone, she paused to make small firm circles with her fingers. Sam moaned and adjusted his weight so his penis pressed against the thin material of her lace underwear.

Leaving one hand massaging his buttock, Del hooked her bikinis with her thumb and attempted to pull them out of her way.

Nudging her face with his nose, Sam said, "Let me." Lifting them both slightly, he skimmed the underwear over her hips. Free of her legs, they dropped over the edge.

Who needed underwear anyway?

"How's your back?" Sam asked.

Killing her. "Fine." She wrapped her hands around his neck and attempted to pull him back down.

"I don't want to hurt you."

"You won't."

She was going be the one doing the hurting if he didn't get moving.

Taking her uplifted hands, he tucked them around his neck. "Hold on." With an arm locked around her waist he swiveled in place until Del was looking down at him. "Better?" he asked.

Actions speak louder than words.

Del grabbed both his hands and placed them on her breasts. Leaning forward he captured a nipple in his mouth. Del bit back a moan as electricity shot from her breast to her groin.

Enough waiting.

Rising up on her knees, she found his erection and positioned it under her. As he sucked on her nipple she edged his penis inside her. She was tight. It had been too long. As he eased into her, she decided she wouldn't make that mistake again.

It felt good, beyond good. She fought the urge to come down fast, taking his length in one quick swoop, but this was too good. The slow in and out. The tease of it. She could feel his breathing growing deeper. He was concentrating too. Both of them lost in the sensation of their bodies bonding together. When he was completely encased inside her, she paused, staring down at him. Even in the dark she could feel his eyes on her breasts, knew he was watching them.

Power came with desire. She reveled in it.

* * *

Del sat astride Sam. His penis throbbed with the need for more, but he didn't move. As she slowly began to slide up and down the length of him, her breasts bobbed and swayed. He felt feverish. He fought the need to grab her by the waist and force her to quicken the torturous pace.

With each slide downward she traced her nails down his stomach. He almost yelled with the pleasure of it. She had him trapped. When he leaned up to take her breast back in his mouth, she pushed him back down. "My game now," she whispered.

For once Sam didn't mind losing.

As her pace increased, he reached out to cup her breasts again, to urge her on at the new faster speed. Faster and harder. She pulled up until he almost yelled from the lack of sensation, then slammed back down, capturing him in one quick move. Again and again. Until he could hold on no longer.

"Del?" he asked.

"Sam." Her breathing was hard. He could barely make out his name. Then her muscles clenched around him and she threw back her head in a delicate shudder. Not able to wait any longer, he followed her, releasing the pent-up desire and yanking her down onto his chest.

They lay there panting, her breath tickling his chest.

"You okay?" she asked.

"Never better."

"I can move." She started to roll off him.

"Don't even think it." With his arm behind her back he locked her in place. "You're the best blanket I've ever had."

She smiled against his skin. "It is a little cool in here, isn't it?"

"Are you cold?" He leaned forward to search for her clothes.

She shoved him back down. "No, you don't. You chose the position. Now you're stuck with it."

He grinned. "Well, it's an awfully good position to be stuck in, don't you think?"

She walked her fingers down his stomach. "One of the best."

"One of?"

Drawing little circles on the sensitive skin near his groin, she replied, "I might be able to think of a few more we could try. Just for argument's sake."

Sam was all for arguing.

"Any come to mind right now?" he asked.

"Right now?" She sounded surprised.

Taking her hand, he placed it on his erection. "Right now."

Hours later, Sam woke to a crick in his neck and a knee near his groin. After adjusting Del's leg so he didn't leave the cave lacking the ability to ever repeat their adventures, he cradled her in his arms. Rooting her nose against his chest, she sighed in her sleep. He brushed her hair away from her face. So sweet in slumber, so demanding in sex. He liked the contrast.

Del was a constant puzzle, ever changing. Kept him guessing. He'd never get bored with a woman like Del. He ran his hand down her hip. And not just because of the sex, which was the best he'd ever experienced, even with a thousand sharp rocks biting into his backside. No, Del was exciting, challenging, but somewhere under all that, soft and inviting. Sam would never get enough.

She shivered in her sleep. She was cold and it had to be getting close to dawn. It would be best if they escaped the cave while it was still dark, before the shooter could see them. He rolled Del onto her side and searched with one hand for their clothes. Almost dawn. There was another reason to leave, but with one arm still wrapped around Del's soft form, he had a hard time latching onto it.

His hand touched Del's pants, just as a thousand little squeaks and the flapping of wings filled the cave. Bats. Bats were the reason. Without thinking he threw Del's pants toward the noise. The resulting din almost sent him into a cowering ball. Bats. They were everywhere.

"Del, we have to get out of here." He shook her shoulder as he yelled her name.

"What?" Still firmly asleep, she rolled back over and shoved him with the heel of her palm. Balanced in a crouch, Sam tipped over and fell six feet to the dirt floor below.

Dazed, he stared up at the swirling bodies above him.

Chapter 14

What a porker . . .

Del awoke to the sound of beating wings and eerie squeaks. "Sam?" In a panic, she jerked upright. She was alone on the shelf of rock, but bats swarmed overhead.

"Sam," she yelled. Where were her clothes? Blindly, she groped through dirt and debris. Sam's T-shirt was shoved into a crevice behind her head. She shook it out and pulled it on.

If Sam had left, he'd left his shirt behind. Scooting toward the incline of rock that led to the cave floor, her foot caught in denim. Her hand closed around the cold metal of an oversized belt buckle. And his pants.

Somehow she didn't see Sam as the streaking type. So where was he?

The shrill sound of the bats lessened as the colony made its way deeper into the cave.

"Sam?" she called. This time she heard something move on the ground below. Crawling on her knees, she peered over the edge.

Sam was sprawled face-up, naked as a plucked chicken, on the dirt. His eyes were open, but he didn't seem to see her. Was he knocked out? Wouldn't his eyes be closed?

"Sam," she yelled again. Dead? Was he dead?

There was no safe, fast way down from there, and Del had to find out if he was alive. She picked up his jeans and dropped them onto his still form.

The belt buckle hit first—right between his eyes.

"Crap," he muttered.

Well, he was alive.

"You okay?" she asked.

He blinked back. "I was."

"Sorry." Feeling around on the ledge, she recovered her own shirt and bra, but no underwear and no pants. Might make getting into her hotel room interesting. With them tucked under her arm, she scrambled down from the ledge.

Sam was tugging his jeans on when she landed next to him. "That my shirt?" He eyed her like he was thinking of repossessing the only thing that stood between Del and complete humiliation. It was one thing to be naked during the heat of sex, but quite another after rational thought returned— especially in the growing dawn.

She stretched the thin material downward, hopefully disguising her hips.

"I'd like my shirt back." Grinning, he held out a hand.

She narrowed her eyes. "Where are my pants and underwear?"

"You lost them? That's rough." His eyes twinkled.

Del wished she'd dropped a boulder on him instead of a five-ounce belt buckle. "It's getting light, and I'm not leaving here without my pants." She caught herself right before performing a foot stomp.

"If I find them, will you give me my shirt back?" he asked.

She had her own shirt tucked under her arm; why would she need his?

"Sure," she replied.

With a grin he sauntered over to the far side of the cave. Her jeans were dangling from a smaller ledge that mirrored the one where she and Sam had spent the night.

"How'd they get over there?" she asked.

He shrugged. "No telling."

Del didn't care. She just wanted to be fully clothed. She held out her hand.

Sam slung her pants over his shoulder. "I think you owe me a shirt first."

"First?"

"First." Sam replied.

"But I'll be . . ." Del didn't complete the thought. The look on his face said he knew exactly what state she'd be in without his shirt. Son of a . . .

Fine. Grabbing the hem of his shirt, she jerked it over her head; with her eyes closed she held it out to him. She knew it was stupid, but she didn't feel quite so exposed if she couldn't see his reaction.

She shook the shirt in her fist. He didn't take it. What was he doing? Exasperated, her eyes flew open.

Sam stood, arms crossed over his chest, analyzing her from the tips of her bare toes to the top of her dirt-encrusted head. The appreciation in his eyes said she had no reason to be embarrassed. Del flushed in places even he couldn't see.

Turning her back on him, she dropped his shirt on the ground and whipped her own over her head.

She'd mess with the bra later; now she just needed covering. The baby-doll tee stopped right at her waist. Great, teach her to try to be fashionable.

She kicked his shirt backward and muttered over her shoulder, "Give me my pants."

"All right, but it's a shame. Like slapping a coat of paint on a Chippendale chair."

Covered, if not fully clothed, she didn't waste more than five minutes searching for her boots. Somehow Sam had his on before she'd zipped her cammies.

Eager to leave the cave behind, she left barefoot.

This man was killing her shoe budget.

Sam smiled as he watched Del stomp out of the cave. She was sans bra, sans underwear, and sans shoes, but she kept her head held high. He couldn't figure what the big deal was, anyway. So he saw her naked. She sure hadn't been shy about that last night.

Not to mention how she was constantly flashing cleavage to get him off his game. He shook his head. Women. There was no figuring them out.

He touched her arm. "You better let me go first."

She graced him with a scathing look and kept going.

Enough was enough. There was still the little matter of a shotgun to consider.

He wrapped long fingers around her bicep. "I said I'll go first."

She stopped, put her hands on her hips, and stared up at him. "You in a hurry?"

Concentrating on how her breasts swayed under her T-shirt, Sam almost missed the sarcasm. "Not really." He could make out her nipples almost as clearly as if she wasn't wearing the shirt at all. Women should never wear bras.

"Hello, I'm up here." She tapped a finger on the sore spot between his eyes.

Before he'd actually seen them, touched them in the flesh, her breasts had been a lot easier to ignore—or at least pretend he was ignoring. There wasn't a heterosexual male who got within a football field of Del who wouldn't notice those breasts.

A finger snap to his sore spot brought him out of his reverie.

"Ow." He frowned at her.

"I said, you in a hurry?"

She was definitely snippy this morning. Sam couldn't imagine why. A night filled with wild cave sex had a calming effect on him. He'd like to try it more often.

With a hrumph she pushed past him, reminding Sam why he'd stopped her in the first place. He lunged forward, grabbed her around the waist, and jerked her against his chest.

"You're about three steps past a reasonable amount of trouble," he whispered in her ear. "But luckily, I'm a reasonable man. I'll give you two choices. Either you step back and let me go first, or—"

Silence and a very unladylike elbow to the gut

answered him. Good thing he kept his abs toned. Before she could get new ideas and go for a less protected part of his anatomy, he slid his arm under her legs and whipped her like a sack of pig chow over his shoulder.

Pig chow. Damn, he'd forgotten all about Toadstool. He needed to get back to his truck pronto and make sure the little porker hadn't eaten his upholstery.

His feed sack came to life. "Let me down." Del smacked him on the back.

"Now, I agree this isn't the best compromise, but I figure if anyone starts shooting, you got a better chance of coming out alive going in butt first."

Her reply was to start bucking. He was sure glad she'd lost her hiking boots. A bare toe and an elbow to the gut he could handle. He wasn't so sure about a boot.

"Hold on." Wrapping his arms around her legs to still her motions, he took off down the trail. Del kept her body upright by putting her hands on his shoulders, but after the third branch whacked her in the back of the head, she collapsed over his shoulder and grabbed his belt for support.

With her draped quietly, Sam took his time. There were no unusual sounds this morning. A squirrel chattered in a tree to their left and in the distance he could hear a hawk screech. As they approached the creek the soft sound of running water greeted them. No shotgun blasts. No crunching leaves as the shooter repositioned.

In sight of the road, he decided it was safe and lowered Del to her feet.

He was wrong. Del landed on her feet, then landed a balled-up fist to his gut.

He grimaced. Toned abs or not, that hurt.

"That's for being a bully." She pulled back her foot. "This is for stealing my pig."

He grabbed her by the shoulders. "I wouldn't do that."

She gave him a haughty look, then let loose with the kick. It was her turn to mutter, "Oww," but she added a one-footed hop.

Sam pointed at her foot, "Bare toes"—then his leg—"leather cowboy boots, you do the math."

Still rubbing her toes, she glared at him.

He'd never seen sex make a woman so cranky. Maybe he needed to work on his technique.

Del turned on her bare heel and stomped toward his truck. Anger seemed to add an extra twitch to her step. As he admired the view of her butt swinging back and forth, he remembered what she wore under those pants.

He couldn't start perfecting his technique soon enough.

Del tried to maintain a steady pace as she strode over the rocky ground. Her days of walking these hills barefoot were long behind her.

She was still steaming from the humiliation of being caught naked as a jaybird this morning. She couldn't believe she'd lost so much control last night that she'd fallen asleep without a stitch of clothes on. It was one thing to flash her assets, such as they were, while fully clothed, but naked? There was no hiding anything then. Del had a strict policy against nudity with an audience.

She didn't even use the public dressing room at the Y. It brought back awkward memories of pre-pubescent girls giggling behind their hands after gym class, and those same girls making catty remarks when the boys shot her an admiring gaze.

Later, Del couldn't help but notice that her body was a little on the full side compared to popular style. Sure, men ogled her breasts, but that was a big difference from seeing her naked and exposed. So she used the covered version to get what she wanted, and made sure the uncovered was never seen.

Now Sam had seen both, and she'd know it every time he looked at her. He'd seen the unvarnished truth of her body, and she didn't know how she'd be able to fool him again. In clothes, she could convert corpulent to curvaceous, but naked? There was no hiding the truth.

Sam's truck was parked by the side of the road, undisturbed. As Del approached, a tiny black snout appeared inside the window. Toadstool. He'd left her pig alone in the truck all night. If she hadn't already tried kicking him, she'd punt Sam into Arkansas.

She tapped on the glass and cooed as she waited for Sam to unlock the door.

"He doing okay?" There was no missing the concern in Sam's voice.

Okay, maybe she'd just punt him a county or two.

With the door open, she scooped up her pig and stroked him under the chin. Sam leaned around her to peer inside his truck.

"Looks like he did a good job," he said with all the pride of a Little League dad noting his son's first hit.

Del rolled her eyes, but the warmth in her chest returned.

"I'd put him down if I were you. It's been awhile since he's been out." Sam gestured to grass.

She'd already paid the price once this morning for not taking Sam's advice. Del lowered Toadstool to the ground. Waving his curly tail, he went to investigate a crop of wildflowers.

"So, who was shooting at you last night?" Sam asked.

Del kept her eyes on Toadstool. She'd revealed enough to Sam; she wasn't letting him in on her suspicions regarding her father.

"How should I know? I just came down here to do a little hiking and some idiot started shooting. Probably just a poacher."

"New pants?" he asked.

She looked at him. Since when had Sam become a fashionista?

"'Cause I don't think I've seen you sporting the turkey hunter look before."

Del did not like the direction this was going.

"I mean, plenty of kids like the look, but it just doesn't seem to fit you. No, I'd think the only reason you'd have on a pair of cammies would be if you were trying to not be seen." He leaned against his truck. "You hiding out here for a reason?"

Toadstool seemed to have located an acceptable spot to do his business. Finished, he began rooting behind an oak tree.

Glancing at the pig, Sam leaped forward. "No more acorns," he yelled.

Del raised an eyebrow. What was wrong with acorns? Pigs liked acorns.

In two strides, Sam reached the runt. As he grabbed for Toadstool, he paused, then leaned over and plucked something red from the grass. He rolled it over in his hands and even held it to his nose for a minute, before holding it up for Del to see.

"Shotgun shell," he said. "Something funny about it too."

Del froze.

"See here?" He pointed to the end of the plastic case. "Looks like some kind of white residue." He held it closer to his face, then looked back at Del. "I'm no expert, but I'd say our shooter was shooting rock salt last night."

Del swallowed. "That's good, isn't it? Means he didn't want to kill us."

Sam flipped the case into the air and caught it. "Might not have been planning on it, but I'd guess rock salt could put a pretty bad hurt on you if it hit you just right, maybe even kill you."

Del was pretty sure her father didn't know that. She didn't even know why he would be mad at her—she was the wronged party—never mind want to kill her.

Sam slipped the shell into the front pocket of his jeans. He was somewhat relieved to know whoever had been tracking them last night wasn't shooting lead pellets. Somewhat, but not entirely. This time it was rock salt, but how about next? Del had some-body ticked off. If he didn't figure out who, what would be coming her way next time around?

"I think I'm going to take a little drive into town. Where's your car?"

Del chewed on her lip for a second, then asked, "What for?"

"So you can drive back to Allentown." He grabbed Toadstool before he could snarf down any more acorns. "You can take the hog too."

"No, I mean why are you going into Docia?"

He raised his eyebrows. "Somebody was shoot-ing at us last night. Don't you think we should report it?"

A look of panic flitted over her face. She covered it fast, but Sam caught it. "But we were trespassing. The sheriff'll probably figure we had it coming." She gestured weakly to where he had found the shell. "Especially considering it was just rock salt."

"Don't guess I have to mention that part, and trespassing or not, nobody has the right to shoot at you."

"Tell them that," Del muttered.

There she went again acting like she was famil-iar with the area, and now that he thought back on it, last night in the heat of things she'd seemed to slip into an Ozarkian twang.

He kept his face blank. "So, you don't think I should report it?"

Relief swept over hers. "No. Just a waste of time. Let's get back to Allentown and forget all this." She waved her hands.

Sam wasn't sure what she meant by "all this," but he wasn't forgetting any of it, especially not their time in the cave. "Tell you what. You get on back, and I'll meet you at the Hutch later. We can talk about 'all this' then."

"You won't go to the sheriff?"

Toadstool tried to wiggle loose. Sam adjusted his grip on the pig and asked, "Where'd you leave your car? Your pet's getting restless, best get him tucked in and head north."

Del gave him an untrusting glance but pointed down the road.

After Del and Toadstool had taken off in a cloud of dust, Sam returned to his truck. She hadn't mentioned the sheriff again. It was just as well. Sam was finding it harder and harder to lie to her. He didn't even want to think about what he would do when he found the Unruh Pig.

Del pulled into Allentown. She didn't know what to do about last night—about any of it. Her daddy'd been shooting at her and she'd had sex with Sam in a cave, of all places. Talk about life-altering experiences. Not only that, but her one and only reason for going to Docia was left undone. She had learned absolutely zilch about the Unruh Pig.

Things were getting difficult here. It was time for Del to find the Pig and get out of southern Missouri before she opened herself up to something that kept her here forever.

But where to go now? Back to Tilde? So far, she'd provided the closest thing Del had to a lead. Of course, there was someone else who had firsthand knowledge of the disappearance of the Pig, and by the looks of things, he was trying to keep Del away from where it had last been seen.

Did her daddy know something about this mess?

Sam's time in Docia wasn't exactly time well spent. The sheriff filled out a report, but not until after he'd lectured Sam on wandering onto other people's property.

Sam did gather one interesting tidbit, though. While he was walking out the door, the woman who sat behind the reception desk stopped him.

"You get everything worked out?" She fluttered nonexistent lashes at him.

Sam paused. The sheriff had been no help. Might as well try a different angle. "Hope so. I was out hunting ginseng and some fool started shooting at me."

"That's terrible." She rested her breasts on the desk. Presentable, but not up to Del's standards.

"I know, not like I was hurting anything. Just walking through the woods."

She shook her head. "Just terrible."

He sat on the edge of her desk. "The sheriff said he'd look into it, but to be honest, I didn't get the feeling it was going to be top priority, if you know what I mean."

She rolled her eyes. "What is?" She whispered, "His brother had the job before him. This county'd elect a skunk if it had the right last name."

Sam grinned. "Don't suppose you'd have an idea who it could have been." He described the area he'd visited last night.

"Oh." She laughed. "That sounds like Jed Mont.

He's always running poachers off all the land around there. He doesn't shoot shot, though. Fills his shells with rock salt. Still hurts like heartbreak if you get a load of it in your pants. He nailed a couple of teenagers last fall. You should have heard 'em carrying on."

Jed Mont, the man who ran the antiques store, and he knew Sam had been headed to the low-water creek. Could he have followed him? Sam pondered this for a second. No, someone had been shooting at Del before Sam got there; at least he thought they had been. He needed to check that with Del.

He thanked the receptionist and slid off her desk. When she tossed out a few hints about lunch, he replied, "I'd love to, but I have to go see a woman about a pig."

At her confused look, he tipped his hat and strode out the door.

Sam should be here by now. Del hated waiting on people, especially men. It lowered her power position, although after last night and this morning, she didn't think her position could get much lower.

She flushed over her long john. Actually, her position last night had been packed with plenty of power. She liked that. It could get addictive.

She gave herself a mental head shake. All the more reason not to get involved with Sam. She knew she couldn't trust him, and she sure didn't need another emotional break. Leaving had been hard enough the first time, but she'd done it. The last thing she needed was another complication, another reason to stay.

She poked the tines of her fork into her pastry. She'd never seen a jelly-filled long john before, but her appetite was gone. There was a first. With a sigh, she stabbed a hunk of doughnut and held it out to Toadstool. The little pig was dressed for a night out in a brand-new rhinestone-studded harness and his zebra lead.

It was awfully nice of Becca to let Del bring him in. Del knew it was against about a thousand health codes, and even if she were blind, it wasn't likely she could sell anyone on him being a Seeing Eye pig.

After tucking a paper napkin under his chin, she scraped some blueberry filling onto her fork. As she held the utensil to the pig's mouth, Sam swung open the door to the Bunny Hutch and strode in.

"What are you doing to him? Look at how you have him gussied up."

Del smiled. No reprimand for feeding a pig at the table, just concern that she had him dressed too girly. You had to appreciate a man like that, and she did. Appreciate him, that was. He'd changed since this morning and, by the look of his wet hair, showered.

The moisture made his hair darker, which made his blue eyes stand out even more. In a fresh black tee and jeans, he was every woman's fantasy. He even smelled sexy. She needed to figure out what that cologne was so she could dab some on her pillow at night. It would make for interesting dreams.

Forgetting her resolve not to get involved, she

wet her lips. "Where you been?" She didn't care, as long as she was invited wherever he was going.

He stared at her for a moment as if unsure where to sit. Del considered moving over so he could sit next to her, but it seemed so high school and obvious. Just because the sight of him gave her a dry mouth and sweaty palms didn't mean she wanted him to know it.

He slid into the booth across from her, and Del suffered a twinge of regret. Maybe being obvious wouldn't be bad, just this once.

"What have you and the pig been doing? Shopping, I'd guess."

"You'd guess right." Were all his shirts this tight? Or was this one just extra clingy? He had the best chest muscles Del had ever had the honor of licking. The thought didn't even cause her to blush. She was that far gone.

"They let him in the stores?" Sam motioned to Becca, who grabbed a cup and the coffeepot and headed in their direction.

"No." The office manager of The Ranch Motel wouldn't let him in her room, either—not even for a quick drink of water. In Del's opinion, the woman took her two-star AAA rating a tad too seriously.

She'd hoped to smuggle him in tonight, but the manager was on to her. Del would have no choice but to leave Toadstool with Sam.

"If I send him home with you, you aren't going to run off with him again, are you?" She tried to look intimidating.

Sam grinned. "You threatening me?" In a lower voice, he added, "You know, I was thinking it might be best if you bedded down at my place too."

Bedded down? Del's mind drifted for a moment. She could do that.

She must not have looked convinced, because Sam kept talking. "You could take care of your pig, and I could take care of you." His voice rumbled in his chest for the last part.

While Del's libido fought with her natural inclination to be independent, Becca arrived with the coffee.

"Who you taking care of?" she asked.

To Del's surprise, Sam flushed. She felt her lips tilt into a smile. There was something sweet about his embarrassment. She decided to save him. "My pig." She scratched Toadstool behind the ear. "They won't let me keep him at The Ranch. Sam's been watching him for me."

A grin split Becca's face. "That right?"

As Sam scowled at his cousin, the bell over the door pealed, signaling a customer. One of Del's many nightmares strolled into the Hutch.

Chapter 15

When pigs fly . . .

Dressed in slim-fitting gray slacks and what had to be an Armani shirt, David Curtis stood with the arrogance of an Arabian surrounded by Shetland ponies. Del dropped lower in the booth.

Sam eyed her for a second, then shot a look over his shoulder. His gaze went straight to David, and like a tomcat sensing an interloper, David twisted on his heel until he was staring right back. The air vibrated with animosity.

Just what Del needed: a testosterone takedown.

"Somebody you know?" Becca murmured. She slid the coffeepot onto the table in front of them and smoothed her apron with her hands.

Del had seen that expression before, from every female from eighteen to eighty who got within six feet of David Curtis. He was good looking and slick, but he was also a snake. In Chicago, Del made it a practice to keep her eye on him. In Missouri, she'd hoped she wouldn't have to.

With a smile as fake as her daddy's Bohemia glass collection, she gave David a wave.

"Friend of yours?" Sam's voice was low and steady.

"Not exactly," Del replied, speaking through her smile.

"Quite the pretty boy." Sam spoke the words while looking directly at David. By David's upraised brow there was no doubt he'd heard them.

Becca leaned down to Del. "I could stand a little pretty," she whispered.

Del didn't reply. In nature the prettiest things were often the most dangerous; besides, for all his looks and smooth ways, Del had never fallen victim to David's charms. They'd always been after the same thing and been willing to take the other out to get it. There wasn't much she'd put past the man.

"Del." David arrived at the table in a cloud of overpriced Aramis cologne. His brown eyes zeroed in on Toadstool, still lapping blueberry jelly off Del's fork.

Del would not be embarrassed. She broke off a piece of doughnut and held it out to her pig. "David, what brings you down here?" Like she didn't know.

"They let you bring pigs in here?" David's gaze switched from Del to Becca. To Del's surprise, when he looked at Sam's cousin his gaze warmed. Maybe he was human, after all.

"Toadstool's a special case." Becca tilted her head as she smiled.

Becca needed to get out more often.

As if sharing Del's thought, Sam snapped at his cousin, "You got customers up there." He pointed to the cash register, where one of the coffee regulars stood shuffling through yesterday's paper.

"So I do." Becca didn't look to be in too big a hurry to help the old guy out, but after another stern stare from Sam, she sauntered off.

"You didn't answer the lady's question." There was no missing the threat in Sam's voice.

David turned an amused look on Sam. "I don't guess I did."

Del rolled her eyes. This posturing was entertaining and all, but there was just so much a girl could take.

"Sam, David's an"—she hesitated. Did Sam already know who David was? There had been that note at Sam's house. If she lied, would Sam know? On the other hand, she did still need to find the Pig, and she wasn't sure what Sam would do when he found out about the potential six-figure item— "acquaintance of mine from Chicago. Would you mind giving us a second to catch up on things?"

The arms crossed over Sam's chest said he would. *Men.* Taking a deep breath, Del steeled herself to switch gears. She didn't feel as comfortable going into vamp mode now with Sam. He'd seen too much of the real her; besides, it felt so false. She was tired of pretending. She wanted to be real with someone—no, not someone, with Sam.

Finally deciding she didn't have it in her, she gestured at David, who was smirking down at them. "Well, sit down." She didn't offer to move over and neither did Sam. After a second, David grabbed a chair from a nearby table and swung it into position at the end of the booth.

This should be interesting.

While Sam and David went through the male ritual of handshakes and stare downs, Del gathered her thoughts.

"So, how are things at work?" she asked.

"Busy, there's that big"—he glanced at Sam—"event coming up. Porter's getting pretty anxious. How are things down here?"

Sam's look was unreadable. He picked up his cup and sipped his coffee.

"Fine. Things are going fine." *Get back to Chicago, you commission-hungry slime.*

"You haven't checked in lately. Any reason?"

"There's no problem. Why check in?" Del stroked Toadstool's back.

"You sure there's no problem?" David glanced at Sam again.

Apparently feeling he'd been insulted in some way, Sam tapped his finger on his saucer. "She said there was no problem. You should believe her."

Moving his gaze from Sam's face to his tapping finger, then back to Sam's face, David asked, "You believe her?"

Okay, this was not going in a good direction. Del dropped her fork with a clang on her almost empty plate. "Well, sounds like everything is fine here and busy at work. You should get on back before something gets screwed up." She gave David a piercing look.

He turned his chair so he could smile at Becca, who was waiting on the booth next to them. "I don't know. I think I might take a little vacation down here myself. I never realized how interesting a place it was."

Turning back to Del, he said, "Besides, the way

things are going, you may decide to just stay here. It'll give us a chance to say good-bye properly."

Del's eyes narrowed. If he thought he was going to take over her sales at Porter's, he had another thing coming. "Nothing is going to keep me here. As soon as I'm done with my . . . collection, I'm heading back north. Count on it."

David didn't look the least bit intimidated. Clearing his throat, Sam picked up his cup. "Strange thing to say. No reason Del'd stay here, is there?"

His look was hooded. Did he want Del to stay?

With his gaze trained on Becca again, David asked, "So where you staying? I'm going to need to get a room."

Before Del could answer, Sam jumped in. "She's staying with me, but I hear The Ranch has some openings. You should check there."

Del didn't correct him. With David here, she needed some allies. Maybe it was time to come clean with Sam. What was the worst that could happen? She sure wasn't finding the Pig on her own.

David gave her a surprised look, then turned an apprising one on Sam. "Well, looks like Del has a few reasons to stay here, doesn't it?"

With steady eyes, Sam replied, "It's for her pig. The hotels around here aren't as friendly as the Bunny Hutch."

David laughed. "Yes, well, everything is for the Pig, isn't it?"

No one spoke for a minute, then Sam gestured at Toadstool. "How long's it been since he was out? You don't want him leaving a puddle."

Del frowned at her pig. It had been awhile, but she

wasn't ready to leave Sam and David alone. Snapping on Toadstool's lead, she turned to David. "You want to walk out with me? I can give you directions to The Ranch."

"I'm in no rush. I'll just stay and chat with Sam, was it?" His wolfish grin told Del she had every reason to be concerned about leaving, but she was committed now.

Putting a light tone in her voice, she replied, "Well, don't talk about me while I'm gone. It isn't polite." Then she lowered Toadstool to the ground and headed for the door.

Mr. Highfalutin' Big-City Auctioneer waited until Del had disappeared out the front before slipping into the seat she'd deserted and addressing Sam. "So, you learn anything?"

Sam stared at him. He liked the man less in person than he did on the phone, and he liked poison ivy more than that. Sam didn't like the familiar way he talked to Del, and he didn't like the wanting-to-get-familiar way he looked at Sam's cousin.

"You didn't mention you were coming to Allentown. When did you get here?"

David ran his thumb along his chin. "This morning."

Glancing at his Timex, Sam said, "Pretty long drive this early, isn't it?"

"Not so. I like driving in the dark."

Sam assessed the man across from him. He had to be lying. No one would leave at three A.M. Of course, he could have spent the night somewhere on the road. But then, why lie? Just to get Sam's goat? Or because last night he was busy shooting rock salt along a roadside near Docia?

David and Del obviously had a rivalry going. How far would he go to stop her from finding the Pig first?

Sam intended to find out.

Becca wandered up to the table right then, giving Sam an excuse to switch topics. "You planning any recreation while you're down here?"

While Becca poured coffee into a fresh cup, David smiled up at her and replied, "Hadn't thought about it. What's fun to do around here?"

"Still a little early for floating, but there's some great scenery for hiking." She slid the cup and saucer in front of him.

"There's shooting too. Becca used to be a member of the gun club." Sam paused. "You shoot any?" he asked David.

Still smiling at Sam's cousin, he replied, "I used to be pretty good at skeet."

A blush formed on Becca's face. "It's been years. I'm surprised Sam mentioned it."

Sam twisted his mouth. He hadn't meant to give them ideas for a date.

"Becca, Evelyn Snider just walked in."

Not even pausing to look, Becca balled up the edge of her apron. "I can still get us time at the club, if you'd be interested, that is."

David gave her the self-assured smile of a predator. "I'd love to, but I don't have a gun."

While Sam wondered if that was true, Becca replied, "No problem. You can use Sam's. He can't hit the broad side of a barn, anyhow."

Great. She'd not only armed the enemy with his weapon, she'd made sure he knew Sam had a terrible aim.

Del stared around the cozy interior of Sam's living room. The walls seemed to be moving in and out like a scene from the *Twilight Zone*. Sam's retro decor did nothing to minimize the feeling.

She, Toadstool, and all their luggage were staying at Sam's. After Sam's announcement to David, they hadn't even discussed her move to his place again. She had just packed up her stuff and gone.

It made sense. She wanted to keep an eye on Toadstool, and she was working with Sam daily anyway. What happened in the cave had nothing to do with her moving in here. She would sleep on the couch. She'd insist on it. She straightened her spine in resolve. She could do this.

"Need a drink?" Sam stood in the doorway to the kitchen, a bottle of gin in one hand, a lime in the other. He had slipped off his boots and removed his belt, even had the top snap of his jeans undone, like he'd just gotten up and forgotten to fasten them. Next thing, he'd probably remove his shirt.

Del swallowed.

"A drink?" He shook the bottle.

Yeah, a drink. Del nodded. She didn't usually drink anything stronger than a glass of wine at one of Porter's fanciest showings. Another thing from her past she'd given up—for good reason. But tonight was a special case. She was going to need something to get through it, to help her decide how much to trust Sam.

Dragging her suitcase behind her, she followed him into the kitchen.

"You have extra sheets?" she asked as he handed her a gin and tonic.

"Somewhere." His eyes flickered.

"I don't want to put you out. I can take the couch." She squeezed her lime, shooting juice across the countertop.

While she pulled a paper towel sheet off a roll hanging by the sink and wiped it up, Sam watched, quietly sipping his drink.

He sat his glass down. "I think we should talk."

Not yet. Not until Del knew what she should do. She scrubbed the counter harder. He placed his hand on hers. "Del, we need to talk."

She stared at the strong fingers that wrapped around to touch her palm.

"About what?"

"I don't know. Why you're here, where you came from, how you know David." He paused. "The Pig."

"Where is Toadstool?" She tried to pull her hand away, but Sam held fast.

"He's outside, and you know that's not what I mean. The other Pig, the one that brought you here."

The tension in Del's body disappeared like air from a balloon. He knew. She didn't have to lie anymore, at least not about the Pig.

"How'd you find out?" she asked.

It was Sam's turn to look uncomfortable. He clinked the ice in his glass, then reached for the gin bottle. "You need more?"

Del shook her head. He was the one asking about

the Pig. Why hide where he'd learned about it? She'd assumed it was David, but now she wondered.

"David call you?" she asked, keeping a close watch on Sam's expression.

It was quick, but she thought she caught a peep of relief flit across his face.

"He did, said you two worked together at some big-shot auction house in Chicago. That true?" Sam lifted his gaze to her face.

Was that hurt in his eyes? So, she had lied to him. He wasn't exactly a choirboy, now was he? In fact she'd bet her entire newly acquired pig collection that he was lying to her right now. Still, his look brought with it a stab of guilt. She just wasn't cut out for this anymore. Time was, when she could lie to her own mother about everything from who had left the milk out to what had happened to her grandmother's Fenton vase and not twitch an eye. Now a little self-preserving fib made her all quivery with remorse.

"Yeah, I work at Porter's." Her tone said, "What's it to you?" She turned her back on him and walked to the box of pig collectibles he had hauled into the kitchen earlier for her.

Pulling the paper-wrapped items out of the box, she could feel his gaze on her. "Whatta you do there?" he asked.

Del kept unwrapping. "I'm an auctioneer."

There was silence for a moment. Del dropped the package she held back in the box and turned. Meeting his eye, she declared, "A good one."

A small smile formed on his lips. "I don't doubt it. You've got all the ammunition: smart, charming, and you can lie with the best of them."

Something inside Del constricted. Not anymore. "I don't lie. Porter's is very strict about being one hundred percent up-front about our merchandise."

"That a fact?" Sam set down his glass and sauntered to the box. "You bought some interesting things. You like any of them?" His hand dipped into the box, pulling out the mini saloon jug she had bought from Izzy. "What's this?"

"Just something that caught my eye." She resisted the urge to grab the item from his hand.

Sam rolled it over in his palm. "I can see why. What you pay for it?"

"I don't remember," she mumbled.

He raised an eyebrow.

"Under two hundred."

He tossed the jug lightly in his hand. "And what's it worth?"

Del stared at her purchase. She couldn't help herself. She was proud of her find. With a grin, she replied, "Seven hundred, easy."

Sam chuckled. "You get this from Izzy?"

At Del's nod, he laughed again. "Serves the old bird right."

As they shared a laugh, something shifted. Sam's eyes, one minute brimming with mirth, suddenly were smoldering with desire. Del saw it, felt the same thing. Sam was wrong. She was no good at lying.

"Sam." She placed her hand on his chest. "It wasn't personal, you know. My pretending, I mean."

"Good to know." He set the jug on the table beside them and put his hands on her hips. "How about everything else? Any of that personal?"

Oh, it was personal all right. And getting more

so by the second. Del tilted her head upward just as Sam lowered his and captured her lips.

The kiss was ferocious, devouring. They couldn't get close enough to each other. As Sam's hands ran down her backside, cupping her bottom, Del ran her leg up his until it reached his waist. With a groan, Sam grabbed her other leg and hoisted her up.

Both legs wrapped around his waist, Del looked down at him. He was gorgeous, and for right now, he was hers. She locked her arms around his neck and met him in another consuming kiss.

Within seconds, she was moving. Sam strode across the room, Del still attached to his waist. She pulled her lips from his and began raining smaller kisses down his neck, then back up again. At his ear, she paused. Blowing softly, she slipped her tongue into the opening. Sam groaned and quickened his pace.

At the bedroom door, he halted and shoved Del against the door frame. The pressure of his groin moving against hers was almost more than she could stand.

"Inside, let's go inside," she panted.

"Not yet." He moved again, causing his erection to rub against her most sensitive part. She felt an accompanying tightening in her groin.

"Now," she ordered.

"Not yet," he replied.

The wooden frame of the door was cutting into her back, but Del was too occupied with the pressure building inside her to complain. Sam ran his hand up her side under her shirt, caressing her breast through her bra, then placed his fingers inside the cup until her nipple was bared to the cool air of his house. Lowering his head, he traced the outline of her areola with his tongue. Del's head lolled backward in response.

"Sam," she urged.

He released the other breast and moved his mouth to suck her nipple into his mouth.

"Sam," she yelled.

"Now?" he asked.

"Now." She was desperate, wanting more, wanting him inside her.

In three long strides, Sam carried her to the bed. Wasting no movements, he stripped off his shirt and jeans, then reached for hers. Del felt Sam's gaze sweep over her. She reached for her shirt to pull it across her breasts.

"No, don't." Sam stopped her.

It was still light. He could see everything. Del tugged on the shirt again.

"No, don't." His voice was softer. "You're beautiful." His eyes were warm, admiring.

Del loosened her hold on the shirt.

"Here." Sam reached behind her, unfastening her bra and pulling it off. He brushed his palm over her breasts, almost reverently. "Beautiful," he murmured. He lowered his head, his tongue darting along her skin, starting at her nipples, then across her stomach to her belly button and lower.

His hand cupped the apex of her legs. Using his fingers, he rubbed the cloth against her already swollen flesh. His finger ran under the edge of her panties, stroking the wet skin below. Del grabbed his shoulders as her body tightened with anticipation.

"Sam."

He ignored her plea, instead tugging the lace down to reveal the triangle of dark hair, and what was hidden beneath it. "Beautiful," he murmured.

As Del gripped his shoulders, he lowered his mouth and parted the skin with his tongue. A groan escaped Del's lips. Sam sucked the tiny bud between her thighs into his mouth, then released it, only to tease it again with his tongue.

"Sam." Del arched against him. "Now."

Again ignoring her demands, he continued to swirl and suck until Del lost all control. As her back arched higher, her vagina tightened, until the pressure overwhelmed her. Letting go, she released herself into the waves of her orgasm.

Sunlight bled through the blinds, dancing across her thighs where Sam still knelt. The old shame filled Del. She pushed her hands against the bed, trying to inch away from him.

"Where you going?" He grinned at her, his chin brushing against the hair at her thighs. "Nowhere, that's where." He lowered his head and retraced his way back to her breast, leaving a trail of kisses behind him.

Del ruffled his hair with her fingers. He made her feel special, worshiped. As if there was nothing to be ashamed of, not now, not ever—past or present. With a sigh she released her inhibitions and pulled his head back to hers.

When their lips met, she twirled her tongue into his mouth and lowered her hand to stroke his erection. Sam froze, panting against her mouth. She tilted her hips upward, as she guided his penis toward her. Holding her breath, she savored the feeling of her body stretching to hold him. Then, thrust for thrust, she matched him. They pounded into each other until another wave of emotion and energy took them both plummeting over the edge.

Later, as they lay tangled together on top of their discarded clothing, Sam stroked Del's hair. She was still holding back, not as much, but still something. They'd both been lying from the beginning, playing each other as best they could.

He was impressed that she had gotten the best of Izzy. Few people ever did. It was obvious Del knew antiques and knew how to work a deal. Just two of the things Sam was beginning to treasure about her. Until they got intimate, he would never have guessed at the vulnerabilities she hid under a facade of sexual confidence.

He couldn't begin to wrap his mind around how someone so obviously beautiful and desirable could be embarrassed by her own nudity. Del should always be naked, here in his bed.

Her fingernails lightly scraped the skin of his chest. "We should get up."

"Yeah."

Neither of them moved. In bed he could relax, not worry about honesty or what was going to happen when one of them found the Pig.

But he needed to find that Pig. Nothing had changed. He still needed the money to save his business and Becca's.

"Del, you want to tell me what you're doing here?"

He felt her tense. "Here?" She laid her palm flat on his stomach. "I thought that was kind of obvious."

"You know what I mean. In Allentown. What brought you to Allentown."

She took a deep breath, her bare breast pressed against his side. He wanted to scoop her against him, bury his face in her neck, breathe in her warmth, and forget his business, the money and the Pig, but he couldn't. He repeated, "What brought you here?"

She sat up, reaching for her shirt. "My boss." As she pulled the tee over her head, covering her nakedness, Sam felt something close off between them. Sighing, he rolled over and began yanking on his pants.

Let the games begin—again.

"For the Pig?" he asked.

Her lace underwear clutched in her fist, she nodded. "Yeah, someone told him it was down here. He sent me to find it. There's a big Unruh sale in a week, now. If I find the Pig, I get the sale. If not, David does."

She stretched the lace between her hands, staring at it as if it held some answer she was searching for. "It's a high-profile sale. It would mean I'd made it. I'd be a full-fledged member of the sales team. Until now, I've never done more than fill in while another auctioneer took a break."

"So? What's it matter? Why play second fiddle at all?" Why not run her own shop, like Sam?

"Porter's has prestige. Nobody questions an auctioneer from Porter's. You're somebody there."

Sam shook his head. She was talking nonsense. "You're somebody here."

She ignored him. "Anyway, he didn't have much information for me to go on. I came down here just fishing, hoping I'd stumble onto something. That's how I found you."

"You stumbled onto me?" He grinned. He wouldn't mind Del doing a little more stumbling.

"Thanks to your cousin." Del plopped onto her bodacious behind and wiggled into her underpants. Sam resisted the urge to hook the white lace under his finger and tug it back off.

"So, you learn anything?" he asked.

She cocked an eyebrow. "Your turn. How'd you know I was looking for the Pig?"

He lay back on the bed to fasten his pants and stared up at the white ceiling for a moment. If he told her about Izzy, she'd realize he'd made a deal with the old trader, that Sam was after the Pig too.

"Your pal David called me," he said.

He felt Del's gaze on him. Not wanting to face her, he swung his legs over the side of the bed and sat up. "He told me you were looking for it. Then I did a little research. Sounds like it's worth a pretty penny." He glanced over his shoulder. Del sat on his bed, her legs folded under her, her lower lip caught between her teeth.

She nodded. "Yeah, it is."

Her wheels were turning. He waited, knowing an offer was in the making.

"Did David offer you a cut?" she asked.

Smart girl—find out what you're up against so you don't overbid. Twenty percent, that's what her buddy had offered, but Sam had never intended on taking it. His plan all along was to sell the Pig himself. Depending on how he located the piece, to split some of the profit with Izzy, but just some. The rest would go toward rescuing him and Becca.

He still needed the boar's share, something Del couldn't promise him.

He steeled himself against the urge to spill everything to her. "Twenty, he offered twenty percent."

He could feel her relax. "That's generous for David." She laughed. "He's known for being on the cheap side." Sam heard her moving behind him. She pulled on her pants, then walked around the bed to face him. "What if I could promise you thirty? Would you forget about working with David?"

Sam gazed into her sweet tea-colored eyes. Two seconds more and he'd forget his own name, never mind that prig David.

Chapter 16

Slippery as a greased pig . . .

Thirty percent—Del wasn't sure Porter would go for it, but she was so relieved Sam had said a figure that was within her possibilities, she didn't hesitate to make the offer. If Porter wanted the Pig for the Unruh sale, he'd cough it up.

Sam stared back at her for a second before his gaze shifted toward the window that overlooked his backyard. "We better check on Toadstool. He's been out there awhile."

Kneeling in front of him, Del struggled not to topple over when he stood up. A stab of concern pierced her moment of joy. "Sam?"

He paused, his hand resting on the door frame they'd been pressed against just an hour earlier.

"So, thirty percent, that's fair, don't you think?"

Without turning back, he replied, "Yeah, that's fair." Then he continued down the hall. Del heard the back door squeak as he pulled it open, then Toadstool's hooves tapping onto the kitchen floor.

That was it. Sam knew about the Pig, knew about

Porter. Two less things she had to lie about. Now if she could just find the missing piece of art pottery and hightail it out of Allentown before she was tempted to risk all and stay.

Sam twisted the kitchen faucet on and filled a bowl of water for Toadstool. The little pig stared up at him, trusting that Sam would take care of him. Just like his mistress trusting that Sam would look out for her.

And he would, he resolved. He might not settle for a thirty percent finder's fee, but that didn't mean he wouldn't watch out for her. There was still the little matter of the shooter at the cave.

Time to address that.

Del padded into the room, her feet bare and her hair tousled. Sam licked his suddenly dry lips. "Just getting the pig a drink; you need anything?"

Her smile was quick and warm. "You have any lemonade? I've really developed a taste for it lately."

"No, but I have tea in the refrigerator." He reached for glasses to keep his gaze off her.

"Have to do, I guess." She plunked down on a kitchen chair. "So, where do we start?"

Right now Sam was more worried about where they would finish. As ice cubes clunked into the glasses, Sam replied, "How about with the shooter. Who else wants the Pig bad enough to take a loaded shotgun to you?"

Del rubbed one bare foot against the other. Her nose twitching, she said, "We don't know that had anything to do with the Pig. Could have been a co-incidence. Probably all kinds of crazies down there."

What was she hiding now? "I talked to the sheriff, you know." He placed a glass of tea next to her.

"Really." She seemed fascinated by a bead of sweat that had formed on the outside of her glass.

"He wasn't much help." Sam took a sip.

"Too bad." The relief on her face contradicted her words.

"But his receptionist was."

She sucked her lip into her mouth. "Really."

"She seemed to think a man named Jed Mont might be involved. Name ring a bell?"

"Not that I can say."

Sam watched for a nose twitch, but she held steady. Her gaze did drop back to the glass, though.

"He runs an antiques shop in town. You didn't notice it when you went through?"

"Didn't go through town."

Still no twitch. Was she telling the truth? Then a thought occurred to him. How'd she find the bridge in the first place, especially without directions from someone in town? Even if she'd learned of the place before heading to Docia, the direct route from Allentown to the bridge would have taken her right through the southern Missouri town. If she had avoided Docia, she had done it for a reason.

"Why'd you go to the bridge?" he asked.

Surprise crossed her face. "Same reason as you. It's where the Pig was last known to be, where the wreck was."

"But how'd you know that, and how'd you find it?"

She expelled a breath. "Met a woman at the Bunny Hutch. We got to talking, turns out she knew about the Pig and where the guy went off the road, simple as that."

Sam thought for a second. "So'd she know you were going there?"

Del furrowed her brow. "I don't know that I said I was, but yeah, she probably guessed." She shook her head. "But there's no way Tilde was the one shooting at us. I can't even imagine her holding a shotgun, much less loading one and toting it around those woods. Besides, why tell me about the place if she didn't want me to go there?"

"Maybe she thought you'd go somewhere else."

"Where else would I go? It's where you went, isn't it? Speaking of, how'd you find out about the bridge?"

Sam still wasn't ready to bring Izzy into this.

"Anybody else know where you were going?" he asked.

She shook her head. "Not a soul."

Sam took a sip of tea. Izzy knew about the bridge too, but he'd encouraged Sam to stay in Allentown, away from Docia. Sam almost smacked his palm against his forehead. He was such an idiot. Izzy had played him like a two-stringed banjo.

But, like Del had said about Tilde, why would Izzy send him there if he didn't want Sam in Docia? Plus, there were still other players to consider.

"How about David?" he asked.

"He just got here."

"Maybe. Maybe not. Maybe he snuck down to Docia first."

Del considered this. "But he didn't know about the wreck." She looked at Sam, suspicion in her eyes. "Did he?"

Sam shook his head. "Not from me." But Izzy? How much had Izzy told the arrogant auctioneer from Chicago?

Del picked up her glass, then set it down without taking a sip. "How about you? Who says whoever was shooting at us was connected to me? Maybe they were after you."

"Who'd want to shoot me?" Sam flashed his most charming grin.

She arched an eyebrow.

Sam pondered her suggestion. Who would want to shoot him? Armstrong was the most likely candidate. He'd come close to threatening it on more than one occasion, but he'd have had no way of knowing Sam was headed to Docia. Besides, Sam couldn't see Armstrong going out of his way to do much, even shooting Sam. And face it, creeping around the woods near Docia was way out of his way.

Sam was back where he started. Whoever had manned that shotgun had to be someone who knew where they were headed. That left three names at the top of the list: Tilde, Izzy, and Jed Mont, with a possible addition of David Curtis. The only way for Sam to find out if David knew about the accident and the low-water bridge was to confront Izzy again.

Del interrupted his thoughts. "Why are we worrying about that, anyway? Once we find the Pig, it won't matter."

It wouldn't matter 'cause Del would be back in Chicago, out of Sam's life. He ignored the twinge this thought brought with it.

She was right, though. They needed to concentrate on finding the Pig. Chances were that their trail would cross with the shooter's soon enough.

"Okay, let's find the Pig." He crossed his arms over his chest and leaned back in his chair.

Frowning, she said, "You don't have to be a smart-ass. If it were that easy one of us would already have it."

True enough, but for some reason Sam thought it was that simple. They just hadn't hit on the right key yet.

"Let's go over what we each know and how we learned it." He hadn't figured out how to cover his deal with Izzy, but he needed to learn what Del knew.

Twenty minutes later, they realized they were both at the same spot. They knew where the Pig had disappeared, that a legend surrounded it, and that no one had spotted it for almost thirty years. Sam had avoided mentioning Izzy by name by saying he'd talked to some old-timers. Del seemed to accept it.

"Maybe we should go back to Porter. He say who called him?" Sam asked.

Del shook her head. "No, I asked, but he wouldn't tell."

That was strange. If the man wanted the Pig found, why wouldn't he give Del all the information he could? More and more this whole chase had a funny feel to it.

"You think he told David?"

Del looked unsure but shook her head. "I don't know why he'd tell him something he wouldn't tell me."

"Well, where do you want to start? Your friend

Tilde, David, or Docia?" Sam knew where he was going. As soon as he could get Del sidetracked, he would hunt down Izzy and shake the truth out of the old buzzard if necessary.

David, Tilde, or Docia. Docia was completely out of the question, and there was no reason to believe David knew any more than Del did, hopefully a lot less. That left Tilde.

Now that Del thought it over, it was strange how the older woman was so generous with her information, even going to the trouble to bring the old newspaper clipping. Maybe there was more to her generosity than just being friendly.

"I'd say Tilde's the best bet, but I don't have her number."

Sam tapped his fingers on the table. "You say you met her at the Hutch?"

Del nodded. Toadstool placed his front hooves on her leg, looking for a scratch.

"She dress like she slipped on a rainbow?"

That was Tilde.

Taking her smile as a yes, Sam continued, "Then I think Becca may just have her number. She should still be at the Hutch, but by now she won't be answering the phone. I can drop you off there."

Del paused midscratch. "Where you going?"

"Nowhere important. Just got some auction business to attend to."

His explanation sounded plausible enough, but Del's untrusting nature resurfaced. "Don't worry about me. I'll take my own car. That way if I need to, I can meet Tilde somewhere."

* * *

Ten minutes later, Del pulled out of Sam's drive, Sam's truck right behind her. At Main Street, he kept going, heading south.

Del circled the block, then pulled her car back onto the main road. She could see Sam's taillights in the distance. The feed store was in the opposite direction. If he had auction business to attend to, it wasn't at his office.

Sam watched in his rearview mirror as Del turned down Main Street. She'd accepted his explanation of auction business awfully easily. Keeping an eye on his mirrors, he accelerated out of town. Sure enough, as he passed the city limits, he noticed headlights behind him.

Untrusting little she-devil, she was following him. He grinned. She wasn't as wily as she thought she was.

The lights to Allentown's most questionable bar were coming up on his right. Perfect timing; Charlie's dad owned the place. With any luck, Charlie'd be behind the bar slinging drinks. He slowed down to a crawl, giving the car behind him plenty of opportunity to pass, but sure enough the other driver slowed too.

He flipped on his turn signal and pulled into the lot. It was early. Only a couple of hardcore regulars would be there now. Sam figured he had a good two hours before the place was full enough for Del to get herself in any trouble. By then he'd be back, or she'd have wised up to his ploy and headed back to town.

He locked his truck and strolled through the front door. It took him only a couple of seconds to find Charlie stacking glasses behind the bar.

"Mind trading trucks for a bit?" he asked.

She raised an eyebrow but pulled a ring of keys from her pocket.

He grinned his thanks. "A good-looking blonde comes in looking for me, I'm in the john."

"How long you going to be in there?" Charlie asked.

"No more than an hour or two."

She raised both brows. "You don't think she's gonna notice?"

"Just keep her here long enough to let me get away." He rapped on the bar with the keys, then snuck out the back. Charlie's beat-up ride was parked inside a lean-to shed. He waited for Del to get in the bar before turning over the engine and heading to Izzy's.

The train car was dark when Sam stopped Charlie's truck in front of it. Sam hopped out and followed a rocky path that led to Izzy's small living quarters.

"Who's a-calling?" Izzy's voice rang out as Sam knocked on the door.

"Samson."

"You got that dressed-up pig with you?"

Sam gritted his teeth. "No."

"Then come in. Nobody's stopping you."

Sure enough, the door was unlocked. Sam pushed it open and stepped into Izzy's kitchen.

What he saw shocked him—oak floors, oak cabinets, and Victorian oak furniture. He felt like he'd stepped into some fancy restored mansion instead of a shack one step above tar paper.

"Can't judge a book by its cover, boy." Izzy leaned back in a press-back chair. He nudged its mate toward Sam. "Have a sit."

Still feeling off-kilter from the unexpected lushness of Izzy's abode, Sam perched on the edge of the seat.

"You here for a reason?" Izzy pushed a plate filled with biscuits across the table toward Sam. "Have one. There's gravy on the range."

Sam picked up a biscuit and weighed it in his hand. Heavy, nothing slice-and-bake about these babies. "You sent me to Docia," he said.

"That right?" Izzy wandered to the stove, where he lifted a skillet and poured the contents into a gravy boat. As always, Sam wondered at his skill.

Returning to the table, Izzy said, "Way I remember it, I told you to stay put."

"Only because you wanted me to go."

Izzy hit his leg with his stump. "You got one suspicious streak in you, don't you, boy?"

Sam didn't say anything. He knew he was right.

Growing serious, Izzy sliced open a biscuit with his hook, then snagged the gravy boat by the handle to dribble the thick liquid over the top. "Now why you think I'd want you to go to Docia?"

"That's why I'm here, to find out."

"Hmm." Over a forkful of dripping biscuit, Izzy watched him. "You still seeing the girl?"

"Somebody shot at us."

Izzy's expression didn't change. "That a fact?"

"Was it you?" Sam wanted answers. He was tired of the cat-and-mouse game.

Izzy laughed and held up his hook and stump. "How you think I'd do that?"

Sam gave him a steady look. "Those don't slow you down a bit. If anything, you use them to get things other people can't."

"Boy, you hurt me. You surely do." Izzy shook his head.

"Give it up, Izzy. There's something going on around here besides a missing collectible, and it's got your markings all over it."

Izzy's watery eyes turned shrewd. "You didn't answer me earlier. You still seeing the girl?"

Del. Was this all about Del?

"Somehow I think you know the answer to that."

Izzy laughed. "You overestimate me, boy. Things change fast when you're young. Hard for an old hound like me to keep up."

"Yeah, I'm still working with her."

"Hmm." Izzy lifted another bite of B and G to his mouth. After swallowing, he asked, "She unpack any of those pigs she bought here yet?"

The pigs? Sam tried to remember which of the motley assortment Del had bought from Izzy. The saloon jug was the only item that came to mind. "A few."

Waving his fork, Izzy said, "You get her to take a good hard look at them pigs. There just might be something there she's missed."

None of this made sense. "Is this about the Unruh Pig or something else?"

Izzy set his fork down and leaned forward. "Love, boy. This is about love. Ain't nothing going on here that don't have something to do with that gut-puncher of an emotion." The old man picked up the gravy boat and held it toward Sam. "You sure you don't want none of this?"

After declining Izzy's offer, Sam got back in Charlie's truck and drove toward the bar. This mess just kept getting thicker and thicker. And Izzy babbling about love. Who'd have thought the old guy was a romantic?

Sam had only been gone a couple hours, but the bar was hopping. Music and light spilled out into the parking lot. He parked Charlie's truck and snuck in through the back. Charlie waved him over.

"She's over there." Charlie motioned toward a table near the pool tables. "She didn't buy the bathroom bit, but she refused to leave. Said you'd come back for your dually sooner or later."

Sam started toward the pool area.

"Sam," Charlie called after him, "get her out of here quick as you can. She's causing a stir."

Del cause a stir in a room full of drunken rednecks? Surely not.

Even in the dim light, he could make out her profile. When they had left his house, he hadn't noticed how snugly her shirt fit, or that it dipped low enough in the front to reveal the crevice between her breasts. The four men gathered around the pool table weren't as remiss as Sam.

He cursed under his breath.

The leader, a young guy in a heavy metal T-shirt and cammie pants that matched Del's shot-dodging getup, sauntered over to her table.

* * *

Where was Sam? Del couldn't believe he'd lost her. She'd been sitting in this rat trap of a bar for over an hour, nursing a now lukewarm beer. The whole experience was bringing back more memories than Del cared to revisit, but this was not the kind of place you ordered wine, and she didn't want to risk hard liquor. She was just about fed up enough to trot out to Sam's truck, steal a spark plug, and tool back to town.

"How about a dance?" A greasy-haired youngster from the pool table leaned over her.

Great. She was attracting jailbait.

"No can do—arthritis." She twisted her arm.

He blinked at her.

God bless the dim-witted.

As he turned to stumble back to his cohorts, a broad chest blocked his way. "I think your buddies are looking for you." Sam pointed his thumb toward the gang by the pool table.

"Huh?" The low-watt bulb flickered. He glanced from the pool game to Sam.

Now Sam had done it—bullied the kid in front of his pals. Del took a sip of her beer. Might as well drink it now; in ten seconds it would be flying across the room.

She started the countdown. *Ten, nine.* Mr. Low Watt's buddies moved as a team toward Sam. *Eight, seven, six.* Sam's muscles tensed. Yep, he knew they were there. *Five, four, three.* Low Watt struck the universal "what's it to you?" pose. *Two, one.* The front-most pal lunged for Sam's arms as Low Watt threw the first punch.

There went that Mont luck again. Del just couldn't catch a break. But she could catch her beer as it skittered across her table. Wrapping her fingers around the long neck, she jumped out of the way right before one of the pool pals picked up her table and flung it across the room.

Oooh. Be still my heart.

This show of machismo was more than Del wanted to deal with tonight, and the last thing she needed was to be hanging around a bar fight when the police showed up. They'd probably pat her on the head and send her on her way, but you never knew. If she got dragged into jail, all kinds of things might be discovered. It was time for her to leave.

She took another swallow of beer and scanned the mass of writhing bodies for Sam. He was holding off two of Low Watt's friends when another tackled him in the gut, sending Sam falling backward. The rest of the gang instantly jumped aboard. Del smacked the beer bottle against her thigh. It had been five minutes since the start of the fight, plenty of time for the bartender to call the cops.

Allentown was small. The police would be here any minute. She really had to leave. She took a step toward the door when the original Low Watt pulled back his foot and kicked Sam in the gut.

Hell. Why'd he have to go and do that?

Setting her bottle on the floor, Del dusted off her hands. There was no choice for it now. She had to get involved. Shaking her head, she prepared for a running start. Two long strides and she sprung onto Low Watt's back. With her arm pressed against his windpipe, she jerked him away from Sam.

The lights flashed on, signaling the arrival of the

cops. Del dropped off the kid's back. He turned on her, fist upraised.

Feet braced, she stared him down. "Don't even think about it."

Taking in whom he was threatening, the kid froze.

Sometimes it was good to be a girl. As Low Watt sorted through what had happened, Del moved forward and shoved the topmost member of his team off Sam with her boot. She was glad she'd taken the time to replace the ugly things before meeting Sam at the Hutch this morning—not that she'd dreamed they'd serve a purpose besides tramping around in the woods.

"Get up." She shoved another team member aside. Sam lay face up, grinning like an idiot.

God protect her from testosterone rushes.

"There's blood on your chin." She pushed him with her toe.

He wiped the stain with his thumb, then stared at the red smear. "Mine?"

"Based on what's coming out your nose, I'd say yes." She stretched forward, offering her hand to pull him up. With another grin, he grabbed hold of it and pulled her down on top of him.

"Anybody tell you you're sexy when you're jumping loudmouthed punks from behind?" He spoke inches from her mouth.

He'd seen that?

With her palm pressed against his chest, she could feel his heart hammering away. He was pumped. People start throwing punches and men get all giddy with the thrill. If Del was going to waste energy getting giddy, it was going to be over something worthwhile like half-price this season shoes or a ten-dollar Wavecrest box.

"Let me thank you." His voice rumbled in his chest. Even sprawled on the grungy floor of the bar, blood dripping from his nose, the offer was tempting. Only the sound of sirens stopped her.

"The police are here. We need to leave." She urged him to his feet.

"It's no big deal. There's a fight here most every week. They just stop by to keep the churchgoers appeased and the damage to a minimum."

The sirens got louder, then whirred into silence. They were here.

"Come on." Grabbing his hand, she tugged him toward the back. "I know there's a way out of here, or you wouldn't have thrown me earlier. Where is it?" She was starting to get panicked. Cavalier as she had been earlier, she had no desire to spend time behind bars, or she wouldn't have left southern Missouri in the first place.

With a quizzical look, Sam led her behind the bar and out past the walk-in beer cooler. Two cop cars sat in the lot, right between Sam's truck and Del's car.

"What now?" she asked.

He leaned against the wall studying her. "We wait."

Yeah, wait. Simple enough. Del paced up and down the short walk behind the bar. "What's back there?" She pointed to a dark structure behind them. "Could we hide in there till they're gone?"

"You got a tissue?" Sam's nose had started spurting again.

"No." Del hopped from one foot to the other.

How long could it take to flush out a few drunks? When would the police leave?

Sam took a step toward the bar's door.

"Where are you going?"

"Back inside. I need a tissue. Besides, I don't like skulking out here. It isn't right."

What was that, bar fight etiquette? "Use your sleeve." Pacing some more, she made a decision. "Come on." She strode toward the building she'd noticed earlier.

Sam mumbled something but followed.

The building was a half-enclosed garage. Inside was a fifteen-year-old pickup, the hood still warm. "So that's how you did it," she commented.

Sam shrugged.

Hidden inside the shed, she felt safer. Remembering why she was caught in a bar fight in the first place, she turned on Sam. "Where'd you go, anyway?"

"Tell you what, you tell me why you're so afraid of the law and I'll tell you where I went." He rested his foot on the truck's rear tire.

She stepped deeper into the shadows to disguise her expression. "I'm not afraid of the law," she replied.

"Sell it to somebody who's buying. You didn't want to report the shooting in Docia, and now you're about to jump out of your skin worrying about the local boys in blue catching you at a bar fight, when all you'd have to do is bat your eyelashes and they'd be falling all over themselves asking to drive you home." He paused. "Unless . . . you've got something to hide."

Chapter 17

*Never trust a pig any farther than
you can throw him . . .*

Something to hide. Del stared off into the darkness, listening to the sounds of drunken pool players being escorted out of the bar: loud voices, followed by slamming car doors and tires spitting gravel, then silence. The police were gone. She could leave now too, but Sam still stood there watching her, waiting for an answer.

She was tired. Tired of hiding who she was and where she came from. Ready to share with someone, she began talking, "Seven years ago, I took a risk, started my own auction service. It was tough going. Being young and female isn't exactly a plus when you're trying to get sale business."

She ran her hands through her hair. "I'm sure you know the auction business is a male business. If you aren't a good ole boy you don't have a crystal compote's chance in an earthquake." She looked at Sam. If she kept talking she'd reveal more to him than anyone in seven years, enough to ruin her. In the dark she couldn't make out his expression. His gaze was on her, but what was the emotion in his eyes? Swallowing, she continued, "Especially in southern Missouri."

He moved slightly but didn't respond.

"Anyway, I did manage to get a sale or two, but nothing worthwhile, then I made my biggest mistake." Her hand clenched the necklace at her throat, pulling so hard the clasp cut into the back of her neck. "I trusted my father."

She walked to the opening at the end of the shed, her back to Sam. "My father is the ultimate good ole boy. He's spent his entire life perfecting his act." Realizing that sounded bitter, she backtracked. "Don't get me wrong, he isn't a bad person, but he gets caught up in the deal and doesn't let the details, like whether what he's selling is authentic, or where it came from, get in his way.

"He started 'helping' me, talked me into running commission sales, made up of lots from multiple sellers. Working the crowd to get the bids as high as they would go. Things started turning around. I had a sale every weekend and my profits were good."

She turned back to face Sam. "I knew better. I grew up with the man. I should have suspected something wasn't kosher." She kicked herself mentally. She was doing it again—lying, even to herself. "That isn't true. I knew something wasn't right— the man can't buy a gallon of milk without conning the grocery clerk out of an extra pint."

Disgusted with herself for what she had done, for denying it for so long, she dropped her gaze to the ground. "One day I turned up at my office to find the place tossed. The police had been there looking for my sale records. I'd been selling stolen goods for months."

She laughed, a low sound without mirth. "Funny how quick people can turn on you. After news got out about the investigation, people started coming forward complaining that they'd been ripped off at my sales, that I used shills or just plain ole called bids that weren't made."

She lifted her head, searching for Sam in the gloom. "That last part wasn't true, leastways not on purpose. There's no telling what all my daddy was doing I didn't know about."

Sam shuffled his feet. "Did you know the goods were stolen?"

"No, but I knew things were going too good and that anything my daddy touched had some kind of con attached. I just never thought he'd go so far as to set me up as a fence for stolen goods." It still hurt.

"They find you guilty?"

Del swallowed, here came the bad part, as if the rest weren't damning enough. "Hard to find you guilty if you aren't there to try. I snuck off before it came to trial, before they even hauled me in. Changed my name, changed my look, and faked my resume. My mama helped, got some people to vouch for me, and I landed the job at Porter's. I've been avoiding southern Missouri and wondering ever since when it was all going to crash around me."

She waited. A condemnation from Sam would be worse than every person in Docia pointing fingers and whispering behind their hands.

"Anything happen to your dad?" he asked.

She shook her head. "There was nothing linking him to the merchandise, just me."

"You could have reported him."

Del jerked her head in surprise. "What, and land us both in jail? Angry as I was—am—with him, there was no reason to do that."

"So, do you know what happened to the case?"

"I know there's a warrant out for my arrest. I get caught and I'll have a whole new window on the world, one lined with bars."

"So that's why you want to avoid the police." Sam's voice was steady, impossible for Del to pick up on his inner thoughts. "You going to tell me where all this happened?"

Why'd he need to know? Would he turn her in? Needing to believe in someone, she answered, "Docia. I grew up in Docia."

Sam rapped his fist against the side of Charlie's truck, hoping the sound would shake something loose in his brain. It was beginning to make sense—how Del knew where the low-water bridge was, why she snuck there avoiding town, why she didn't want him to go to the sheriff—but there were still a few gaps.

"Your father. He's Jed Mont, isn't he?"

Del's voice was weak, exhausted. "Yep, the illustrious Jedidiah Mont. King of the good deal."

Her tone was bitter. Sam guessed she had reason. He'd asked if she'd turned her father in, but what he hadn't asked was whether her father had stepped forward to shoulder the mess he'd dumped on her. Based on Del's rigid shoulders, Sam guessed he hadn't.

"You think it was him shooting at us the other day?"

Rolling the thought around in her mind, Del seemed to relax some. "I thought so at first, but that time of day he's usually at his shop. Besides, why shoot at me? I'm the one who took the heat."

Sam nodded. He'd come to the same conclusion.

"Except . . ." Del started, then shook her head.

"What?" Sam encouraged.

"Well, Tilde, the woman I told you about, she had this picture from an old newspaper. It showed a group of men standing around that dead collector's car. My daddy was front and center. . . ." She let her words trail off.

"You think he might have the Pig?" A flicker of excitement twinkled in Sam's stomach.

Del shook her head hard enough to make her hair dance. "No way. If my daddy found that Pig, it was gone two minutes later. He could no more hold on to something that valuable than a starving dog could save a steak."

Del had covered for her father before. Could she be doing it again? Sam didn't think so. The hurt in her voice had been too real. Remembering that pain, he strode forward and touched her arm.

"You okay?" he asked.

When her gaze dropped down to the cracked cement floor, Sam tilted her chin up with his finger. "You were young and you made a mistake. There's no reason to spend the rest of your life paying for it."

Tears glimmered in her eyes. "I haven't paid for anything. I ran away."

"Del, sweetheart, I'm guessing you paid the biggest price of all." He resisted the urge to press his lips to hers. She was vulnerable. He didn't want her thinking he didn't mean his words.

She spoke softly. He had to strain to hear. "Delilah. My name is Delilah Mont, but everybody called me Lilah."

"Delilah," he murmured. It fit her. Del was so mannish and Sweet Tea was anything but. "You mind if I call you that?"

A slight smile curved her lips. "You don't hate me?"

Her question jolted him. He'd been so busy concentrating on her story and how it tied in to what had been happening, it hadn't occurred to him that she might worry about his reaction, his judgment.

With a low laugh, he cupped her chin in his hand. "Delilah, I feel a lot of things when I'm around you, but hate isn't even in the running." Then he gave in to the longing and dropped his mouth to hers.

This kiss was different than the others they had shared. The desire was still present, but there was more. Comfort, longing, and . . . love.

Sam pushed the thought to the side. Del couldn't love him. How could he betray her if she did?

Sam didn't hate her. Del relished his words. It seemed impossible; she'd spent so much time hating herself.

When he lifted his mouth from hers, she stayed wrapped in his arms, her forehead resting against his chest. With each outward movement of his chest, she grew stronger.

She could handle this. She could find the Pig, and she could face her past; with Sam she could do anything.

He spoke into her hair. "Let's go home."

Del wanted to drag him down into another kiss to show him how much his casual acceptance meant to her, but instead she just nodded, with what felt like a permanent smile on her lips.

Back at Sam's house, Del let Toadstool out for a stroll in the back and plopped down on Sam's slimline couch. It was ugly, but pretty comfy. Her feet propped up on the cushion, she allowed herself to relax. It had been a long seven years. She could wait until tomorrow to figure out what she wanted to do next.

Sam peered into the living room. Del was asleep on the couch, her head thrown back and her blond hair spread over the olive-green end cushion. She looked like a mermaid washed ashore after a long struggle against the waves.

He suspected the analogy was somewhat apt. Del'd been fighting for a long time. He resisted the temptation to sneak into the room and cradle her against his chest, to carry her to his bed and make love to her the rest of the night.

He resisted because what he was about to do was hard enough without adding more sex to the mix. Returning to the kitchen, he pulled her box of purchases into the center of the table and began unpacking. A stab of guilt caused his hand to shake as he set a salt shaker shaped like a smiling pig onto the wooden surface.

When he was done the entire tabletop was filled with swine: big, fat, and cutesy; creamers, vases, and figurines. Every type of pig collectible he could imagine, and not a one that held a clue he could see to the Unruh Pig. What had Izzy meant?

One by one, Sam picked up each piece and rolled it around in his hand, checking for any hint that would lead him to the Pig. Nothing. The salt and peppers matched the set he had bought Del at her father's shop.

Sam smiled at the irony of that visit. The man had been giving him such a hard time about showing up with a pig and the woman who owned it, and all that time he was Del's father. If Sam had known then what her father had put her through, he would have . . . He let the thought die. No, he couldn't claim any right to defend Del, not when he was planning on stealing the Pig right from under her kissable nose.

Sickened by himself, he grabbed up the pigs and shoved them back in the box. In his anger, he almost dropped one—the ugliest of the lot. Picking the malformed object up, he decided it wouldn't have been any great loss, except he'd have to explain to Del how it came to be broken. He held the piece up to the light.

What possessed her to buy this thing? It was a smashed-looking mess constructed of bumpy gray clay. Only the snout identified it as a pig. Turning it over, he saw initials on the bottom: D.M., Del's initials. Maybe that's why she bought it. Shaking his head, he replaced its paper wrapping and set it back in the carton.

After retrieving the gin bottle, Sam poured himself a drink. The hunt through Del's stash was a bust, but there were a few more leads they hadn't followed up on yet, the most obvious being Del's dad. He had been near the car when the Pig disappeared. Del admitted he wasn't the straightest ruler, and he was known to shoot at trespassers.

Carrying his glass, Sam wandered into the living room and gazed down at Del. Tomorrow Sweet Tea was going to have to face her past.

The next morning, Del rested her head against the Naugahyde booth.

"How long's it been since you saw your father?"

Sam's question caught her off guard. When he had suggested they discuss their next step over breakfast at the Hutch, she had assumed it was so they could get Tilde's number from Becca.

"Seven years. Why?"

"That's a long time."

"Not long enough." Del picked up the creamer. Empty. Setting it back down, she looked for Becca.

"Don't you want to put everything behind you?"

She gave Sam an incredulous look. "You been watching *Oprah* when I wasn't looking? I thought you were helping me find the Unruh Pig, not sorting out my family problems."

He looked uncomfortable for a minute, then, crossing his arms over his chest, replied, "Okay, I think your dad is the best lead we have toward finding the Pig. I don't care if you make up with him or dropkick him. But we need to talk to him. He's been involved in this legend for thirty years, and he's the best candidate we have so far as the shooter goes."

"Well then, you talk to him." Del wanted to put her past behind her, but she wanted to do it on her own time and after she returned to Porter's victorious— Pig in hand. Maybe next Christmas. It was a slow time for the auction business. Maybe Porter wouldn't notice if she was missing for, say, five to seven years, possibly three with good behavior.

"I say we talk to Tilde first," she stated with as much authority as she could muster around a mouthful of banana cream pie. The Hutch was out of doughnuts, and Del had been through a lot of stress lately. She needed sugar. "There's Becca. Let's get the number." She waved her fork at Sam's cousin.

As Becca approached, Del noticed something different about her. The hangdog look she'd been sporting since Del met her was gone, and if Del wasn't mistaken, Sam's cousin had added eyeliner and lipstick to her morning ritual.

"You need your gun back?" Becca greeted Sam. Not waiting for his response, she continued, "Because David and me were going back out to the club tonight."

David. That explained the extra makeup, but the gun part left Del wondering.

"He's a great shot." Becca topped off their cups. "Didn't do too bad myself, either."

Del raised an eyebrow at Sam. Busy frowning at his cousin, Sam missed it. "You don't know enough about that guy to be spending time with him."

Becca snorted. "You're the one who suggested the gun club."

"Not really. I just mentioned the place and you jumped on it like a frog on a fly."

Looked like Becca had an interest in David, and cousin Sam didn't approve. He was just keeping way too busy trying to keep other people's lives in order, if you asked Del. Deciding to help Becca, Del waved her fork again. "David's okay." For a weasel—but Becca was a big girl. Sam should let her make her own mistakes.

Sam turned his frown on Del. She shrugged it off. "Listen, Becca, I was hoping you could give me someone's number." While Del described Tilde, Sam continued to glower.

After Becca skipped off to get the number, Sam spoke. "What do you think you're doing?"

Man, he was in a snit. "Getting Tilde's number. Isn't that obvious?"

His expression said his patience was beyond strained. "Encouraging Becca to see that slimebag from Chicago."

Del pressed her shoulders against the back of the booth. Sure, she thought of David as a slimebag, but Sam had met him only once. Seemed a short acquaintance for such an intense dislike. Remembering the note with David's number on it, she said, "You have a history with him I don't know about?"

"Did you know he shoots skeet?" Sam countered.

At her "So what?" look, he continued, "With a shotgun?"

"What do you expect him to shoot it with—a pool cue?" She raised both hands. "You think

David was skulking around the woods near Docia, shooting at us?" She laughed. "The man wouldn't risk his Gucci loafers."

"Not even to get the Unruh Pig?"

Del stopped laughing. David had to want the Pig as badly as Del, and she wanted it pretty darn bad. "How would he have found out about Docia?"

Sam lowered his gaze, but not before Del saw the look of uncertainty in his eyes. Suspicion pierced her like a bayonet. Was she trusting the wrong person again?

"He could have done some research, found the same newspaper article Tilde showed you."

Del wasn't buying it. She doubted seriously if the *Docia News* was cataloged today, much less thirty years ago. The chances of David falling over a tip that led him to the low-water bridge without spending time down here, or talking a lot to someone who did, were slim.

She studied Sam. How much had he talked with David? Had he told Del the truth when he said her co-auctioneer offered only twenty percent, or was Sam working both of them?

Her emotions too on edge to argue the point, she tried to keep her tone as noncommittal as possible. "Not likely."

As he stirred his coffee, Sam's shoulders seemed tense. Her suspicions piling higher, she prodded some more. "When he offered you a cut, did he mention working with anyone else down here? You know, try and get you for less because he had other options?"

Sam looked her in the eye. "No, no, he didn't."

Now she knew without a doubt he was lying.

Whether David had other options or not, he'd always claim he did. It was just his way.

She pushed her pie away. She'd lost her appetite. Just when she thought she'd found someone to trust, she discovered the rattle on the end of his tail. Would she never learn?

At least she learned in time, before she did something stupid, like risk her heart. Biting her lip, she forced her hand not to stray to her pearls.

Damn tell. Now she couldn't even lie to herself.

Chapter 18

Driving hogs . . .

Sam swilled down the last of his coffee. Even lukewarm, it hit his stomach like a bomb. Too bad he couldn't blame the bitter taste in his mouth on his morning cup of joe.

He was worse than Del's pal David. At least the other auctioneer wasn't pretending. Del had no doubt he was out to get the Pig, just like she was, but Sam she trusted.

Pushing his cup across the table, he said, "You get the number. I have to hit the john." Without waiting for Del's response, he stalked toward the bathroom.

Inside, he locked the door and pulled out his cell phone. Maybe things weren't as bad as he thought; maybe he could buy more time with the bank.

Mike, his loan officer, answered the phone with an upbeat tone. Sam forced a similar cheerfulness in his own voice before replying.

"How's the bank business?"

"Good, good," Mike said with a note of caution. "How's the auction business?"

Sam took a deep breath. "Could be better. Listen, I was wondering if I could get an extension on my loan payment."

There was silence on the other end of the line, then, "I don't know, Sam. We've already given you three."

"I know." Sam caught a glimpse of his reflection in the pink-edged mirror that hung over the sink. An air of desperation hung around him. Balling his fist, Sam flattened it against the bathroom wall. "How about Becca? You give any thought to her loan?"

"You know I can't discuss Becca's loan with anybody but Becca." Mike paused. When he spoke again, his voice was full of apology. "I'd like to help you out, but there's not much I can do, not without some kind of assurance you'll have money coming in soon. What about that deal you mentioned? You getting close on that?"

The man in the mirror stared back at Sam with hollow eyes. "Yeah, I'm getting close."

"Well, see, you're still in the game. Don't worry. It'll work out. Just give me a call when you can tell me more details, and I'll go to the bosses for you."

After pushing "disconnect," Sam stared at the lost soul in the mirror. Yeah, he was still in the game.

Del had Tilde's number now but wasn't sure what to do with it. Did she want Sam tagging along while she hunted down the Pig?

He returned from the bathroom looking like somebody just swiped his bid card. Del's fingers ached to smooth the stress lines from between his eyes.

"You okay?" she asked. She wished she didn't care, but there was no denying she did.

"Fine." His response was terse. "You got the number?"

Clasping the scrap of paper in her hand, Del nodded. "I was just going to call her."

He motioned with his hand for her to go ahead. Tilde answered on the first ring. "Tilde. Start yapping."

Del smiled at the older woman's vinegar, then stammered trying to explain the reason for her call. "You remember that story you told me about the Unruh Pig? I . . ." Where had all of Del's skills for smooth talking gone? "I was wondering if you might know something else."

"Something else—like what? You go down to Docia?"

"I went to the place pictured in the news clipping." Del couldn't keep a note of defensiveness out of her voice.

With more than a hint of exasperation, Tilde asked, "You didn't talk to nobody?"

Del shook her head, then remembered she was on the phone. "No."

The other woman muttered, "You can lead a horse to water—" She broke off with a curse.

Del stared at the phone. She was getting the distinct feeling Tilde was annoyed with her.

"Kid, how you expect to learn anything if you don't do some talking? I gave you all I have to give. My part's done. You need to haul your *heinie* back to Docia."

Barely waiting for Del to say good-bye, Tilde hung up.

What had she meant by her part was done?

"She give you anything else to go on?" Anxiety shone in Sam's eyes.

"I'm not sure. She said I should talk to people." Del touched her pearls. "People in Docia."

"That's what I said." Sam didn't look particularly pleased that Tilde had backed him up.

"I know." Docia. All signs pointed to Docia.

Neither of them spoke for most of the drive. Del was busy plotting a quick entry and exit. She'd borrowed one of Sam's hats and put on her sunglasses. She looked like a country-western star avoiding the paparazzi, except her trackers would be armed with badges and handcuffs, not microphones and cameras.

She fidgeted with her glasses. She could do this. Sam was right; her dad was their best lead. If he knew anything about the location of the Pig, he owed her enough to tell her.

She had given up her life, had to start over from scratch because of him. The least he could do was give her some information.

Unless he had the Pig and was behind the shooting. Then she might be walking into a nightmare. Del stared out the window at the trees whizzing past. No, she still couldn't bring herself to believe that.

She glanced at Sam. His hair was mussed from his hat. Even with her uncertainties, she wanted to lick her finger and smooth the locks back into place. The way he'd been scowling at the world since they'd left the Hutch, she didn't think he'd appreciate the gesture.

She leaned her head back against the top of the seat. She could handle anything her father threw at her, but what about Sam? Could she handle it if what she suspected more with each avoided gaze was true? Could she handle it if she meant nothing more to Sam than a road to riches?

Her head hurt. She wished she could keep the pain there, away from her heart.

"Almost there." Sam glanced at her, and she thought she caught a glimmer of concern in his eyes. Maybe he did care.

She pushed away the thought and concentrated on the approaching confrontation. What did you say to a father who handed you stolen merchandise, then turned his back when you took the blame?

"Del?" Sam touched her arm to get her attention. "You see that?"

Del turned her gaze toward the small parking area in front of her father's shop. "The sheriff."

Sam gave her a searching look, then turned into the bank's lot across the street and eased the truck into reverse.

"Where you going?" she asked.

"Home. Finding the Pig isn't worth losing you"— he paused and Del's heart soared for a moment, then—"to jail."

Nice. At least he didn't want to see her behind bars. That was something, she guessed. Not the lifelong commitment of love and fidelity most girls dreamed of, but felons had to take what they could get.

As they drove back past the store, Del strained

to catch a glimpse inside. The windows were large but grimy. She could see bodies moving around inside—two male, one female. Even without seeing her face Del knew the woman, could tell by her stance, feet apart, hands on her hips. She was reading the riot act to the two men, and if they knew what was good for them and their privates they were taking it and keeping quiet. Her mama rarely spoke up, but when she did, even the devil kept his rear end in hell and out of her way.

A tear beaded to the surface of Del's eye. She brushed it away with her hand, only to have another one follow. Stupid, this was stupid. Crying was for people who had regrets. Del didn't. She'd built a good life for herself in Chicago. Sure, leaving Docia had been hard the first time, but now? The only reason she was here was to make sure her daddy didn't screw up her second chance like he had her first.

Del slept on Sam's couch, or tried to. Even the fact that he hadn't fought her on her sleeping choice depressed her. He'd just dug in the linen closet for clean sheets and laid them on the green cushion before slipping away to his room.

As she stared into the darkness, listening to her pig snore, surrounded by the smell of sheets left too long on the shelf, another tear dripped down her cheek. Her life was at an impasse. When she had left Chicago everything had been simple and perfectly planned: retrieve the Unruh Pig, secure the sale, and be made a full-fledged member of the auction team. Then security and contentment would follow.

But now she realized it wouldn't. Even if she found the Pig tomorrow, she wouldn't be happy. She'd still be hiding from herself, her inability to face her father and her own past mistakes. Hard as it was for her to admit it, she was tired of living life as Del Montgomery. She wanted to be Delilah again.

Rolling over, she buried her face in the pillow. Sam had pulled it off his bed, and unlike the sheets, it smelled of Sam and his unique lemony cologne.

The scent brought on a new wave of self-pity.

He didn't love her. He wasn't even working with her—not really. He was pretending, using her. She didn't know exactly what he was up to, but she knew whatever it was involved getting the Pig for himself and not helping her.

She should leave, right now. Pack her bags and her pigs and scurry out before dawn.

Her head didn't move from the pillow. She should, but she couldn't. Some tiny little piece of her still held out hope that she was wrong, that Sam wasn't just using her to line his pockets.

Alone in the bed that less than a day earlier he'd shared with Del, Sam fought an inner battle. Del was lying less than twenty feet from him, hurt and confused, and he couldn't comfort her, touch her.

When she had asked for sheets for the couch, he'd been relieved. He was already too close to her, too concerned. Another night in bed together, breathing in her warm scent, stroking her hair, and he'd be completely lost—along with his business and Becca's.

Now, though, he couldn't sleep. The impulse to go to her, to pick her up and carry her to his bed was almost overwhelming. With a curse, he stood up. He just needed to check on her, then he'd sleep.

He padded into the living room, his bare feet cold from the floor. Del lay face up on his couch, her arm thrown across her face. He stepped closer and kneeled down next to her, watching as her chest moved up and down in even breaths.

See, she was okay. She'd be okay. She didn't need the Pig like Sam did. She'd go back to Chicago and her life would be the same. Maybe she wouldn't get the promotion she was hoping for, but she wouldn't really be hurt any.

She murmured something in her sleep and dropped her hand from her face. The tracks of semi-dried tears showed clearly against her pale skin.

The sight hit Sam like a sucker punch to the gut.

Damn. He couldn't do this any longer. He had to get Del out of southern Missouri and back to her life in Chicago. It was the only way to keep strong and go forward with his plan.

He could find the Pig without her, and that's what he would do. Tomorrow she was leaving. Running the back of his fingers over her damp cheek, he wiped all visible signs of pain from her face. He just wished it would be as easy to remove all of it—especially what was sure to come with his betrayal.

Del blinked at the cheery light streaming in the front window, another beautiful day in the Ozarks.

A beautiful day to what? Run back to Chicago, tail between her legs? Hide the hurt under a layer of pearls and fancy clothes? Forget Missouri, forget her daddy, forget Sam?

"You up?" Sam looked down at her, dark circles under his eyes.

Good. Let the sinners suffer their own torments.

She pushed herself to a sitting position, letting the sheet fall down below her breasts. She didn't need the cool air against her skin to tell her that her silk nightie had slipped in her slumber, barely covering her nipples. The fire in Sam's eyes said it all.

His gaze searing into her, Del reached for the sheet to cover herself, then paused. What was she doing? Why was she hiding? The bright sunlight seemed to bring her back to her senses. It was like being pulled out of a well after seven years of entrapment. Enough cowering—it was time to take names and kick some fannies. The only question was, which one first?

She tossed back the covers and stood up. Sam had seen it all before. Why not give him another good look before she trotted out the door, collected the Pig, and left him behind in her dust?

Striding past Sam in a whirl of blue silk, she flipped her hair for good measure. No more victim. It was time to get her life on track, and if anyone—Sam, her daddy, or some mysterious shooter—thought he could take her down and keep her there, she had a lesson to teach him.

"Del." Sam sounded unsure.

Ignoring him, Del yanked open the cupboard and pulled out a mug.

"Del," he spoke again.

With her head in the refrigerator, she reached for a Dolly Madison box. Cinnamon crumb, a month-old by the looks of it—not exactly perfect, but she'd make do.

Realizing Sam was standing behind her she swished her hips side to side before standing up, box in hand.

Sam took a deep breath. Del reached back in the refrigerator for butter. Swish to the left, swish to the right. At Sam's soft groan, she grinned. It felt good to be back—and maybe a little large, but definitely in charge.

"Del." His voice tense, he stood in the corner by the sink, his hands flat on the cabinet tops beside him. "With everything you've told me and what we saw last night"—he glanced down at the floor—"I think you should get back to Chicago as quick as you can." He paused. "Today."

He wanted to get rid of her. Del's heart dropped a few inches. No, she wasn't going to let it get to her. She was taking control of her life—the good, the bad, and the painful.

"That a fact?" She wrapped a length of blue silk around her wrist and pulled, revealing her thighs. After a pause for effect, she settled onto a chair and crossed her legs at the knees.

She wished she had some fluffy, feathery mules to add to the look. After buttering a slice of cake until it held a nice solid layer, she held it to her lips and took a big bite.

Some things were better than thin thighs, especially when your day was off to such an inspiring start.

"Del? Did you hear me?" Sam asked from his corner.

Over the coating of butter, Del glanced at him. He was getting antsy. At the moment Del couldn't work up the teensiest bit of sympathy for him. In fact, she thought some termites in his pants might be a nice twist to the old cliché.

A hunk of cake laden with butter and cinnamon dropped into her cleavage. Waste not, want not. Del rescued the fallen tidbit with her finger. Popping it in her mouth, she looked at Sam again.

He turned his head as if in pain. Del was trying to decide which spaghetti strap to let fall slowly from her shoulder when the front bell rang.

Giving her a last heated glance, Sam strode from the room. Del sashayed after him. Maybe she would forget the Pig and just concentrate on seeking revenge on Sam. So far it had been darn entertaining.

"It's your buddy David. You better get some clothes on."

Del alternated between elation and annoyance at Sam's proprietary tone, but since she had no desire for David to see her in a negligee, she shrugged and sauntered to her suitcase. After grabbing a pair of jeans, she tugged them on under her nightgown.

Sam stood by the door, hand on the knob, bristling with impatience. Changing into a bra and shirt offered a bit more of a challenge, especially if she wanted to maintain any pretense of modesty. Glancing at Sam over her shoulder, she remembered her earlier resolve. She was done cowering.

She whipped off the blue silk, then picked up her

bra. Back still turned, she brushed her hair over one shoulder and looked back at Sam. "Could you fasten this for me?"

He stared at her like Superman eyeing kryptonite. She half turned toward him, bra straps edging down her arms, breasts overflowing from their cups. "I seemed to have strained something."

The doorbell pealed again.

"In a minute," she called out. With a smile she walked to Sam's side. "You mind?"

With shaking hands, he hooked the two pieces of lace-covered elastic together. Before Del could gloat, she felt his knuckle trail down her spine. When his hands touched her shoulders, she was ready to forget her mission and fall back against him, back into his bed. Five short insistent dings of the doorbell stopped her—Sam, really. He dropped his hands, breaking the spell. With a quick yank she pulled a T-shirt over her head.

"Decent?" Sam asked, his gaze on the oak door.

Del laughed. "Decent as I'll ever be. It's not something I plan on striving for from here on out."

Sam took the time to send her a quizzical look before jerking open the door. Becca and David tumbled inward, knocking into Sam.

Looked like they'd been practicing a little indecency of their own.

"What took you so long?" Becca made a good stab at sounding indignant, but David's hand cradling her butt ruined the effect.

Apparently Sam agreed with Del. "Where's your son?" He eyed David as he said the last word.

Becca smacked Sam in the stomach with the

back of her hand. "Lay off. David knows about Clay. In fact, we all had dinner last night."

"Together?" Sam's dry tone brought a smile to Del's lips.

"Yes, together. Like I'd hide Clay from anyone." His cousin stomped past him, heading to the couch. At the rumpled sheets, she paused. "Looks like you could use a little 'together' lesson here."

"What are you doing here?" Sam pulled the door wide and stood in front of it, his expression saying "don't let it smack you on the way out."

Del was happy to see spunk in Becca's step and color in her cheeks. It was nice to see someone enjoying a little hanky-panky without fear of repercussions. However, she didn't want to talk about her sleeping arrangements any more than Sam did. Striding to the couch, she gathered up the sheets and tossed them in the corner.

"What's this?" Del's nightgown dangled from Becca's pinkie. "Maybe there was more 'together' here than I thought."

Before Del could reach her, Sam yanked the nightie from his cousin's hand and threw it at Del. "Like I said, what brought you here?"

Pulling the blue silk off her face, Del frowned at Sam. Becca thinking they had sex couldn't be that embarrassing, could it? Perturbed, Del dropped the garment on the floor. If he ever saw her in sleepwear again, which he wouldn't, she'd wear a granny nightgown complete with buttoned-up neck and wrist-length sleeves.

"Got a call from Porter. He wanted me to pass along a message to Del." David folded his arms over his chest.

"Why didn't he call me himself?" she asked.

"He did, last night. He got voice mail."

Del dug into her suitcase to remove her phone. It was dead. Her call to Tilde yesterday must have used up the last of her battery power. She'd been so caught up with pigs, her family issues, and Sam, she'd forgotten to charge the darn thing all week.

"Oh." Del had never forgotten to charge her phone before. In fact, in the past it had been like an umbilical cord attaching her to the auction house, that's how connected to the place she'd kept herself. She realized that in the past few weeks she'd thought of Porter's Auctions less and less. Sure, she'd thought about the Unruh Pig, but not really the business itself. She suddenly realized she didn't care if Porter's sold another silver teaspoon, much less the art pottery find of the past fifty years.

"So, what did he want?"

David raised an eyebrow at her disinterested tone. "He said for the two of us to quit playing games and to find the Unruh Pig. He wants us to work together."

Del pursed her lips. Another thing she'd forgotten—what a pain in the ass Porter was. Why had she ever thought working for the self-important prig was a good idea? Maybe she wouldn't even go back. With the Pig under her arm she could get a job with any auction house in the country—criminal record or not. Mulling this over, she missed David's next question.

"Hmm?" She realized everyone was waiting for a response from her. "Sorry. So, Porter wants us to work together, why don't you tell me what you have?"

David smirked. "You first."

Del rolled her eyes. She was tired of the lot of them—well, except Becca, but she was wrapped so tightly around David's well-toned leg, Del couldn't really count her as a separate being. With a shrug, Del strolled into the kitchen and began unpacking her pig collection.

Sam stomped in right behind her. "What are you doing?"

"Looking at my pigs." Where was the mini-jug? She'd left it right on top.

"I mean about your pal David."

"Is he? My pal, I mean. I've been thinking more and more that he might be yours." She kept her words casual, continuing to remove pieces from the box.

"He's no pal of mine. I can barely stomach having him in my house."

Del peeked at Sam. He looked sincere enough, but she wouldn't let herself weaken. He was up to something; she could smell it all over him, like cigarette smoke and stale beer after a night out drinking. Whatever he was doing might rip her up later, but she wouldn't let him see the signs.

"So, you're totally in my ball field?" This time she stared him in the bright blues.

His gaze wavered but held. "Of course I am. You can't honestly think I'd choose David over you."

He was good. There was no arguing that. Remembering him trailing his knuckle down her spine, she revised the thought: not just good, too good for safety.

Chapter 19

Common as pig tracks . . .

Del dug deeper in the box—still no jug.

"What are you looking for?" Sam asked.

"Just looking," Del murmured. Then she noticed the items were all messed up, not wrapped in the tidy, loving, tucked-in manner she'd left them. "You been going through my pigs?" she asked more with surprise than accusation.

David and Becca roamed into the kitchen, but Del ignored them. Sam had been going through her purchases—why? One by one she unwrapped each piece and set it on the table. Were any missing?

"Is this what you've been doing down here?" David picked up the ugliest item, the hand-formed vase. "I don't know what this is, but it isn't Unruh."

"Give it to me." For some reason, Del didn't want David holding the disfigured little pig.

With a shake of his head, he released it into her hands. The piece was heavy, definitely not made by an experienced artisan, but there was something touching about it, something that made her feel warm, safe, and loved. How had she missed that before?

She ran her fingers over the grooves of the snout. It was almost familiar. Searching her brain for a lost memory, she turned the vase over. On the bottom were the initials *D.M.*

Her initials.

"Del, we need to discuss what we're doing," David broke in.

"Del, what is it?" Sam asked, his hand on her arm.

The memory was vague, but it was there—this ugly, malformed vase sitting on the windowsill behind the kitchen sink of her childhood home.

But just a couple weeks ago she had found the item at Izzy's. How did he get it?

She twirled the piece in a circle on the table. Hideous as it was, it did hold a remarkable resemblance to what the Unruh Pig should look like. She glanced at the initials again. *D.M.* Had she made this?

"Del, what is it?" Sam asked again, this time with concern.

It wasn't until she heard his voice that she realized how hard she'd been concentrating. Still holding the vase, she turned to him. "I'm going back to Docia."

"But what about . . ." Sam motioned with his hands.

"It doesn't matter. I'm going back."

It took some doing, but Sam convinced David and Becca to stay in Allentown. Now he and Del were traveling south for the second time in a little over a day.

Del sat in her seat, the strangest of her purchases clutched in her hand. She hadn't let go of the thing since she had pulled it out of the box this morning. Something about her expression as she held the vase made Sam feel even lower than he had.

Izzy had said the key to the Unruh Pig was in the box of purchases. This had to be the piece he was talking about—meaning in a matter of hours, Del could be holding the real Unruh Pig instead of this ugly replica. Except she wouldn't. Once it was clear where the Pig was hidden, Sam would get there first.

Lost in thoughts of her own, Del rubbed the pottery snout. Sam gritted his teeth. This mess kept getting worse and worse. If only he'd realized from the beginning how tough the end of this deal was going to be—he never would have opened his office door to Sweet Tea in the first place.

Del was beginning to wish she had never left Chicago. Not that life was great there, but the realization she was about to face her father after seven years of avoiding him and all her feelings toward him was making her sick to her stomach.

She'd let Sam bring her. She wasn't completely sure about her reasoning behind that, either. He seemed to assume he'd drive her, and she didn't want to face this alone, but there was a deeper motive too. She needed to know if Sam was another betrayal in her life, or the partner she hoped for. The only way to find out was to take him along.

The parking area in front of her father's store was empty. Sam pulled the dually into the space and turned to look at her. "You ready?"

Del nodded. Ready as she ever would be. Still holding the vase, she opened the door and hopped down onto the sidewalk. She let Sam go first. Just because she had steeled herself for the meeting didn't mean she was eager to get it started.

"Well, if it isn't the pig wrangler." Her father strode forward to grab Sam's hand.

Del stood back. Sam hadn't mentioned knowing her father. She swallowed the questions that sprung into her mind. Just another example of why she couldn't trust her supposed partner.

Her father hadn't changed a lot. He was still big and loud, and wearing that squirrel-eaten Confederate hat. Why he refused to believe some people might actually be offended by the sentiment eluded Del. She grasped the pig vase tighter. He had exchanged his usual overalls for jeans and red suspenders.

Probably going to church later.

She tapped down the bitter thought. She was here to learn something; coming off mean right at the get-go wasn't going to help her.

"Is this the little lady that loves pigs?" Her father stepped around Sam to include her in his bigger-than-life grin. His lips froze in place.

"Hey, Daddy. Long time."

"Lilah, girl. That you?" Her father's voice was no more than a hoarse whisper.

If she didn't know the old faker better, she'd think he cared.

"In the flesh." She waited for a joke, a comment

about her pants size, or a laugh at how much flesh she actually filled out.

Nothing. Her father just stared at her with hang-dog eyes. "You look just like your mama."

This loving-father routine was wearing on Del. She tromped past both men and sat the little vase on the counter. Her father didn't even glance at it. His gaze stayed on Del.

"Big sale, now there's a surprise." Del flicked a faded sign with her fingernail. "Any big deals in the works?" She folded her hands over her arms.

"Where you been, Lilah girl? Your mama's missed you sorely."

A jolt of guilt knocked into Del. Three times she'd been in Docia now and not once had she contacted her mama.

As she stared at the BIG SALE sign, something hit Del. He was doing it. He was putting her in the low-man position, making her the one who needed to apologize.

It wasn't going to work. She'd been trained by the best. She studied the man she'd spent a life-time emulating. He hadn't even bothered to lie and say he'd missed her. She was nothing to him but a body to be clothed and a mouth to be fed, and every penny that went her way was one less he had to spend at some auction.

"This ring any bells?" She held up the vase.

His gaze lingered on her face before flitting to the object in her hand. Looking at her again, he asked, "You staying for a while? Your mama will like to kill me if you don't."

She was not getting off topic. "The vase—you know how Izzy got it?"

That got his attention. She should have known mentioning one of his trading buddies would do the trick.

"Izzy? You been visiting with that old cuss?" Her father stepped forward to take the piece. "I think he took you, sugar. This don't have no age on it." He rolled it over and glanced at the bottom. "Well, look, it's got your initials on it, don't it?"

Del wanted to scream. He was talking to her like nothing was wrong between them, like she'd just been gone a day, like the law wasn't after her—thanks to him.

"How much you give him for it?"

Del closed her eyes and breathed. She was losing control. She was one casual comment from pitching the biggest hissy fit this side of the Mississippi. When she opened her eyes, Sam had moved forward, his blue gaze soft with concern.

She didn't need concern. She needed retribution.

"You talked to the sheriff lately?" she asked, her voice calm.

The change in topic seemed to surprise her father. "Matter of fact I did, just the other day." He glanced at Sam. "Your mama called him."

Del waited for him to go on, but he didn't. *Fine.*

"How about shooting—you been doing any shooting?"

A frown creased her father's face. "The sheriff asked about that too. Said some big guy . . ." He turned to Sam. "You who he was talking about?"

Sam gave an almost imperceptible nod.

"And you were with him?" her father asked Del.

Del took the vase he still held. "Wasn't that the point? To shoot at me?"

Her father's mouth dropped open a notch. Twisting the pottery pig in her hands, Del kept her gaze steady. "We found the shell."

"You can't tell nothing from a shell, not like I buy 'em monogrammed," her father mumbled.

"It had rock salt in it." Del said this with the finality of a judge declaring a defendant's guilt.

Her father took a step backward. "And you think it was me. Following you out in them woods and taking potshots at you." It wasn't a question, more like he was talking to himself. He shook his head slightly and dragged a beefy palm down his face. "Lilah girl, why would you think I'd do that?"

Spurred by pent-up emotion, Del held the pig vase between them. "Because of this. Tell me now, how did Izzy get it?"

Her father looked at Sam again. "You know what she's talking about? Cause only 'bout ten percent of what's coming out of her mouth makes a molehill's worth of sense to me."

Del came embarrassingly close to stomping her foot. "I made it. Don't you remember anything? It sat behind our kitchen sink for at least ten years and you don't even remember it." Her voice petered out along with her burst of adrenaline. What was she thinking? It was a wonder he remembered her.

She stumbled to a chair and sat down.

Looking even more confused, her father bent down beside her. "I know I missed a lot when you was growing up, Lilah girl, but you can't expect me to remember every rock you painted and called a pet or every glob of clay you smashed together and named a vase. You was always making something or the other."

Del exhaled. "But why this? Why make something that looks like this, and how'd Izzy come to get it?"

"I don't reckon I know the answer to either one of those questions." Her father raised a hand as if to grasp hers but at Del's look stuck it behind his suspenders.

Keeping her words measured, she answered him, "Don't you think it looks a lot like the Unruh Pig?"

Her father pulled back so he could see both of them. "That's what this is about, that lost piece of pottery?"

He was good. She had to respect that. The extra note of incredulity really added to the effect.

"Where've you kept it all these years? That cave? Is that why you run kids off there all the time, why you were shooting at us?"

"I don't believe it. My own girl thinks I'd be shooting at her over some puffed-up piece of art pottery. And not only that, she calls the sheriff on me, sends him over here to give me a hard time. Like I don't have problems enough." He laughed, but without humor.

Oh, that was rich. Poor Daddy. His little girl done him wrong.

Seven years of anger spilled out. "You're one to talk. You didn't think about me seven years ago, did you? Setting me up with stolen merchandise, committing fraud in my sale room." Fury sent her to her feet. "And when the police tossed my office, when the sheriff came and shut me down, where were you? Standing there behind me, explaining how I was the innocent party?" She snorted. "Not likely. I bet you weren't even late to dinner that night. Your world went on uninterrupted, but what about mine? Everything I worked for was gone. Even if I'd beat the jail time, these people weren't ever going to trust me again. You set me up and left me with nothing."

Afraid of what she might say or do next, she spun on her heel and stalked toward the door. Her father let her go—big surprise.

Standing on the long wooden porch that ran in front of her father's store, Del blinked to hold back the tears. This was a mistake. Why'd she ever think coming back here would be a good idea? As soon as Sam got his lazy butt in gear and moseyed out of the shop, she was leaving—for good.

No more southern Missouri, no more Unruh Pig. If what she suspected was true and Sam was after the legend, he could have it. She'd go back to Chicago, tail between her legs—wasn't like it would be the first time. Porter would be ticked, but he'd get over it. She'd have to kowtow to David awhile, but she'd deal with it. She'd miss Sam, but she'd . . .

She kicked an old washer that stood beside her. Why didn't anything ever work out in her favor?

"Lilah Mont, that you? I got a call saying you were in town. I think we need to talk."

She looked up to see the drab tan uniform of the sheriff's office.

Damn, her daddy had done it again, but this time he'd gone an extra step. He'd actually called the law on her.

* * *

Sam watched as Del's father pulled a blue bandanna out of his pocket and ran it over his face. "I didn't realize she hated me so much," the older man said. "Her mama warned me, but I didn't listen."

He collapsed onto the chair Del had just vacated.

Sam wasn't sure what to say. He couldn't believe Del hated her father. If anything he thought her anger showed she still cared, that she was hurt and waiting for someone to make it right.

"Did you do it?" Sam asked.

Jed Mont dropped the bandanna and shook his head. "I didn't shoot at you'uns."

"No, I mean the stolen merchandise, the shilling, letting Del take the heat." Sam wanted to know. He wasn't sure why he cared, but he did.

"You think I'd set my little girl up?"

"Did you?"

"Hell, no." Jed slapped his palm against his leg and leaned forward.

Sam ignored his aggressive stance. "Then how'd the stolen goods get in her sales? And why'd people accuse her of cheating them?" Sam was sure of one thing, Del wasn't a cheater, at least not in the trading world. Sure, she might do things that in the real world were seen as shady, but that was because regular folks didn't understand the way of the deal. But out and out cheat a buyer? Or sell stolen goods? No way—not if she knew about it.

Her father folded like compressed bellows. Head in his hands, he said, "I may have been a bit eager, trying to get her business going and all." He looked up at Sam. "I didn't know them goods were stolen." He fiddled with his bandanna again.

"I just might not have been real particular about asking questions."

Sam let the statement sit for a couple seconds before asking, "And the shilling? Were you upping bids on people?"

The man grimaced. "There might have been a time or two when a friend of mine thought something was going a little low. There's some rich folks around here. Know it doesn't look it, but there's a few. They can afford to pay what something's worth."

"Did Del know?" Sam knew the answer, but he asked anyway.

"No, she'd have pitched a twenty-ton fit if she'd have caught us."

Instead the sheriff caught her.

"She going to forgive me?"

Sam let go of a low laugh. He was the wrong person to be asking. He'd been spending a lot of his own time wondering about Del's forgiveness quota. There was one thing for sure though.

"Not if you don't ask her."

Her father gave a tired nod. "I can see that now. Well, I don't think she's going to do it today. She's like her mama, once she gets a good head of steam going, you're best off to lay low till it peters out. I'd say we got at least twenty-four hours before she'll let me within spitting distance—even then I may get a little wet." A weak grin showed he hadn't given up all hope.

Laughing, Sam slapped him on the back. "You're okay, Jed, but you're right. Del needs a little time. What you say I talk to her, either get her to come back down or set up a time to meet somewhere on neutral ground?" Again, Sam questioned if Del would listen to his advice, but all he could do was try. Her dad wasn't a bad sort, and she deserved to put the ugly feelings behind her. Maybe he could figure out a way to help her with the charges against her, if there even were charges. Sam just couldn't see that she'd done anything worth arresting her for—hassling, sure, but arrest? That seemed extreme.

Sam walked onto the shop's front porch steeled for a tongue-lashing from Del. The boardwalk was empty. So was his truck. Where could she be? Wasn't like she could catch a taxi back to Allentown.

Sam rubbed his chin. There was only one place he could think Del would be—after the Pig. Sneaky. He'd thought she was all caught up in reliving her past problems, but instead she was plotting how to get out of the shop without him and swipe the Pig from under his nose.

He shook his head at his own stupidity. He had to stop letting this woman distract him like she did. Might not matter anymore. She might already have the Pig and be on her way back to Chicago.

No. He hadn't been inside that long, and she wouldn't leave Toadstool. He just had to figure out where she had gone. She must have decided her father didn't have the Pig. But if he didn't, who did?

Del stared across the army-green desk at the evil elf of a sheriff. From his twinkling blue eyes to the toes of his turned-up cowboy boots, he looked like he'd just left Santa's workshop. Probably specialized in lumps of coal and bunches of twigs. Arms crossed over her chest, she waited for his pronouncement.

"You sure you don't want to call somebody? Let them know you're here?" he asked.

Del frowned. Why couldn't he just get on with it? Lock her up, throw away the key? "I told you back at the shop. There's nobody here that'd care. Besides, you haven't done anything yet. Don't you have to read me my rights or something?"

"You seem to be in an awful big hurry to get thrown in the pokey." His gaze darted from her to the phone, then back at her.

Couldn't the man even concentrate on her? He was seconds from ruining her life and acted like he was waiting for a big-money phone bidder to check in. "Seven years doesn't seem like that big a hurry to me." *Come on, already.*

"Seven years?" His fingers crawled toward his intercom.

"Yeah, seven years." Nice to know the good folks of Ozark County were equal opportunity, electing such a mental midget and all. She stifled a yawn. The closer the clampdown came, the less she cared. She let her gaze drift around the office. This wasn't how she'd envisioned being arrested at all. No snapping dogs, hushed crowds, or handcuffs. Not even a pat-down. Looking at her interrogator again, she said a quick prayer of thanks for the latter.

"Maybe things would go quicker if you just told me why you think I brought you in here today," he said.

He wanted her to tell him? What was this, some kind of a trap? "Don't you think I should talk to a lawyer first?"

His fingers reached the curly cord of his phone. Wrapping the red plastic around his thumb, he answered, "Do you think you should talk to a lawyer?"

Hell, yes. 'Cause in twenty seconds, she was going to yank that phone cord out of the wall and string the little pain-in-the-butt elf up.

Chapter 20

In a pig's eye . . .

A scrap of a yard stood between Sam and the Pig. He was sure of it. He'd left Jed's shop and just driven, seeing where his gut took him, and it brought him here, about two miles past the low-water bridge where the Pig had disappeared.

It was hard to miss the mailbox, surrounded by black-eyed Susans and proudly hand-lettered with MONT. When he saw the name he knew, Del's childhood home. That was where this story had to end.

An ancient iron fence that had to have been scavenged from another older and much grander home circled the yard. The house, no more than two bedrooms, Sam guessed, sat on the crest of a small knoll. Not far away, an abandoned barn rotted into the ground and a few chickens pecked at the dry earth.

He lowered his body to the ground, half expecting gunfire to ring out. Instead, four hounds of indeterminate origin came barreling around the corner of the house, sounding an alarm. Hoping they were more blow than go, he strode forward. The smallest, a beagle mix, positioned himself between Sam and the house and promptly bared his mastiff-sized canines.

Sam froze.

"It's always the small ones you got to watch out for, you know that?" An older woman squeaked open the screen door and held her hand above her eyes as a shade against the sun. "It's a good trick. You're busy watching the big guy and the little feller sneaks in and snaps a hole in your pants."

Keeping his gaze on the dogs and a hand on his jeans, Sam gave her a curt nod.

"Not many folks make it all the way out here. Don't think we've even had a Jehovah's Witness for a couple years, not since Petunia there helped herself to an armful of brochures. Was like a ticker tape parade."

The slathering beast was named Petunia? As if knowing she was being discussed, the beagle edged closer to Sam. He concentrated on looking firm and unafraid while calculating the distance between him and his truck.

"Females are the worst too, you know that? Don't call 'em bitches without reason." The woman stepped farther onto the porch, then looked him up and down.

Sam couldn't tell if she liked what she saw or not.

"She could have done worse, I reckon." The woman slapped her thigh and called, "'Tunia, come here, girl."

The beagle gave Sam one last warning snarl, then turned and trotted to her owner, tail wagging the whole way. Sensing the show was over, the other three hounds collapsed on the ground and began to snooze.

"Might as well come in. You aren't going to learn anything out here." The woman turned and disappeared inside the house.

Sam picked his way past the prone hounds, giving Petunia a last wary gaze before following the woman inside.

The place was packed floor to ceiling with knick-knacks, old books, and magazines. Leaning in the corner by an oak hall tree was a double-barreled shotgun.

He paused. The woman stood in a doorway. He could see the kitchen behind her. "Do much shooting?" he asked.

"Only when I have a cause. It's Jed's." She motioned him forward. "Have a seat. I just fried up a new batch of doughnuts. I was hoping my girl'd stop by. They're her favorites." After rolling a ball of fried dough into a sugar mixture, she placed it on a plate and slid it in front of him. "Don't guess you'd know what's keeping her."

"Del?" he asked. Their introduction had been a bit lacking; even with the name on the mailbox, he wasn't one hundred percent sure he hadn't wandered into the wrong farmhouse—or alternate reality.

"Del. What caused her to ruin a perfectly good name, I ask you." Del's mother shook her head and nibbled at the side of her doughnut. "Eat while it's hot. That's when they're the best." She nodded to his plate.

"Mrs. Mont . . ." Sam began.

"Geraldine. Now, did I curse Lilah with a name

like that? Did I name her Jedidine? No, gave her a perfectly acceptable name and she changes it. Just shows you can't please your kids no matter how you try." She pointed to Sam's intact dough-nut. "You going to eat that?"

Not sure what else to do, Sam picked up the pastry and popped it into his mouth. He got lost for a minute in the heady flavor of sugar, cinna-mon, and fried pastry.

"Good, isn't it?" Geraldine beamed at him, then shook her head. "Sure wish Lilah was here. Don't know what else I could have done to get her here though. Did she at least stop by her daddy's?"

Sam nodded and eyed the bowl of doughnuts.

"Have another. If you're here and she isn't, I'm guessing she ain't coming today. I'll have to make a fresh batch tomorrow."

As Sam bit into his second doughnut, something occurred to him. "Do you know who I am?"

She laughed. "Of course I know who you are. Don't think I'd let my daughter spend the night in a cave with just anybody, do you?"

Sam lowered his doughnut. "You mean you were the one . . ."

She laughed. "Don't play coy. You already knew that. That's why you're here, isn't it?" She rolled an-other pastry in the sugar mixture, then held it up.

Sam shook his head. She had just admitted to shooting at him and her daughter. Was he alone with a crazy woman?

"Don't go getting all jittery. I wasn't about to hurt you. It was just rock salt."

"I know, but why . . ."

"Shoot at my little girl?" She picked up their

plates and stacked them in the sink. She turned back, a wet cloth in her hand. "She didn't leave me much choice, now did she? That girl could out stubborn a mule."

Sam lifted his arms from the table to avoid the angry swish of the dishrag. "For years I tried talking her into coming back home, facing whatever problems she had with the law, talking things out with her daddy, but when she could tell what direction I was going, she'd hang up on me. Hang up on me." She scrubbed at a spot on the scarred wood.

"So I come up with an idea, found out what she wanted the most, or leastways had herself convinced she wanted the most, then set the trap and waited. Sure as shooting, she trotted on down. I thought everything was going to roll into place like baby ducks behind their mama, but no, not my girl. She doesn't take any of the clues I set for her. Goes off on her own, hiring you, then stomping around in the woods instead of going to see her daddy like I'd planned. She left me no choice but to shoot at her. Figured for sure she'd guess it was Jed and go after him. But even that didn't work." Geraldine fell onto her chair. "I'd about give up when I saw your truck bumping down the drive, but here you are all on your lonesome—still no sign of Lilah."

She exhaled, blowing a strand of mousy hair out of her eyes.

"So you arranged everything?" Sam could feel his future slipping away.

She nodded.

That was that. There was no Pig. The whole thing had been an invention to lure Del back home. A strange elation erupted in Sam's chest. There was no Pig. He didn't have to steal it away from Del. He was going to have to forfeit his dream and all his cash, maybe lose his house, but . . . his mood dropped again. He was totally screwed.

Depressed, he strived to maintain an interested look. "How'd you do it?"

"It was easy. I've known Bennie Porter since we were three—went to school together over near Black River."

Porter of Porter Auctions was from Black River? Sam grinned. From what Del had said about him, he doubted she realized that.

"I called him up and told him about the Pig, but said if he wanted it, he had to send Lilah. I wasn't turning it over to anybody else. The hardest part was getting him to do it my way. He always was an impatient sort. Wanted to send her straight here, have her grab the Pig and head back to Chicago. But that wouldn't work. Knowing Lilah, I knew she needed some time down here—near home, but not at home, to remember where she come from and who she is. I have friends near Allentown, so it fit the bill perfect."

Poor Porter—he didn't realize there was no Pig, either.

"Course when she got there, she gummed things up good by hiring you, but then I realized meeting a good-looking man with a business close to her heart might not be all bad." She looked at him from under a raised brow. "Still not sure if I was right or not."

Sam squirmed. He hadn't felt this analyzed since

his dad quit checking behind his ears to see if he had washed.

"Anyhow, with help from my friends, I threw some reminders out." She paused. "How's the piglet, by the way?"

Startled by the change in subject, Sam blinked at her.

"I heard she named him Toadstool." Del's mother smiled. "She tell you she had a pig named Toadstool when she was little? Her toting that thing around was about the cutest thing you ever did see." A frown replaced the smile. "Then her daddy, the big galoot, sold him for sausage. I could still kick the man for that." She shook her head, and for a minute Sam was afraid she was going to cry.

"He's fine—Toadstool, I mean. We left him with my cousin. He gets carsick—Toadstool, that is. My cousin's a woman." He was stammering like an idiot. *Shut up and let the woman talk it out.*

She nodded, using a calloused hand to wipe away the moisture in her brown eyes. She did look like Del, Sam realized—smaller, more birdlike, but their features were the same and they shared the sweet-tea color of their eyes.

"When Tilde told me she bought the pig, I was real hopeful."

"Tilde?" Sam prompted.

Laughter jumped into Geraldine's eyes. "She's one of the friends I mentioned. Once you meet Tilde, you don't forget her."

That was right, anyway.

"Tilde found out about a hog farmer that just had a new litter of Hampshires—just like the original Toadstool. So, she arranged for Lilah to make a little trip out that way. Lilah did just like I hoped and brought the runt home. How many fancy city girls you know that keep a Hampshire hog?"

Sam couldn't name a one.

"Then Izzy, you know Izzy." There was no question in her tone. Sam had the feeling this woman knew as much about his comings and goings of the past couple of weeks as he did.

"Well, once I heard about Lilah working with you, I knew you'd have to take her to Izzy's. She might have avoided him on her own, but with you steering the way she'd have to wind up there. Anyway, Izzy agreed to take a little pottery pig and mix it in with some other collectibles." She paused again, shaking her head in disbelief. "I still can't believe she forgot that vase. She made it, you know, and she was so proud of it for so long."

That explained the initials. "How old was she when she made it?"

"About four."

Sam thought Del's mother overestimated the staying power of a four-year-old's mind.

"Izzy said he even prodded you a bit, but it didn't do any good. I was sure she'd take a good look at that vase, add everything up, and show up at Jed's shop to at least guilt him out of the Unruh piece. I had Jed and the sheriff all lined up, ready to be on their best behavior, but she never showed."

So the sheriff was there for Del. Why would her mother do that? "We did, but we left."

"What?" The look Geraldine nailed him with made him inch back in his chair.

"We drove down, but when we saw the sheriff's car we turned around."

Del's mother let loose with a very unmotherly string of words. "I could have had this settled yesterday."

Afraid she'd turn her temper—or worse, her dog—on him, Sam kept silent.

"So, I've told you my story. Did you get what you came for?" With a low laugh, she continued, "Of course not. You came looking for the Unruh Pig, didn't you?"

Sam held his breath. Did it exist?

Her eyes hard, she tapped her fingers on the tabletop. "You care about my daughter at all?"

The question stopped Sam. Not that it wasn't something he hadn't been thinking about himself, but he'd also been avoiding it. When it was laid out like that, he didn't know how to answer. With the truth? That he cared more about her and her car-sick pig than he'd ever cared about anybody? That even though he did care, he was going to crush her by looking out for his own hide and Becca's, while leaving her with nothing?

The phone ringing offered him a reprieve. Geraldine hit him with another piercing gaze before leaving the table to answer the call.

What was keeping the evil elf? Del was pretty sure detaining somebody at the sheriff's office without filing charges wasn't legal.

Course, she couldn't complain. He'd shoved her out of his office and into some tired meeting room. The carpet was stained and the windows dirty, but a treasure trove of pastries occupied the center of the chipped conference table.

She flicked open the pink cardboard box and pulled out a bear claw. If she was going to jail, there was no reason to worry about a few extra calories. When she finished this, she just might chase it with a chocolate-frosted long john.

She hoped the doughnuts came out of the good sheriff's pocket; maybe she'd eat the boxful.

"Well, let her go." Impatience laced Geraldine's voice. "I don't care what she's expecting. She needs to get her *heinie* home."

Sam tried to look like he wasn't listening to the phone conversation. The sharp stare Geraldine stuck him with told him he wasn't succeeding.

"Go ahead and tell her. Keeping her wondering won't do any good."

It was obvious she was talking about Del, but who was on the other end of the line? Were they going to tell Del the Pig was a myth?

"Just make sure she understands she has to come home or the deal is off."

Sam's ears perked up at the mention of a deal. His heart couldn't take much more of this yo-yo ride. Unruh Pig. No Unruh Pig. He just needed to know. Was he a callous creep willing to sell Del down the river? Or an out-of-work auctioneer who pinned his dreams on a myth and failed his only living relative?

He was pondering which would be harder to live with when Geraldine returned.

"So, you didn't answer my question. You care about my little girl? Or were you just treasure hunting?"

Sam tried, but he couldn't keep his gaze steady. After two seconds, it dropped to a spot on the table.

Geraldine sighed. "That's what I was afraid of. The last thing Lilah needs is to tie herself to a man who cares more about hunting down the next rare find than loving his family."

She pushed herself away from the table. "Might as well get this over with." Motioning to him over her shoulder, she opened a door that led to a small enclosed porch.

Inside was a chest freezer and shelves full of jelly jars. Sam adjusted his weight from one foot to the other.

For her small stature, Geraldine seemed to fill the space. "I don't have much worth anything. What I do have I had to squirrel away to keep my fool husband from trading it off, and the most important thing I ever had left seven years ago. I'd give up everything I own, melt down my fillings if they were worth anything, just to get that one thing back." She leveled her gaze at him. "I'm telling you this so you'll understand how easy it is for me to let go of things that ain't as important."

Without another word she reached into the freezer and pulled out a burlap sack.

Sam held his breath as she pulled the tie that closed it.

Del was polishing off a jelly doughnut when the sheriff returned. Strawberry, not her favorite, but better than bread and water.

He glanced from her red-stained face to the

empty pink box, his eyes round. Del shot him a warning glare.

She was in no mood to discuss her eating habits. "You ready to get on with this?" She looked around for a napkin to wipe the jam off her fingers. Not seeing anything, she picked up some papers and scraped the red goo onto them.

The sheriff pulled the remainder of the stack away. "You can go."

Thinking maybe she was delirious from excessive sugar to the brain, Del leaned back in the chair and stared at him. "You mean to a cell?"

"No, home, wherever. Not here." He removed the sticky page from her hand and made a shoo-ing motion.

"But the charges . . ."

"There are no charges; they've all been dropped." He took a step backward, watching her with wary eyes.

Dropped? "When did that happen?"

He edged closer to the door. "A few years ago."

A few years ago and nobody told her? "I've been hiding out in Chicago for seven years and nobody told me the charges were dropped?" She put her hand down on the half-eaten doughnut squishing jelly onto the dingy wood.

The sheriff stared at it like she'd spit in the White House.

"Do you think it might be a good idea to let a person know when charges have been dropped against them?" She grabbed the paper back to swipe at her palm again.

The elf squared off. "Only if the person isn't hiding out where the sheriff's office can't find them."

Oh, yeah, there was that. "How about my mama? You tell her?"

He nodded. "Yep, and she said if you got a problem with it, you better go talk to her in person."

Del stared at him through narrowed eyes. "Who were you talking to all this time?"

With a superior smile, he held open the door.

She was halfway into the hall before she remembered. "Wait, I don't have a car. How am I going to get back to the shop?"

"Your daddy's sitting out front waiting on you."

Del opened her mouth, but the sheriff waved away her protest. "And your momma said to tell you to be nice or the charges could be undropped just as easy."

Undropped? Her mama didn't have that kind of power—did she?

Deciding it wasn't worth the risk, Del trudged down the hall to the waiting area.

Her daddy sat on an old church pew that served as a bench, his Confederate hat in his hands.

Del cranked down the window of her father's fifteen-year-old Chevy truck and sucked in the smells of fresh cow manure, dust, and sunshine. Together it was more alluring than expensive French perfume.

"I met your pig." Her father's gruff voice broke the silence that had stood between them since leaving the sheriff's. "He's a good 'un."

For what, lunch? Del snorted and leaned her head out the window, letting the breeze catch her hair.

"Your mama said you named him Toadstool, after the other . . ." He let the words trail off, adjusted in his seat a bit.

A hawk glided on the breeze above them. It was a beautiful sight. The bird shrieked and lunged toward the earth. Yeah, a beautiful sight—if you weren't a mouse.

"I could turn on some music, but the radio don't come in out here and my tape player broke last year. Besides, you never liked my music."

His music. He listened to the same crap Sam did. Something clenched in Del's stomach. Sam. When she suggested her daddy drive her back to the shop and she'd go back to Allentown with Sam, he told her Sam was gone. He'd left the shop not long after Del and hadn't come back. She got the feeling there was more to the story, but her father clammed up and Del wasn't sure she wanted to know the rest anyway. She was pretty sure she wasn't going to like the ending.

"I'm sorry about the other little hog, Lilah girl. I don't have no excuse, except I was just thinking of keeping food on the table. Never occurred to me might be better to go hungry for a while."

Del glanced at her father. Or skip an auction? He didn't see his addiction to junk as part of the problem. To him trading was more essential than food, air, or her.

She crossed her arms over her chest and looked out the window. The hawk was long gone, probably dining on Mickey or Minnie's cousin.

With a huff she turned in her seat. "You still found money to go to sales though, didn't you? Still found money to buy more junk."

Her father looked at her with unsure eyes. "I never said I was perfect, Lilah girl." Gaze back on the road, he mumbled, "Guess I messed up more than I realized."

His somber tone cut into Del, past her years of anger. Damn. She wasn't ready to forgive him, to put all her resentment behind her.

She glanced at him again. There was definite moisture in his tired eyes. She knew he wasn't a bad man, in a lot of ways not even a bad father. He spent time with her. Sure, he was always at a sale or B.S.ing with a group of men, but he'd taken her along.

And the first Toadstool? She shook her head. Her daddy was raised to think of livestock as food. It was natural for him to treat an animal as a pet and then turn around and eat it for breakfast. It wasn't fair of her to hate him for it. It would be like blaming a rooster for crowing.

With a sigh, she spoke. "How about the stolen merchandise? Why didn't you speak up and tell the sheriff I didn't know about it? That you and one of your buddies arranged it?"

The look he gave her held nothing but surprise. "But then we'd have been admitting we done something wrong. Way it shook out nobody knew for sure. Was just rumors."

Del let her head fall back on the seat. Her father was a rooster. She'd have to remember that.

Chapter 21

Living high on the hog . . .

The Mont's chickens replaced the dogs in sending Sam off. A glossy-feathered rooster flapped his way to the top of an old metal wagon wheel and crowed his good-byes. Sam got the feeling the cocky creature was glad to see him leave.

Sam was glad too. Glad to leave Del's mother and her knowing gaze behind. Wishing he could leave the guilt behind too. He glanced at the rough sack tucked under the passenger seat. It held the answer to all his and Becca's problems. No more worrying about banks and mortgages, no more thoughts of losing his house.

No more Del.

Sam jammed a Hank Williams Sr. CD into the slot and turned the volume to vibrate, but even Hank's croonings couldn't silence the guilt thumping in his chest.

Del's mother had given him the bag. It and what was hidden inside was his. There was no reason to feel guilty. Del would understand, eventually. How long could she stay mad?

Sam thought of her father, sitting in his shop, tears filling his eyes. A long time, maybe forever. Sam had to face facts. Del wasn't the forgiving type. If he kept going, took the Pig and sold it, Del would be gone before the final hammer clapped down.

The little yellow house Del had grown up in looked smaller and run-down, but it sat on the small hill bathed in sunshine like a pot of gold at the end of a rainbow. Just looking at it made her chest go tight and tears fill her eyes. Her father reached across the seat and clasped her hand. With a sob, she threw herself across the space and wrapped her arms around his neck. Rooster or not, he was hers.

Squeezing her tight, he said, "I'm sorry for everything, Lilah girl. I'll try to do better."

She rested her cheek against his shoulder and replied, "I'll try harder too. It's my own fault. I should have stayed and fought for what I wanted, not run off." Pushing away, she grinned at him. "Next time, I'll just call you on it."

"I'd like that. I surely would." He yanked her into a giant bear hug and pulled her from the truck. "Your mama's gonna have my hide if I don't get you inside."

While her father fussed at the pack of hounds that came charging around the corner, Del dragged herself up the walk. Admitting you were wrong was a hard thing to do. As much as she wanted to see her mama, she wasn't sure how she'd find the energy to do it again.

The front door swung open and her mother, hands on her hips, stood facing her. "'Bout time you got here. I been frying dough all day."

Del grinned and ran into her mother's outstretched arms. She was never going to be so stupid again. Some things were worth fighting for, even if you thought the battle was lost.

Inside the house, her mother fussed and flitted, rolling freshly fried doughnut holes in cinnamon and sugar and plopping them on a platter in front of Del.

Del stared at the pastries like they might explode, which they would if she stuck them in her overextended stomach.

"I ain't never seen a day when you couldn't eat at least a dozen of my doughnut holes." Her mother tapped on the plate.

Del shook her head. "I'm just too happy to be home."

Her mother smiled. "Not as happy as we are to have you."

Del sat in silence for a while, enjoying the warm smells and feel of the kitchen. She'd spent most mornings of her childhood sitting at this table eating doughnut holes. She couldn't believe she'd left this behind for so little.

"You did it all, didn't you?" she asked her mother.

Her mother nodded. "I found that Pig day after all those fools cleared out. Got itself wedged under an old log. I was hunting rocks for my garden. Brought it back home and cleaned it up. I knew right off what it was, but didn't see no sense in turning it in. Didn't really have an owner anymore. Why shouldn't I keep it? So, I tucked the little guy away like a bank account. Times have always been tough, and I knew sooner or later, I'd be needing a nest egg."

"But my vase, it was modeled after the Pig, wasn't it?"

Her mother grinned. "Yeah, guess I've got a bit of your daddy in me. I'd kept the thing hid for years, but after you came along, I had someone I could trust. Couldn't resist showing you my find— even if you were too young to understand its worth. When your daddy was off doing whatever he did, I'd take the Pig out and let you hold him. After you made your own though, I stopped. You were getting old enough, sooner or later, you would've said something to the wrong person, and my nest egg would've been gone."

Del relaxed against her seat, amazed that her mother had kept the Pig from her daddy for so long.

Her mother continued, explaining how she had contacted Porter. Del was surprised Porter was not only from Missouri but apparently also an old friend of her mother's. He'd certainly never given Del any preferential treatment—unless you counted hiring her in the first place, which apparently her mother had set up too. Del still wasn't clear how much her boss knew about her past, and she didn't want to be. Thinking of him as an arrogant snob was a habit she didn't care to break. Learning he'd known every-thing all along, and maybe even watched out for her, wasn't something she thought she could swallow just yet.

After getting Porter to send Del south, Del's mother had arranged for Tilde and Izzy to push her toward Docia. Del would say her mother should have just called her, told her the charges were dropped and she'd have come home, but she knew it wasn't true. She'd built up a big bunch of crap in her brain and let it take over.

If she'd known there was no warrant, no threat of jail time, she still wouldn't have come home. It would have just made it easier for her to settle into her life in Chicago—no fear of the past, nothing to keep her looking over her shoulder.

And shooting at her and Sam? How could she be angry at her mother for that? It was the final push she needed to get closer to Sam—a lot closer.

Sam. She tapped a fingernail against the platter. Where was he?

"You thinking about that boy?" Her mother leaned back in her chair.

Del sighed. She'd have to get used to her mother's uncanny ability to read her mind again—no use lying. "Yeah."

"You love him?"

Del shrugged. Did she? Or were they just caught up in the hunt together? They would be a horrible match. He'd never accept that she was the better auctioneer. She smiled at the thought.

"You going after him?"

Del looked at her mother in surprise. "He's been here?"

"Left about fifteen minutes before you got here. Must have taken the long way to the highway, if you didn't pass him." She shook her head and mumbled, "Can't count on nothing anymore."

"What was he doing here?" Del asked the question, but she didn't need to hear the answer. Something was already clutching her heart before her mother replied.

"Not sure he knew, but he left with something."

"Something I need?"

Her eyes unreadable, her mother nodded. "Yeah, I think it is."

The Pig. Her mother had given Sam the Unruh Pig. Del's hand shot to her pearls. She'd been right. He had been just using her, just looking out for his own interest.

Well, she wasn't putting up with it. He had something she wanted, and she was going to hunt him down and take it.

The burlap sack looked out of place on Sam's counter. He ran his hand over the rough cloth. He should open it, make sure it was undamaged. The thing had been stored in a freezer for thirty years. There was no telling what might have happened to it.

He didn't know why he hadn't opened the bag yet, hadn't even sneaked a peek. Back at Del's parents, the phone ringing again had interrupted her mother before she could untie the sack. When she came back, she just shoved the burlap package in his hands and pushed him out the door.

He didn't even know for sure the Unruh Pig was inside. Taking a deep breath, he pulled out a pocketknife and flipped it open. Time to find out.

"Sam, you in here?" The sound of his cousin's voice almost caused him to shove the three-inch blade into his palm. Damn. He should have locked the door.

With a snap, he returned the knife to his pocket and tromped into the living room.

Toadstool trotted forward, his curly tail twitching when he saw Sam. Despite the blast of guilt that hit Sam when he saw the pig, he dropped to his knees and scratched him between the ears. "You been a good hog?"

"Happy as a pig in mud." Becca grinned at him. "Wait, he is a pig."

"But we avoided the mud." David sneaked in the door behind her.

Sam resisted the urge to look over his shoulder into the kitchen. The last thing he needed was Mr. Hot-Shot Auctioneer discovering the pig in a poke on his countertop. As if sensing his worry, Toadstool twisted away and took off for the kitchen.

"He's probably thirsty. We've been driving around for a while." Becca threw David a cross look. "I'll get him some water."

Before Sam could stop her, she'd followed Toadstool into the kitchen.

He stood in front of David, blocking his path. "So where you been driving?" Sam asked.

"Nowhere." David took a step toward Sam. "You going to invite me in?"

"Wasn't planning on it," Sam replied.

David grinned. "It's hell losing, isn't it?"

"Who's losing?" Sam kept his back to the kitchen.

"He's all cocky 'cause we talked to Izzy." Becca stepped back into the living room.

Sam released a breath in relief. Smiling, he watched David. "Help you out, did he?"

"He's going to." David's tone challenged Sam to deny it.

Sam didn't feel the need. "Well, can't win them all, can you?" He flipped his palms up.

David's eyes narrowed. "Where's Del?"

"Visiting family." Sam was amazed at how naturally the words came out, especially after working their way around the knot in his throat.

"She coming back to get the pig?"

Sam started at David's question. The Pig?

"She's just visiting, right?" Becca asked, then to David, "She wouldn't leave without Toadstool."

Toadstool. Sam forced his fingers, which had clenched at his sides, to relax.

"What's in the bag, anyway?" Becca cocked her head at him.

Damn. "Nothing important." Sam attempted to stare her into silence.

"What bag?" David perked up like a bird dog flushing a covey of quail.

Becca looked a question at Sam. He was cursing under his breath, when a fourth voice interrupted, sending the hairs on the back of his neck shooting skyward.

"More importantly, where's my pig?" Hands on her hips, toes together, cleavage front and center, Del looked like a forties pinup girl on a mission.

Sam's mouth went dry, his usual aplomb evaporating as his adrenaline soared. Del was here and she looked hot—in more than one way.

"Toadstool's in the kitchen," Becca said, looking with curiosity from Sam to Del and back again.

"Good to know." Del kept her gaze leveled on Sam. "You planning on taking off with my pig again?"

Del hoped she looked confident, because she'd never been closer to collapsing from nerves in her life. Sam stood in front of her, his tight tee a little dirty and his dark hair a little mussed. If she wasn't mistaken that was cinnamon and sugar dusting his shirt, proving he'd been at her parents'. She licked her lips. He probably tasted just like one of Mama's doughnuts. It took all Del's resolve to keep from flinging herself across the room and finding out firsthand.

"You here for the Pig?" His tone was light, but she could read the tension in his eyes.

"What do you think I'm here for?" She cocked one hip, then sashayed into the room. "They dropped the charges."

"Really?" A spark of joy shot through his eyes. She noted his reaction but tucked it away to analyze later.

"And I made up with my daddy." She took another step toward him.

"He isn't a bad sort," Sam murmured, his gaze on her lips.

"He means well. Just like my mama." She stopped an arm's length away.

"They mean well," he echoed.

With a slow smile she licked her index finger,

then ran it through the sugar grains on his shirt. "You been eating doughnuts?"

The air between them seemed to thicken. Del's heart thumped in her chest. He was a liar and maybe a cheat, but he was a liar and a cheat she loved. The question remained: Did he love her more than the Pig?

She flattened her hand against his chest to feel his heart too. The resounding thud reassured her. He could act cool, but he was no more immune to their attraction than she was.

"So, you ready to hand over my Pig?" She kept her expression neutral, watching for his reaction. It was subtle, but it was there—tiny lines formed on the sides of his mouth. He was thinking—hard.

What would he decide? Would he keep the Unruh Pig and throw away their relationship, or would he choose Del? Wanting it to be his choice, Del waited.

The lines by his mouth grew deeper. Del could feel Becca and David watching them, but she kept her concentration on Sam. This was it. Just once she needed to be put first.

"It's in the kitchen."

She almost didn't recognize his voice, it was so low and gravelly.

"I'll get him." Becca took off at a trot into the kitchen.

Del pulled back her hand. Becca was on her way with Toadstool and Sam wasn't going to correct her.

Would he just let Del walk away? Choose the Unruh Pig?

Becca returned with a grunting Toadstool.

Stepping away, Del looked Sam in the eye. "That's my pig, all right. I wouldn't want anyone to steal him. That would be unforgivable, don't you think?"

"Sometimes people have good reasons for doing bad things," Sam replied, his voice low.

Damn him. He was choosing the Pig over her. Biting her lip, Del dropped her gaze. She could call him on it, insist he hand over the vase, but for what? Money? That wasn't what she wanted, not really—and she could tell by the way Sam avoided her eyes, she'd already lost what she really valued.

Del picked up Toadstool and concentrated on keeping tears from welling in her eyes. With one arm around her pet, she reached behind her neck and unhooked her pearls.

"Here." She dangled them toward David. "Give these to Porter. I don't need them anymore."

"You can't be serious." David stared at the necklace like it had fangs and a rattle.

She shook it again. "Take it."

"But what about the Unruh sale, the Pig?"

Sam stood in silence, studying a spot above their heads, his hands shoved into his pockets.

Grabbing the handle of her rolling suitcase, she gave it a yank and replied, "I hear some things are more important. I intend to find them and start enjoying them."

Without looking at Sam, she turned and strode from the house. She made it to her car before the tears rolled down her cheeks.

* * *

The door clicked behind Del with the finality of an auctioneer's gavel ending a sale. Sam closed his eyes and let his shoulders slump. He had done it. He had let her leave.

"What was that about?" Becca stared at him, one hand on her hip.

"Nothing." Sam turned and walked toward the kitchen, not caring if David and Becca followed.

Becca stopped him. In a tense whisper, she said, "Is this about that burlap bag on your counter? 'Cause if it is, you're an idiot."

Sam studied her face. "Did you look in it?"

Shaking her head, Becca said, "No, but David's been talking about it enough. Then Del's performance. Somehow you got that Pig, didn't you?"

"It can solve all our problems."

"Our? Don't be sucking me into your mess. I can solve my own problems."

Sam glanced at David, then nudged Becca closer to the kitchen. "Don't be stupid. I didn't do anything wrong. I didn't steal anything. It was a fair trade."

Becca gave him a sad smile. "A fair trade. You got the Pig, and what did you give up to get it?" She stepped away from him. "You want to keep it, fine. But don't be saying it's for me. Anything you gain from that thing is totally on your head."

Turning around, she grabbed David by the arm and pulled him toward the door. "Come on. We better check out that lead Izzy gave you."

Sam was alone, totally alone—well, except for the burlap bag on his counter. He walked the twenty steps to his kitchen to stare at it. All he had to do was open that bag, print up some sale bills, and his business would be out of hock. It would be more than out of hock. He'd be pulling in bidders from New York to California. People who couldn't find Missouri on a map would fly in to attend his sale.

He lowered his body back onto the stool and reopened his pocketknife.

Chapter 22

Go whole hog . . .

Del gazed out over the crowd. Not huge, but respectable. The July sun blared down on her, causing a trickle of sweat to run between her breasts. Balancing on a makeshift chair constructed from an old tractor seat and a milk keg and nothing but a child's Porky Pig umbrella over her head to cut down on the heat, she'd come a long way from Porter Auctions. Some would say the wrong way, but Del didn't doubt she'd made the right decision—at least about Porter's.

She sighed. It had been a month and she still couldn't get Sam out of her mind. Every time she passed a phone, her hand drifted toward it—just to check in, she told herself. But then her daddy would come home with some beat-up bargain or he'd polish up some of Mama's silver to sell at the shop and she'd remember why she walked away, why she owed it to herself to stay away.

"You about ready to start?" Her daddy peered up at her. "I got the crowd all warmed up for you."

"Daddy . . ." she warned.

He sighed. "Don't be worrying about me. I'm behaving—just charming the ladies is all." He flashed her a carefree grin, and she smiled in return. Life was easier with her daddy now that she accepted him for who he was, but it didn't mean she wanted to rope herself to a man with the same addictions.

She clicked the trigger on the bullhorn and said, "Five minutes till we start. Grab your wallets and forget your limits, it's almost auction time."

Laughing along with the crowd, she almost missed her mama herding a red-faced Porter toward her. Curious, she scrambled down from her perch.

"Bennie came looking for you."

Del still wasn't used to the idea of her mother and Porter being buddies. She nodded at her old boss. "Sorry for skipping out like that on you. I know it was short notice."

Porter twitched his lips like he was going to agree, but a firm look from Del's mama seemed to stop him. "I'm not here to talk about old problems."

That was good, she guessed.

"I'm here because I need you."

By the look on his face, Del figured the statement hurt pretty badly. "You don't need me. You had one too many auctioneers-in-waiting anyway."

Porter picked up a sale bill and used it to fan himself. "Not anymore. David left."

"Left?" She was enjoying Porter's discomfort.

"He's staying in Missouri, southern Missouri." He spit out the words like they left a bad taste behind, then glanced at Del's mother. "Sorry, Geraldine."

She just patted his arm. "That's fine. I know how you feel."

"With Becca?" Del couldn't believe David was giving up the conveniences of Chicago to run a diner in Allentown, Missouri.

"I didn't catch her name, but yes, there was some woman involved." Porter looked completely mystified by the thought. Explained why there wasn't a Mrs. Porter.

"There's more, though. He's going in with some auctioneer down here."

Del's amusement vanished.

"That's what brings me here," her ex-boss continued.

David and Sam? It couldn't be. They were like two tomcats sharing the same alley whenever they were together.

"His partner . . ."

"Sam?" she asked.

"Yes, that's it." Porter looked relieved he didn't have to exert any energy on remembering the details. "He made me an offer, but he has some conditions I have to meet first."

Sam had called Porter—about her? "What kind of offer?"

"He's located the Unruh Pig. You remember, the item you were sent down here to retrieve."

Now would be a good time for her mama to smack her old friend into line. Del looked at her mother, but the older woman didn't seem in a hurry to defend her daughter.

Del tried a cross look of her own. It worked. Porter continued in a hurry, "Anyway, he's offered the Pig to Porter Auctions, if you are the headlining auctioneer."

Nice try. So Sam thought he could escape his guilt by giving her the publicity, while keeping the money for himself? Yeah, that was going to happen.

"I'm not interested." She turned to climb back on the tractor seat.

"But you have to be." Porter dropped the flyer he'd been using as a fan to the ground. "This will be one of the biggest auctions of the year. Do you know what this could mean to our careers?"

"Yep, and no. Not interested. Now pick up that flyer before you forget it. We can't be littering up a perfectly nice hay field."

"Don't you even want to see it?" Sam's velvety voice sent chills running up her spine.

Without turning, she could feel him behind her. "Well, I am from Missouri. Don't believe much of anything until you show me."

"Seeing is believing." Sam stepped into view, a burlap-wrapped package tucked under one arm. "I brought everything you need with me."

Del steeled herself against the flutter in her stomach. "You think?"

His blue gaze drilled into her eyes. "I do."

"What about you? What do you need?"

"Sweet Tea, you definitely have everything I need." A slow smile warmed his face, causing his eyes to look sultry and inviting.

She pretended she didn't notice the awareness pulsing between them. "Well, let's see what you've got." She nodded toward a wooden table to her left.

A glimmer of amusement told her he didn't miss the double entendre.

Flushing, she brushed aside a collection of porcelain birthday girls and motioned for him to set the package down.

Despite the many lectures she'd given herself about not caring about the Pig or Sam, she felt her heart skip a beat—or twenty. The close proximity of both objects of her desire was making her a little light-headed.

With a solemn nod at Porter, Sam unwrapped the rough cloth and set a small statue on the table. It was blue and green and brown, like a child had mixed too many watercolors together and dribbled them down from the top, ending in a mottled mess at the bottom. The form itself wasn't much more impressive to Del's eye. It was obviously hand-formed into a rough representation of a pig, nothing but his snout and ears sticking out of a bag not much different than the one the statue had been wrapped in.

Del could see why as a child she thought she could do better.

"It takes your breath away, doesn't it?" Porter gazed at the Pig with unconcealed lust.

Sam looked at Del in much the same way. "It does," he murmured.

Del felt her face flush and her resolve weaken. He didn't have to insist she take part in the sale. He was giving her something.

No, the ignored child inside her screamed. It wasn't enough. She shook off the blush and gave Sam a level stare. "I told Porter I wasn't available."

Sam gave her an inscrutable look. "Not for any offer?"

Her heart made up for beats lost earlier by pounding against her chest.

"No," she replied. "I'm all booked."

"That's too bad, 'cause the owner insisted on you selling the piece or it goes back in its bag." He flicked the burlap sack. "Be a shame to tuck something like this away for another thirty years, don't you think?"

She glanced at the statue, her palms clammy. "The world will survive."

"Don't be so sure. There are some people whose world may depend on seeing that Pig sold, seeing things set right." He placed his hand on the table near hers. She stared at the masculine hand that had roamed her body just a month before.

Swallowing hard, she replied, "Maybe that's something the owner should have thought of before he made a demand that couldn't be fulfilled."

"She."

Del blinked at him.

"She, the owner's a she."

Del frowned. Had he sold the thing already?

"I've just been holding it for her, making sure it didn't fall into the wrong hands. You know, some people can get downright stupid when presented with the opportunity to make a few hundred grand."

"That right? I've never run into that myself." She ran her finger over the Pig's half-exposed snout and attempted to stamp down the hope that was bubbling in her chest.

"Yeah, downright stupid. I even heard tell of a

fool who let the best thing he'd ever had a hope of having walk out the door."

"That does sound stupid." She stroked the statue between his little pottery ears. A small smile formed on her lips. "How'd he see the error of his ways?"

"It took him awhile. He even went so far as to make some phone calls and pile on some promises, but then he was sitting all alone in his house and he realized something."

When he didn't continue, Del looked up at him. "What was that?"

The intensity of his gaze caused a new wave of heat to flow over Del, but this heat she didn't mind. This one she longed for.

"That it's better to have nothing but dreams with someone you love than to have everything you'd dreamed of, alone."

Del sucked in a breath.

Pulling her away from the table, Sam said, "I love you, Delilah Mont, and an offer of two thousand Unruh Pigs couldn't change that."

She wanted to believe him, to throw herself into his arms, but she had to know for sure. "Who owns the Pig?"

"As far as I know, your mother. I told her a week ago I couldn't keep it, even if you wouldn't ever speak to me again. She thought maybe you would." His eyes blazed. "Was she right?"

Del smoothed the dark T-shirt on the chest in front of her. She was so glad that when he'd changed his ways, he hadn't changed his wardrobe. "Well, I don't know if I can completely forget the pig."

Sam stared down at her, then looked away. "I guess I can respect that."

Reaching up, she turned his face back to hers. "'Cause Toadstool, he expects full rights to the bed—no more sleeping on a pallet for him. Makes him hard to forget."

With a grin, Sam replied, "I've been meaning to buy a new bed anyway—you think a king is big enough?"

Feigning concern, she shook her head. "I don't know, but if we're going to do this—"

"Why not go whole hog?" Sam finished. Lifting her off her feet, he spun her around. "Sweet Tea, we're going to make a hell of a team."